MICHAEL PRESLEY'S

BLACKFUNK

Dedicated: To my mom for being such a wonderful guide.

Revised Edition 2

Blackfunk Publishing
PO Box 23782
Brooklyn, NY 11202

BLACKFUNK-Book.com

Presley

Printed in Canada

Copyright © April 19, 2000

Library of Congress Copyright office

ISBN: 0-9705903-0-x

BLACKFUNK

**IT'S ABOUT WHAT
YOU'VE GOT AND
HOW YOU USE IT...**

**In a world where love is dying,
Sex is used as a weapon,
Jealousy and hate feed on each other
And dreams and reality
Become nightmares-
A man and a woman
Will try to beat the odds
Before the worms have their say...**

Acknowledgements

I would like to acknowledge the following people for their help and words of encouragement in publishing my first book. Val, you were there from the beginning and throughout the creation of Blackfunk, much thanks to you. Debbie, you have been very helpful, your constructive criticism and words of encouragement helped make this work possible. Shawina, even though you came along at the end of the project, your assistance was invaluable. Fabia, thanks for helping me stay focus and being there when I needed you. Hazel, thank you for being there at my weakest moments to make sure I kept my head up. Rose, thanks for the help in the final revisions. Kyle, the bond was created in college and it has never waned, much thanks and appreciation. Al, I appreciate your words of encouragement. Thanks for being a good friend. Frantz, your help over the years have been greatly appreciated. Good luck in your future endeavors. Brian, thank you for being a good friend going way back to fighting in the park in Grenville. Ken, thanks for the words of encouragement and your faith in me. Sherry, Kareem, and Tiffany, thanks for the headache. Tech crew, thanks for the input. To the rest of my family and friends, thank you.

"Get the hell out," Andria screamed at the figure lying on the bed, naked except for a red condom on his penis. "Why the hell did you have to go and do that?" She stood, holding on to the doorknob, "I told you, Paul, I don't want this shit. I am twenty-six years old, and I am tired of the games." A stream of tears flowed from her eyes. "And—look at you—thirty-six years old and still doing the same old shit you use to do when you were twenty."

"Andria, can I explain?"

"Explain what? Paul there is no need for an explanation. The picture is as clear as day."

"Don't we all make mistakes?" Paul leaned back on the headboard. He felt like a cigarette right now, even though he had recently given up smoking. "I never said I was perfect."

"You know what, Paul, just get the fuck out." She couldn't stop the rain from bathing her cheeks.

"Okay, I understand you're a little bit upset, but I want to come back when you've calmed." He got off the bed.

"Who the hell do you think I am, Paul? Do you think you've gonna walk out and come back two hours later and everything will be okay?"

"Listen to me."

"Paul, get the fuck out before I stab your ass!" This time she started to make her way toward the kitchen, her eyes red and bulging. This was not the life she had envisioned. Everything was all fucked up.

"Crazy bitch," Paul muttered under his breath as his eyes swept the room looking for his pants. He took a swipe at the rest of the colored condoms that lay on the night table. There were six remaining from the pack of a dozen he brought two days ago. He turned and looked at her with a smirk, not a hint of remorse. He had given her two years of his life, maybe not totally, but she was always his number one. His body felt hot and sticky. He put his pants on without his underwear; he hadn't the faintest idea where they were or what Florence had done with them. And of course, now was not the right time to go looking for the fucking underwear. He had other things to worry about, including his love standing, threatening to call the police. He was angry that she was telling him to leave. It may have been her apartment, but he was paying half the rent.

"Paul, I gave you everything! Why? Why? Look at me. There is nothing left to give."

"I'm sorry," he said as he looked at her, silently agreeing with her statement.

He couldn't understand what went wrong. He thought he had played it safe. Andria was supposed to be at work until 5:00 P.M. He estimated it took her about one hour to get home. Florence had called him fifteen minutes after eleven; saying she was hot for him. The last time Florence was in heat he had to wear an ice pack on his dick for hours, but it was worth every bit of that ice. He called Andria's job to make sure she was there. Mrs. Patterson, the short, plump secretary on Andria's job, had said that Andria was in a meeting. City workers were always in meetings, meetings being one of the main reasons that there were few competent city agencies. He wondered how the city workers ever got anything done when they had this excessive paperwork to muddle through and always had to attend meetings. He pressed the talk button on the phone and praised God that Mrs. Patterson's high-pitched voice was a distant memory. He hadn't given Andria her customary good-bye morning kiss because he heard her coughing last night. It didn't make any sense for them both to have a cold. Besides, she'd had that cold for more than a week already, and it seemed to be getting worse. He hated colds. They made him feel like shit, though he didn't know exactly what shit felt like. He had told Andria that he wasn't going in today because he was feeling a little bit under the weather. He also had to fix the car to get it ready for their trip on Sunday. She knew his mechanic, a Jamaican immigrant named Rupert. Rupert was an excellent mechanic, but his rambling made a simple ten-minute job take almost an hour. He told everyone who came to do repairs his life story, and boy did Rupert have a fucked-up life story.

Paul actually did go to see Rupert who told him his car brakes needed a minor adjustment. Fifteen minutes later and twenty dollars poorer, he was back at his house relaxing, watching *Love Connection*. It was after the show that Florence called. She was surprised to find him home, and she wanted to know if she could stop by on her way to the supermarket. She was going to bring Peter, her son, but she thought it might be better if she left him with her neighbor.

Paul had met Florence about a year ago when her husband had introduced his second half to him at a community meeting. He hated those community meetings but Andria had insisted that he attend. She told him he should get to know the people in the community that he was living in. So, he did his usual: He sat in the back of the room and voted with the majority. To him, the most exciting thing about community meetings were the bored housewives. There were plenty of them tired of 365 days of that same old loving. Actually, depending on the marriage, sometimes there weren't even twenty days of loving in the year. There were all different kinds of marriages: arranged, prearranged, "you do your thing, I do mine," "let's stay together for the kids," "my spouse is gay." America is a land of opportunities and sometimes if you don't do your job, another person will do it for you. Paul knew he took care of business at home, and occasionally, he was willing to help another brother take care of his shit. As soon as Andria introduced him to Florence, he knew Florence's man wasn't taking care of his business; So Paul had to do the honorable thing. It was in her eyes. Her words were short and courteous, but her eyes were telling him about the quivering between her legs. Paul knew it, and Florence wasted no time giving him her telephone number to discuss this new action committee.

Paul's interest in the community made her feel so proud, but now she knew why. She watched him as he stood and put his clothes on. He was the gentlest and most loving man she had ever known. He knew how to make love to a woman. Their lovemaking usually left her grasping for air. Even when he wasn't up to par, he used his hands and his mouth to open the sky for her, but most of all, she liked when he cradled her in his arms when they were finished. She liked the fact that he brought her flowers at least once every week. He would sometimes get down on his knees and clip her toenails. He would make dinner for her at least three times a week. And he would go with her shopping and not once would he complain, even when she went to ten different stores and left without buying anything. Paul was a good man. He made her feel safe and secure. In bed, he would do anything to please her, and obviously, he was willing to do the same for other women. Over the years, he had learned her body to the point that he

3

could make her have orgasms at his will. Her friends had always been leery of him but they didn't know what she thought she had. She never told her friends about how good he was because she was afraid that they might want him. No, she didn't want to share him with anyone.

Florence had already flown through the door, hesitating only briefly to hoist her sleeping son over her shoulders. She knew the little boy should be getting up about now. Her girlfriend had told her that the pill she had given her son, crushed and mixed with juice, lasted approximately three hours. There were no side effects, but Florence had seen her girlfriend's kids looking like they were doing everything in slow motion. She had wanted to ask Andria if she was going to tell her husband, but she thought better of it when she saw the look on Andria's face.

Paul stood six-feet-two inches tall and weighed 230 pounds. Thick muscular thighs supported his stomach hanging over his genitals. He was a big man by anyone's standards yet he never tried to intimidate people with his size. He reached inside the brown dresser drawer and pulled out a rumpled gray shirt, Andria had bought for him two years ago.

"Make sure you take everything, you fucking bastard, because I don't want to see your fucking face in my life again." Her face seemed contorted as if ice-cold water ran through her veins. She started to shiver, desperately wanting a blanket, but she didn't want him to see her breakdown. She had to be strong a little while longer.

"What do you want me to do, Andria? I said I was sorry and I am leaving! Okay?" He became agitated and as he looked at her he wondered what would happen to them. The face that he enjoyed so much was now twisted in hate.

He remembered the time Andria brought him that shirt. It was about the same time they had pledged their undying love to each other, promising to talk to each other instead of talking to others. They felt it was important to leave the lines of communication open because they knew other relationships where the couples did not talk at all. They had seen how unhappy these people were, living in the same house but living two different lives. They both had their share of meaningless sexual flings. They had talked about them openly, but

4

he always got upset when she spoke of her past. She took that to be a man thing. He never wanted to admit that anyone had been there before him. He never wanted to believe that anyone had touched his sacred woman; she was going to be his wife one day. But he had gotten over that. He had come to realize that she had a life before him, the same way he had one before her. They had made plans to get married the following year.

He was doing really well, too, but then Cassandra from his job had invited him over to her place after work. He didn't plan to do anything even then, but that changed once he saw the ass on Cassandra. He wondered where she was hiding it before. God must have given her extra helpings. It started with her, and once the mold was broken, the women started to pile up. After Cassandra came Joyce, Florence, Beverly, and Maria. He used a condom religiously with all the women; only once was there an accident. The condom broke while he and Cassandra were doing it doggy style. The following five weeks were hell until Cassandra got an abortion. She already had four kids; another one would bring her close to having a basketball team without a stadium for them to play in. Her husband was already raising one of her children from an affair.

Damn, Paul had a woman for every night of the week. Hell, this was the nineties and women outnumbered men five to one. And God knew enough of these men were fruitcakes so they didn't count. The women all knew Andria and they spoke very highly of her. Two were married with kids, and the other three were just beautiful, educated, horny black women. Maybe something was missing from their lives; who knows, but then that wasn't his problem.

Florence was a crazy bitch but she was an excellent fuck. She could do things to a man's dick that would make his toes wiggle, and she was always willing to try anything new. Paul and Florence's husband played basketball in the park on Sundays. Florence would always be there, smiling at her husband as he ran down the court, and opening and closing her legs when Paul looked at her. Florence's husband told Paul that his wife was the best thing in the world. She was always cheering him on no matter what he was doing. Paul agreed with him down to her bald pussy. Paul had told Florence that they had to cool it. Twice a week was getting too dangerous, and sometimes he had to do double duty. He wasn't twenty-one anymore, and she was starting to push the envelope. He once fucked Florence in her kitchen while her husband was upstairs sleeping. He had come over to pick him up to go to the park, and Florence had answered the door in a long T-shirt. She asked him if he wanted something to drink, and she guided him into the kitchen. There, she poured him a large glass of Tropicana orange juice, just the kind he liked. A minute or so later, she bent over the kitchen table and slowly she lifted her T-shirt, exposing her beautiful curvaceous ass. Paul took a quick look upstairs and realized he was trembling. Florence slowly spread her legs apart; she took her hands and parted her ass. The Pope would have had trouble making a decision at this point. Paul had two choices. He saw the remaining used oil in the frying pan next to Florence's right hand. He touched it, it was warm, he dipped his hand in and slapped it between her butt. All she said was "oh." His penis had already saluted the entrance, something of a surprise considering he had just finished making love to Andria about a half hour ago. He was also taking chances with his life. The act was dangerous, and the risk outweighed the pleasure. He should've turned and walked out, but he knew it was too late. His other head was doing all the thinking. It was pussy power at its best. He was risking his life for a shot. Yet, he wasn't going to disrespect his woman by opting for the first hole. No, he had to go to the second. When he entered, Florence said thank you. He did not exactly finish the orange juice, neither did he wait for her husband to come downstairs to go play ball. After they had finished, Florence told him that her husband got a little bit too much for him to handle this morning. She smiled wickedly as the words left her mouth. However, she would be happy to go and wake him up after she had cleaned up. When Paul called her a "fucking bitch," she told him she would see him next week and he knew she would.

Damn Florence. She had to fuck things up. He tried to tell the bitch not to come over, but trying to tell a woman who is not thinking with her head something logical is impossible. He had concluded that a woman in heat was worse than a man. A woman in heat *had* to be fucked, and if her man wouldn't do it, she'd simply find someone else who would. Moreover, if that wasn't possible, electronic noise would sound or a cucumber would disappear from the refrigerator.

Paul wished Florence had found someone else today. As he continued to get dressed, he couldn't help but look at Andria. Florence had nothing on Andria who was beautiful all over. She had short black hair cut so that it barely touched her ears. Her face had enviable brown skin with small, black eyes accented with full lips. There wasn't a blemish on her whole face. Oil of Olay should pay her millions for not using their products. Her walk was confident but with an undeniable sensuous sway. Her nose was small and straight. She stood five feet seven inches with a shape that his friends compared to Coca-Cola bottle. It was her body that first attracted him, but the rest of her qualities he found out were even more precious than her body. He fell in love with her after six weeks of platonic dating. At that time, he didn't mind waiting for her because he still had a few booty calls from ex-girlfriends. He was so happy with her the first year they were together, but then things started to change.

He could not put his finger on exactly what it was but something changed. He used to bring flowers home to Andria every Friday. They would go to plays, movies, and sometimes clubbing. He loved the way she danced. Then interest started to wane like it had with so many women before her, yet he tried to hold on because he knew she was special. He kept telling himself it was going to get better. It was at that time that he discovered that her beautiful body and nice personality was not enough. Many of his friends commented on her hint of pure sexuality, something he reveled in when he first met her. Her body was curved in all the right places, a slim build accentuated by a well-rounded butt. It was a model's body that he had the pleasure of imaginary molding. Two years ago, he thought she was the most beautiful woman in the world, but now as he pulled his pants up, she was just another angry bitch, but God, what a sweet pussy. As he thought about her, he felt himself begin to rise. The condom dropped off into his pants and rolled all the way down his leg. He knew he had fucked up this time, but maybe she would let him eat first and fuck later. He looked into her eyes and realized the faster he got out of there, the healthier he would be.

"Help me. Lord! Help me, Jesus," Andria said as she walked out the room. She was still reeling from what had just transpired. Her hands and knees still trembled. Only half an hour before she had walked into the apartment and heard sounds coming from the bedroom. She wondered if Paul had left the TV on and the sounds were coming from a washed-up soap queen. But as she reached the bedroom door she heard the voices. It was unmistakably Paul and Florence.

"Come on, baby. Come on do that shit," Paul encouraged Florence, "you are the fucking best."

Andria's hand had frozen on the silver plated doorknob. She wanted to scream but the words remained deep down in her throat. She felt herself gasping for air and sank to the floor, weakened by the thoughts that reality had brought forth. In the process, she had slightly opened the door.

"Fuck me, fuck me," Florence's high-pitch voice squealed. Paul had seen Andria fall down to the floor, but it was impossible to stop. Florence was on top of him, her back facing the door about to have an orgasm for the second time, and he was about to send millions of helpless sperm to their death inside a large, red monoxol nine lubricated condom. He looked at Andria as Florence continued her aerial stunts on his pole. He wished Andria would close the fucking door, join, do something. If not, the least she could do was wait until they were finished.

"No! No! No!" she whispered to herself, as she lay in front of the door. There was a pain deep inside of her throat, choking her. Her face felt wet and sticky. Her nose had stopped running and even that constant cough had disappeared. The world had suddenly stopped turning and she wanted to jump off. She mustered all her strength, pushed herself up off the floor, and ran to the kitchen.

"Motherfucking bastard!" Her mouth had begun to accept that salty-tasting fluid coming from her eyes. She held on to the kitchen cabinet as she rummaged through the knife drawer. Fourteen inches of pure steel settled in her right hand, but she barely had the strength to hold on to it, and it fell to the floor. She pushed herself off the white Formica kitchen cabinet. The tears had stopped; now her face had become wrinkled and contorted. Her body shook, but she wasn't sure if it was due to symptoms of the cold or the present situation. Still, her course to the bedroom was set. Suddenly, she had thoughts of her mother coming to her room when she was six years old, a crazy thought because her mother was covered in blood. As quickly as the thoughts came, they vanished and Andria continued on her path to the room.

Now she lay slumped down on the sofa in the living room.

She had forgiven Paul once before. Even though she had never caught him, he had admitted to having an affair with Cassandra. Love had made a fool of her and now her heart was feeling the pain of believing in a fool's paradise. He had told her it was a mistake that just happened, and he promised it would never happen again. With tears in his eyes, he had asked her forgiveness and sworn on his mother's grave his undying love for her and his commitment to make her his wife one day. After that, he had shown her more love than she had ever felt from a man. He did everything she wanted and treated her like a queen.

For a long time after that, she didn't trust him. Their great sex life had become a battle of insecurities; her thoughts of him doing the same things and saying the same words to another woman became constant. She had lived a lie. She started to think about all the things they did together. Did he really go on a trip with the company? How many times did he actually stay to work overtime? Did Cassandra visit him at work? Did all her neighbors know, and had she become a big joke at dinner? People say once you do it the first time, the second and third times became easier. How many women was he sleeping with?

She had gone to the doctor and taken every sexually transmitted disease test that was available. Yet, the doctor informed her that certain STDs had no immediate symptoms and some took a long time to show up. Andria made Paul take the tests, too, and he was clean. Now she had to go and do it all over again. How could he do that to her? How could he do that to someone he claimed he loved? But time, the healer of all things, made life and love go on. In time, she forgave and in time, she learned to trust again. Maybe she had forgiven him because she never actually witnessed his infidelity. There is a saying "a picture is worth a thousand words," but that wasn't true. This picture was worth a million words, and they were all flying around inside her head. Without a picture, the memory disappears with time. Now she had the pictures videotaped in her mind, forever etched in her memory to be eternally replayed. She now wondered how many other women Paul had brought to their bed, on his so-called days off. The questions kept pouring through her head. Each question raced the other for importance. How could she have been so gullible? Maybe he never had lunch during the day; maybe his lunch break had become a fuck break. Her anger and pain felt like daggers through her heart, slowly breaking it with deep-wrenching pain. She felt used, betrayed, and put on stage to be the butt of a comic's jokes. Slowly, she was losing control. She needed to be away from there.

All her friends were either married or in relationships headed to the altar. She had invested three years in this man. She wanted a home with children, and she didn't want to go back into the dating game. The dating scene plagued with AIDS and all the other sexually transmitted diseases, had become a game of Russian roulette. Yet she didn't want to be alone. She realized now that home could be the most dangerous place of all.

"Why me? Why me? Haven't I been good, Lord?" The emptiness in the room let her echoed words match the space in her heart.

"Fuck you!" she screamed to the room. Her heart had become empty and heavy and the tears once again streamed down her cheeks, depositing their moisture inside her gaping mouth. She again screamed, "fuck you" to the empty room. The voice came from deep down in her heart and tore at her already tender throat. If it was exhaustion, she didn't know, but her mind had begun to drift to a better place . . .

Once more, thoughts of the incident when she was six came to the forefront of her mind. Her mother had come into her room, bloodied and crying, pulled her into her arms, and steadily repeated, "I couldn't take it anymore. I couldn't take it anymore." Tears flowed freely down her mother's face onto hers. Andria kept asking what happened, but her mother held her tight and kept rocking her. Then her aunt came in and pulled Andria away from her mother. Andria remembered screaming for her mother and fighting to get away from her aunt. Her aunt held on to her and carried her out of the house. As she sat in the car, the police sirens bellowed in the distance quickly coming into view. Among the commotion of yelling men and crying women, her uncle emerged, lifted her up, and took her away. She did not get the news that her father was dead until a week later. She went to his funeral but couldn't see his face because the casket was closed. At that age, she did not know what death meant and for months, she waited for her father to return home. He never did and neither did Mommy.

Reality of the moment awoke Andria with a cough. She felt the phlegm rising in her throat. Her face felt hot and her body was shivering. It was that nasty cold that made her leave work early. Mr. Burke was very understanding. He saw that she was in no condition to work; he put her in a cab and sent her home. She resisted at first because she had some work she wanted to finish, but he insisted. Once in the cab, she realized Mr. Burke was right. She felt horrible. She couldn't wait to get home to seek the warmth of her bed. The Haitian cab driver, with his fake smile, gave her his home remedy for getting over colds. He told her to stop in the liquor store and pick up a pint of 100% proof Haitian rum, mix some of that with honey and bula. The bula she should be able to get at any of the Chinese vegetable stores. She was amazed at the Chinese stores. They supplied the black community with everything it needed except music. For a second, she thought about a Chinese rap group and it brought a smile to her face. Wherever there was a West Indian, there was a Chinese vegetable store. She thanked the driver and left him and his remedy in the cab. All she wanted to do was find her bed and slip under the covers. Unfortunately, her bed was already occupied.

Andria pushed herself off the couch and made her way to the armchair located at the edge of the carpet facing the Zenith twenty-five-inch floor-model TV. Somehow, the weakness she felt earlier had disappeared, but the lump in her throat constantly threatened her with nausea.

She dialed the numbers without feeling her fingers touch the phone, the same phone Paul probably used earlier to make his plans.

"Hello?" The voice on the other line sounded tired and hoarse.

"Hello, Robin," Andria said fighting the nausea that had begun to increase its upward flight.

"What's wrong, Andria?" Robin asked, immediately sensing the pain in Andria's voice.

"It's Paul, I . . ." Andria's voice trailed off to an unidentifiable whisper.

"Andria, what did Paul do to you? Did he hit you?"

"No, he did not hit me."

"What did he do?"

"In my own bed, he was doing it in my own bed."

"Andria, what are you talking about?"

"Robin, he and that fucking bitch were doing it in my own bed."

"Calm down, Andria. Everything will be all right. Now tell me what happened."

Robin listened to Andria tell her story, not once interrupting to ask any questions. Robin had known about Florence for a long time. When Andria was finished, Robin sat back almost tipping her chair over in the process. She was a big girl these days, thanks to her husband's seed. Robin had told Andria to dump Paul when Robin found out that he had slept with Cassandra. She believed that once a dog, always a dog. She knew how well Andria treated Paul, and she knew Paul wasn't shit. Robin didn't believe in second and third chances. Once a person did something, the likelihood he or she would do it again was ninety-nine percent. Character flaws were hard to treat. They just keep coming back. She told Andria to cut him loose and move on, but now was not the time for "I told you so." Andria needed a friend to hold her hand. Robin was expecting this day to come eventually. She believed Paul was closer to dog-shit than a real dog. But she also knew he made Andria happy, and she couldn't fight that. She believed that Andria should thank God she got out alive without catching AIDS or something. Robin told Andria she would come over and see her as soon as Jack, her husband, came home.

Andria took two swigs of the Russian vodka she had in the liquor cabinet and laid back on the brown antique couch in the dining room. At 6:30, a pounding awakened her. She shook her head to stop it, but it only got louder.

"Andria, Andria, open the door, it's me." The voice came from the direction of the front door. Andria took one step in the direction of the door, but her head started to spin and she fell back into the sofa. The second time she heaved herself up and ignored the spinning in her head, and swerving she finally found the doorknob.

Robin's stomach pushed into the door, each breath trying to catch the other. These days her stomach was always the first to reach her destination. She was eight months pregnant. It was her first child, and each day she prayed for the delivery. She desperately wanted the baby, but the changes her body had gone through were driving her crazy. Robin had wanted a baby since she began having sex at fourteen. Her mother didn't find out she was sexually active until Robin was twenty. When she was in high school, her friends were having babies as if the summer season was dropping time. They would get pregnant in early September and have the baby in the middle of the summer. Robin, herself, had a few close encounters with bringing life into this world. Once she had a miscarriage, and then there was a false alarm. She wondered where the losers that tried to make her a mother were today. As she grew older, she realized that having a baby involved more than making goo-goo eyes and rocking. It wasn't until Robin was twenty-eight and married that she got pregnant again. Now little Robin was kicking and turning inside her stomach.

Andria's hair was uncombed and seemed glued to her face. The remaining half of the cheap Russian vodka was nestled in the corner of the couch. Robin never knew Andria to drink any kind of liquor much less vodka. Yet, this time it was different. Andria was trying to chase that lump in her throat away. She was trying her best to exit a world that gave the illusion of a lifetime of happiness but only gave pain. No, Andria was hurting and Robin saw it in that haggled face without the assets of make-up to hide the lines. As Andria flopped back onto the sofa, her head rested against the sofa armrest with her right foot on the floor and her left foot completely on the sofa.

Robin headed to the kitchen to prepare another of Colombia's addictive export. In a few minutes, the strong smell of coffee had replaced the stale aroma of vodka.

"Sit back here and drink this," Robin said, trying to support Andria's head as she brought the coffee cup to her lips.

"No, I don't want that shit," Andria said as she tried to pull her head away from the ever-threatening cup of coffee. The curse word sounded strange coming from those perfect lips. "I just want to lay here and die," She said her voice rasping in its urgency and pain.

"Come on, Andria, drink this. Then we'll talk about how you're going to kill yourself. Remember, that could be a very painful task, which would require sober thinking." Robin's faint attempt at humor did nothing for Andria's mood. She held the cup as Andria took the hot coffee in gulps.

Andria felt the constant throbbing etching out a pattern in her brain. She tried to rise, but the pain swimming in her head made it impossible. The most alcohol she had ever drank was a small glass of cheap sweet Canei wine, and she had hated the taste of that too. However, this feeling was new to her, and her thoughts strayed to an old cliché: "Mama never told me that love would hurt so much." With all the different thoughts going on in her head, one kept recurring to her. Why did he have to do this? She gave him everything she had. Was everything ever enough?

"The fucking bastard brought her into our bed. He didn't go to a hotel or anything," Andria said, trying to think of circumstances that would make the pain less. She knew this was the nineties, but these things didn't happen to her much less twice with the same person. "Granted, we haven't been having sex as often as when we first started seeing each other, but the passion was still there. We still had a lot of fun together, going places, doing things. What the fuck do men want, Robin?"

Robin wanted to say to Andria, " You knew this fucking two-timing bastard was no good, so why are you acting like if he was some kind of saint" But instead she said, "I'm really sorry about what happened to you and Paul, but maybe it's all for the best." Paul was a player. He would fuck anything in a skirt. Robin had heard so many stories about who Paul was fucking that she stopped listening to them after someone told her about Andria's next-door neighbor Phyllis. Phyllis was fat and ugly, two adjectives that should never be used to describe a person in the same sentence. If Andria only knew what Paul did, she would send him away with a bullet in his dick, kneel down, and praise God she was still alive. Robin did not tell Andria about Paul because she was afraid of losing a good friend. Besides, Andria would never believe her—many friendships had ended like that. Andria also forgave Paul before for messing around on her, maybe she would have just forgiven him again. So had Robin told, who would be hurt the most? Still, Robin hated seeing Andria like this. She did not know if it was better to tell a person of infidelity, or have that person find out from a doctor. By that time, it's usually too late because by then the doctor started talking about either getting rid of it or how much time you had to live with it and the advances in modern medicine. Stress lines had taken up residency under Andria's eyes. Her face was a mask of confusion and anguish as she lay whimpering in Robin's arms below her distended stomach. Robin knew the phone calls would come much more regularly now, and she would have to spend countless hours telling Andria things that Andria already knew. But she didn't mind. She was happy to be there for her. She knew only time healed the wounds of the heart.

Andria's head lay in Robin's lap, as Andria slowly drifted in and out of sleep. Robin's legs had started to get stiff so she took a couch pillow and put it under Andria's head. Robin then got up and eased herself into the big brown leather TV chair next to the couch Andria was sleeping on. Within ten minutes, Robin was in dreamland, walking on the beach with her family.

They must have slept for about five hours before the loud ringing of the black rotary phone woke them up. Robin saw Andria getting up, motioned her to lie back down, and went to answer the phone. She had looked at the stand for the cordless but the handset wasn't there. She looked at the oval off-white clock that hung against the wall, then at Andria. She felt she needed to spend more time with her friend. Her husband had gotten the note she had left on the refrigerator and wanted to know how she and Andria were doing. Andria was one of Robin's friends that he actually liked. He asked her if she wanted him to come and pick her up. She told him to give her two more hours before coming.

Andria had finally gotten up and started attacking the dishes Paul and Florence had left in the kitchen. There were two plates with floral embroidery on them and two tall glasses from the Hard Rock Cafe—the glasses they had received on Paul's birthday. Andria and he went to the cafe for dinner before going to see the Broadway play *Love Nest*. That afternoon was completed with a carriage ride through the city. Andria must have spent more than five hundred dollars that night, but she really didn't care. This was her man, who would one day be the father of her children, her life rotated around him like a carousel. As Andria washed each dish and glass with liquid soap, she threw them to the floor. The breaking plates brought Robin to the kitchen. She ran over to Andria and grabbed her hands; once again, tears flowed from Andria's eyes in an effortless stream. Andria threw her hands around Robin's neck as her body heaved and the pain returned.

Robin's hands circled Andria's waist from the sides and supported the three of them back to the room. Andria tried to apologize for her emotional outbursts, but Robin did not want to hear of it.

"Andria, you will get over him," Robin said as she guided her friend to her bed. She laid Andria down on the mattress and discreetly swiped a plastic condom wrapper from the edge of the bed, looking at Andria to see if she'd noticed. Andria's eyes were following Mr. Spock on a mission to another planet. Robin secured Andria on the bed, elevating her head with two pillows just in case the vodka got her a little bit restless. Andria muttered thanks to her and sank into a restless sleep.

Robin turned the channel on the small cable-ready digital Sony thirteen-inch TV that rested on Andria's dresser. Channel 4 was showing the latest news headlines. The biggest story of the day seemed to be a woman claiming to have gotten AIDS from a date set up on the TV show *Blind Ambition*. Robin shook her head and wondered, her mind became filled with questions of loyalty. Should she have told her friend about Paul and risked losing her friendship forever? Maybe she could have saved Andria from the sudden fall or worse a painful death. Before she was able to justify herself to her conscience, Robin's thoughts were interrupted, by the loud ringing of the doorbell. She opened the door after her husband identified himself. She was relieved to see him and was happy because he was not Paul. She looked at Andria sleeping peacefully, but she knew that when she woke up the pain of consciousness would send her into misery. She kissed Andria good-bye and made a mental note to call her before she and her husband went to bed.

It was 11:30 that night when Robin, Andria's mother, the super, and the police opened Andria's door and found Andria's body bent over the toilet seat. The right side of her face was lying across the toilet cover and her hands were dangling over the sides of the bowl. There were two tablets left in the bottle of Actifed. Upon seeing her daughter, Andria's mother began to wail. It was a loud eerie sound that echoed through the apartment, a mother's cry for her only child. Andria was her only good remembrance to a bad past. She had spent five years in prison on manslaughter charges. Andria's father was the only man she ever had in her life. She held her daughter's hand tightly as the EMS technicians loaded her onto the ambulance. She prayed to God, asking Him to take her life but spare her daughter's, because Andria's life was her thread.

The ambulance raced down Highway 16 with its siren blaring and Andria's mother holding on to her hand. The paramedics had revived her, so there was at least a weak pulse. If Andria's mother looked out the window for a split second, she would have seen Paul's car parked in front of a two-car garage, attached to a house belonging to Joyce. Andria had also introduced Paul to Joyce and now Paul was about to enter Joyce's comfort zone. Andria had found notes that Joyce left for Paul. They had a big argument over Joyce, one of the many promises Paul didn't keep. Actually, he stayed away from Joyce for two weeks before he started servicing her again. During that time,

Joyce had met a cop with a very possessive personality, who claimed that she was his woman. She agreed with him; after all, she was approaching thirty, and it was time to settle down. But old friends with Paul's talent were very important to her and she needed some variety to add some spice in her life. Her man was always grunting as if he was doing something special, but he was only tickling her. Paul, on the other hand, made it be known that size does make a difference.

The doctor stopped pumping Andria's stomach at the hospital about the same time Paul stopped doing the backstroke. When they were finished, Paul told her his situation and Joyce told him hers. There was no match to be found, but the release from the tension was good for Paul. Two hours later, as Andria lay resting in her hospital bed, Paul pulled out of Joyce's driveway, and headed back to the forty-five-dollar-a-night motel just off Linden Boulevard. Tomorrow he would look for Cassandra. There are eight million stories in the naked city—this one was just beginning.

FUNK 3

He stood in front of the full-length bathroom mirror, an antique one with gold-plated trimmings and a metallic stand. It was a gift from his mother. His pinpointed black eyes, matching the color of his skin, pierced his reflection. His mother once told him he was the blackest boy she had ever seen. When he was growing up, his friends called him Blacky. On dark nights, Blacky could be right next to someone and they couldn't see him. As a boy, he hated himself, always standing out with his black self. When you are a black person in a group of black people and you stand out because you are black, then you know tar has nothing on you. He hated the name Blacky, but it came so natural to people that he stopped fighting every time someone said it. His friends rarely called him Rashaun. The only time he ever heard himself called Rashaun Jones was from strangers or teachers. Dating in his teens were very difficult, not for him but for the girls he went out with. They were called names like Miss Blacky and Charcoal Lover. He once went out with an Indian girl whose parents refused to let him come inside their house. He had to wait on the steps at the front door until she came outside. When he was outside the door, he could feel their eyes on him. He believed the only reason they allowed her to go out with him was because she was their only child, and they were afraid of her reaction if they said no.

Rashaun became very self-conscious, and he spent a great deal of time getting to like himself. It was a difficult process, especially when he constantly felt everyone's eyes riveted on him. It was funny though, most dark-skin black women were ready to go back to Africa, but they weren't interested in dating a black man, therefore, most of his dates were with light-skinned black women.

He looked to books for his escape from a world that made him special because of his color. There wasn't a damn thing he could do about it. It just was the way things were. He read almost everything he could find, including books on making love. He learned self-control and to depend on only himself. By the time he was ready to graduate from high school, he was valedictorian of his senior class but his academic accomplishment did not keep him away from the streets, where he spent plenty of time learning that way of life. He quickly earned a reputation as a smart boy nobody wanted to fuck with. Blacky could beat you with either his words or his fists. He was his mother's pride and joy, and she never wasted an opportunity to tell everyone about him. He loved his mother, more than himself sometimes, and he was sure that one day he was going to make her very proud of him. He was the first and darkest of four children, two boys and two girls. A firstborn in the West Indies is always looked upon as a guide for the rest to follow. He took pride in his family and kept a tight reign on his brothers and sisters. His relationship with his father was cordial at best, yet he respected him for his financial support of the family. Rashaun wasn't sure where he was going or what life had in store for him, but he strived to be the best at everything he did.

"Rashaun Jones." He said his name as if he expected acknowledgement from himself. He would be turning thirty-one in June, whether to be happy or sad about that, he couldn't decide. His inspection started with his eyebrows, making sure that they still held their groomed look. He ran his hands over his face searching for a hint of a pimple. He broke into a smile and his perfection glittered white like a ray of light in the darkness of the night.

As his eyes inspected his body in the mirror, his hands traced the outline of his body. He was six-feet-three-inches tall and his weight fluctuated from 210 to 215 pounds. At the age of seventeen, he took up bodybuilding and never relinquished the sport. His triceps were formed by sets of four and repetitions of ten push downs and triceps presses performed twice a week. He worked his body to exhaustion and became totally focused on its development. He would sometimes break dates to complete his workout. His right hand now touched his left biceps, there was a little nudge there, and he would have to increase his biceps sets to five. His hands left the hugging of his body and he flexed his muscles pushing his chest forward.

"Rashaun," the feminine voice interrupted his vanity. Her name he could barely remember. Her date of birth followed by her life story was told to him as he whisked his car down Seventh Avenue. She said that she had never been with such a pretty, black-as-tar man in her life. This was the third time he was going to bed with her. Her complexion was light, almost white. She had long hair reaching way beyond her shoulders, and her body was small but compact. Her breasts, which no child had sucked, were firm and pointed as the pyramids of Egypt. And of course, she had to have "back." That was one of his prerequisites in a woman. She worked at a hospital in downtown Brooklyn, another unimportant fact as far as he was concerned.

"I'm coming," he said in his American accent with a slight trace of his West Indian roots.

"Rashaun, come here, baby," the voice said taking on the urgency of feminine passion. She had already started.

He made no motion toward the locked bathroom door. His face barely acknowledged the voice. His pecs jutted over his washboard like stomach, made possible by a half hour of stomach exercise each morning. His hands traced the outline of his body. He believed the secret to lovemaking was anticipation and readiness. When he went into the room, he had to be ready. His hands went down to his waist then he brought them in. Then he started, patiently and knowingly.

The lights were on in his bedroom when he went in. He saw her look at him and smile. He hit the switch on the side of the door. He instantly became one with the room. He touched his night-table lamp, which came on in one of three settings. He touched it again; it went one level higher. The room was now illuminated.

The room was large enough to accommodate three king-size beds. His king-size bed was located in the middle, a black lacquered four-post structure that went as high as six feet. The headboard was made of a one-inch glass that went four feet high. The same mirror continued with the same height to both sides of the bed. The mirror was interrupted briefly on the corners of the headboard with two touch night lamps built in. He had the bed custom made about two years ago for nine thousand dollars. On the right side of the bed was a built-in closet that contained about twenty Italian suits and an assortment of jackets, shirts, and pants. The dresser on the left side contained his undergarments, jerseys, T-shirts, and summer wear. He had a second dresser next to it containing his sweaters and an assortment of winter wear.

The off-white walls were adorned with six large pictures placed in different locations. The picture at the right end of the back of the headboard was one of four African paintings in the room. It

21

depicted a naked black couple entwined in lovemaking on a white background. He had brought the painting for six hundred dollars at an art show in Soho. Opposite, a painting of a black family walking through the desert adorned the wall. The man had a child on his back while his wife carried the food and water. The left side of the wall showcased two paintings, one of Bob Marley and the other of Harriet Tubman. The other side of the wall contained a painting of black people dancing, and the other, of a black band playing. The room was completed with a desk and a Panasonic cordless telephone with caller ID and a note pad. The carpeting in the room was of a light grayish color. There was nothing on the recently vacuumed floor except for a pair of men's slippers.

Rashaun knew something most men did not know—that presentation meant everything. He had learned to present himself with confidence bordering on arrogance and unwavering manliness. He walked in his confidence, ego, masculinity, pride, and his penis ready from the foreplay in the bathroom. To him fucking was an art and he understood all the intricacies of that special talent. He stood at the bottom of the bed, waiting for her eyes to adjust to the light. He looked in her eyes as they feasted on him. A smile broke his lips apart. As he walked to the bed, she lifted her body off the mattress and knelt with her arms open.

He took her right hand and put the two middle fingers into his mouth. He tasted the depths of her womanhood. She had already started.

She was ready.

She brought her face close to him, expecting a kiss but instead he hugged her, almost squeezing the breath out of her. He felt like a god and she was his offering. She was his to mold and shape with his hands, mouth, and whatever else he might wish to use. He felt her hardened nipples against his bare chest. He methodically kissed behind her right ear, making sure both lips touched her neck simultaneously. He started with feathery kisses all down her neck and continued down her back. His tongue traced the track of her spine. She lay on her stomach, spread eagle for him or a thousand men. His tongue and lips continued to trace lines from her neck to her toes. She started to wriggle her body as she accepted his touches. She tried to turn around, but he held her down with his powerful arms.

She begged him to turn her over to enter her, but he wasn't

listening to her mouth, he was only responding to her body.

He pulled himself away from her, at the same time turning her over. She hardly felt her back touch the blue silk sheets. He took her hands from her side and spread them wide, then did the same to her legs. She was again ready to be sacrificed. Her body, the holder of her mind, was his to do as he pleased. Only a yearning that left her paralyzed to the king-size bed bonded them. He pulled himself up as swiftly and lightly as a ballet dancer with his knees between her legs and his hands by his side, his head bowed. Once again, he was unborn. She looked at him motionless waiting for what she knew had to come.

His actions took about fifteen minutes, yet it seemed like an hour. He put his hands next to her outstretched arms; his knees next to her waist followed them. His manhood barely touched her womanhood. She attempted to grab him to pull him inside her, but he quickly brought his knees up and stood over her. His fingers and toes were the only things touching the bed. A small dark spot on the sheet under her buttocks had begun to expand. He brought his hands to her face and gently held them with his palms. His face followed with his tongue barely visible in his half-opened mouth. Then he started . . .

His first kiss was a soft one with his lips lightly touching her right cheek. Another one followed, this time his tongue darting out to lick her eyebrows. She moved her hands toward his shoulders, but he stopped them in midair. He tightened his grip on her wrist and rested her hands back to their original position. She ignored the pain she felt in her wrist because the kisses were coming much faster now. The kisses with the flickering tongue traveled the length of her body. They finally settled on her left breast. First, he barely touched her nipple with his tongue as she heaved her body toward his perched mouth. Then all of a sudden, he had quarter of her breast in his mouth, his right hand finding its way to cover her womanhood. He moved his hands back and forth around her eagerness. Then his tongue traveled from the left breast to the right. Simultaneously the right middle finger had found the pulse to her pleasure.

Her eyes were closed and her mind lingered on the perfect marriage of mind and body. His right hand and his mouth continued their assault on the moving body, and his left hand knowingly reached for the Saran Wrap. He hated to use it, but life in the nineties had its dangers.

His tongue had left her nipples and was now tracing her belly button on its way down. Seven-inch- by six-inch Saran Wrap fitted perfectly over her womanhood. As he slipped his finger out, his tongue bored into the plastic.

Her upper body continued to rise and fall, as his tongue became her world. His tongue maneuvers resonated for more than twenty minutes, ignoring the three times her body broke up in convulsions. Her bottom had been off the bed for over fifteen minutes. Once more, he reached to the left of the headboard, his hands settling on a small white package. He withdrew his tongue and threw the Saran Wrap to the floor. He ripped the covering off the package and pulled the ring out of its case. In the meantime, his big right toe had taken over the maneuvering of his tongue. When the condom was finally in place, he removed his toe.

His right hand had slipped back inside her.

She had recovered enough energy to scream for him. She wanted to control his body the way he had controlled hers. With a powerful thrust, she willed her pelvis upward and smiled. Then she took him inside her. As soon as he entered, her body trembled with rapture.

Then he felt it. He had felt it before, the feeling of worthlessness; the thoughts swarming in his head.

...How meaningless was it all? This was the third woman in two days and he still felt nothing. He got up and pushed her off his body. She threw herself at him only to fall on the floor as he went into the bathroom. She followed him. Her words were obscene; they were angry and thrown at him with piercing vengeance. She attacked his manhood, his mother, and his sexuality. He didn't hear a word of it. He was in his own world, a world she would never understand, and one he had created, void of feelings and emotions. His world had just closed in on him. He felt small and weak. He wanted so much more from life, but the life he had was the one he had chosen. He thought about calling his mother, and then dismissed it with the ignorance of pride. He sank down onto the cold bathroom floor. He wanted to cry but he couldn't, the tears lost in his eyes. He had created a meaningless sexual world and every woman was vulnerable to his charm, but no one knew his name, and he didn't care to let them know.

For the first time he was afraid of what he had become, a runner fleeing the life he feared. He missed the closeness of loving. There were no emotions involved now and he had become what he once hated. The superficiality of the moment sank him deeper into himself. He was a performer in a recurring movie, with costars changing and little else. He listened to their bodies but never looked at their hearts. He gave them answers to their physical longings and ignored their hearts' desire, and in most cases that was enough to keep them coming back. For those who wanted more, he sent them fishing, but with each new conquest, he lost a little bit of himself.

Rashaun put on his red silk boxer shorts and stepped out onto the patio. It had started to rain again. It was sunny one minute, and raining the next. Like a bad woman, the weather was constantly changing. He took a deep breath and looked up at the sky; somewhere up there were plans being made for him. His script was already written, and it was up to his conscience to follow it. He did not know where his journey would take him and what he had to do, but then again, that was not for him to know. A man never knew what was expected of him until those expectations were not met.

"Fuck you, asshole!" She slammed the door as she stormed out.

"**W**hat's up, man?" George asked in his deep Trinidadian accent.

"Nothing much," Rashaun replied as he shifted the car from second to third and sped along Kings Highway. He loved driving, envisioning his car like blood racing through his body.

"So—did you bust her out?"

Rashaun didn't reply.

"Come on, man. Was it good to you?" George kept on, pushing his waist back and forth on the black leather seat.

"I didn't finish it."

"What?"

"I said, I didn't finish it."

"Yo, I hate when a woman do that to me. One time she want it, then some kind of fuckery goes on in her head and she don't want it no more. What the fuck she think we are, robots or something"

"It wasn't her. It was me."

"What?"

"There's got to be something more."

"You mad, boy." George paused a second to contemplate. "You get top sirloin like that and you fess. Blacky, you must be losing it." George leaned back on the seat with a look of exhaustion and rolled his eyes. He was disappointed he wouldn't get to hear some lurid, detailed sex story. "You mean that girl came by your house, opened her legs to you, and you went to the corner of the room and started crying. Rashaun, one day your ignorance is going to kill you!"

"Not exactly, I went to the bathroom."

"Damn, man, you making me ashamed of you, giving up pussy like that. One day, when you're seventy, you'll say to yourself 'I should've had this pussy and that pussy.' "

"I just couldn't go through with it. George, there must be more to life."

"Oh, shit, don't tell me you couldn't get your dick hard." This time he turned to look at Rashaun.

"Nah, that wasn't it," Rashaun said. With relief, George patted Rashaun on the back.

"Man, you were supposed to hook me up with her friend.

Now you don't get pussy and I don't get pussy. You fucked up."

"Like you need more pussy. How many girls you fucking? Ten? Eleven?"

"That's not the point, man. The thing is, you should never let the pussy go to waste."

"You don't understand, do you?" Rashaun glanced at his friend, hoping to get him to see where he was coming from.

"Let me hear," George said, sitting upright in his seat. "Let me hear one good reason why you give up good pussy."

"It just didn't feel right," Rashaun explained, sounding almost apologetic.

"You know what, Rashaun, I think you are ready to get married," George said exasperated. "You want what I have."

"No George, I'm definitely not looking for what you have," Rashaun insisted as he made a left turn onto Sumpter Street. "What you have is a security blanket that allows you the option of testing all the other girls who come along without having to commit yourself to anything but a fuck. Your wife, Joanna, is a nice girl, a little bit too nice for you."

"What do you mean she's too nice for me?" George's voice took on an irritated high pitch.

"What I mean, George, is that the damn girl just had a kid for you and during six months of her pregnancy when the doctor said she couldn't have sex because of complications, what were you doing?" George eased up a little from his seat. Rashaun continued, "You were fucking Saundra who lived downstairs from you, and you were fucking that other girl on the job. What's her name again?"

"Debra," George said.

"Have you ever been with Joanna at least one year without fucking around?"

George scratched the top of his head andsmall flakes of dandruff fluttered onto his shirt.

"But I treat my woman good. I take care of my woman," George maintained. "Joanne has no complaints in or out of bed. This is one black man who takes care of his family."

"You do take care of your family, George, but you are also exposing the woman you love to a whole lot of shit."

"Rashaun, you don't understand women, and one day if you don't protect yourself, you will be destroyed. You have a good heart,

Rashaun, a tender one, and one day if you don't put some lead in it, you will be sorry."

Rashaun pulled the car outside of his friend's two-car garage and parked next to George's black Lincoln Navigator, the vehicle George referred to as the pussy finder.

"Forget about me, George. You need to check yourself because what you are doing to your wife is not right. Our people have made unlimited sacrifices in our fight to be given a choice, and you are taking that basic right from her. You need to grow up and be a man, whose masculinity is not measured by the amount of conquests he has made, but his ability to keep one woman content. Look at me." They walked toward the house. "I could fuck a different woman every night, but do I? Well, sometimes I do, but that's not the point. I am jealous of you, George you have . . ."

"Hi, honey." Joanne opened the front door, her face smooth and sensuous. She was beautiful by any standards. Her hair was cut in a short fade, low on the sides and high on the top; it was similar to a flat top except the top was more rounded. Her stomach did not have the pouch that was a telltale sign of recent childbirth. And for a woman relaxing at home, she was remarkable groomed. Her perfectly rounded teeth lit up her face, reminding Rashaun of the model/actress Shari Belafonte. Rashaun was always pleased to see Joanne. She had a way of making him feel welcome.

"I don't know how you do it, Joanne, but you just had a baby and look at you."

"That's my girl." George held Joanne in his arms and kissed her on the lips.

"You have a beautiful woman, George," Rashaun said as he pushed the door closed.

"By the way, honey, Debra called. She wanted to remind you of the four-day conference in June."

"Thanks. honey," George said. "Where is my little man?"

"George, you didn't tell me about that conference, must be real important." Rashaun smiled as he saw his friend grimace, "Is Joanne going?"

"You know I hate flying, Rashaun?" Joanne said as she led them up the stairs.

George told Rashaun that the technique to getting away with cheating was to introduce your woman to the woman you were cheating with. Therefore, everything is always in the open. If he went out to lunch with her one day and his wife saw her, there was no explanation necessary.

As Rashaun watched George and his family together, he wondered if he would ever have a family like that. He had lost his trust in women a few years ago. He and his ex-girlfriend used to live in an apartment building in downtown Brooklyn. He had been seeing this girl for four years and they had plans to get married. Rashaun lived for that girl; whatever she wanted he would give to her. Then one day he was taking the stuff out of one of the drawers she used for storing junk so he could put away a lovely necklace he had just brought for her. He was going to surprise her. He had asked her about the drawer before, and she said it was shut tight and couldn't be opened. She said she had some junk in there so it didn't matter anyway. She already had more space than she needed. He took a knife, shimmered all around the drawer, and pulled it open. It was then the letters dropped onto the floor. They were labeled to my love, honey, my endless love. In addition to the letters, there was videotape and audiocassettes. Rashaun ripped the letters open and read with a vengeance. His hands became clammy and his body hot. Even though the letters were addressed to his girlfriend, they were signed with different initials. He didn't want to cry because a man never cried, but the tears came anyway. After finishing reading the letters, which were very explicit in their sexual content, he picked up the videotape and went to the VCR.

The videotape had blackfunk written all over it. The first person he saw on the videotape was his best friend with whom he had spent countless nights in his apartment with his girlfriend. They would study for law school exams and talk about their future after graduation. Rashaun's mother never liked him because she said there was deceit, jealousy, and envy in his eyes. Rashaun told her he was one of his best friends. His mother's remark was that she couldn't tell him who to be friends with but to watch out for him. The video had a date written on it, a date he remembered very well. He remembered his girl saying she couldn't be with him for two weeks because she was bleeding. In fact, she could hardly sit properly. He had felt so sorry for her. She said she went to the doctor and he told her there was nothing to be worried about, so he gave her some antibiotics and told her to abstain from sex. Now he watched her come into the room in a pink teddy with the buttocks and the crotch cut out. The video had to be taken by someone in the room because the person was zooming in for closeups and zooming back out for the wide-angle shots. The video told tales the letters and the audiotapes couldn't. He recognized his friend's apartment from his frequent visits. He and his friend once slept on the bed when they had come home drunk after a party. His woman always said she hated his friend's apartment because it was always so dirty.

He watched with a throbbing pain in his head as his woman jumped into his friend's arm and stuck her tongue in his mouth. For the next hour and a half, Rashaun watched his friend totally destroy the insides of his woman's vagina. His friend seemed angry, almost mad the way he used her body. There was no lovemaking on the TV screen, only hate and vengeance. As Rashaun watched the tape, he could feel the pent-up anger almost as if his friend was trying to kill her. He seemed to be avenging everything that was done to him from the time he was born to now. When he left, her vagina was bloody and deformed, and then he went to her butt. He took the blood from her vagina and slapped it between her butt and looked into the camera smiling. Again, the cameraman came in for a close up. Rashaun knew his girl would not let him do that because she had told him she would never have anal sex. He watched as she took her right hand and parted her butt for his friend. When they were finished, his friend couldn't move and neither could his girl. The cameraman came in for one last closeup of his woman's butt that showed blood running all the way down the crack of her ass. Then the cameraman came back out for the wide view of them sleeping together on the bed.

After viewing the tape, Rashaun packed up some of his clothes and left. He took the tape with him and the gift he had just bought. That night, he slept at his mother's house with the videotape under his pillow. The next day he sent his friend a copy of the tape and with a note reading Thank You For Keeping Me From Making A Mistake. He never spoke to his girlfriend again. He saw his friend one more time, but they didn't say anything to each other. From that day on, sex was the only thing a woman could give him.

"I tried to do it right. I listened to my grandmother," Andria said as she pulled on her white dress.

"Go on," Dr. Wagner encouraged as she sat at her desk taking notes.

"You don't know what it's like growing up without your mother. I love my mother. I love my father, and I didn't have either one of them. Yet I still try to do my best."

"What do you mean by do your best?"

"I was a good girl. I did my schoolwork. I stayed away from boys and all that shit."

"Do you think that was expected of you?"

"Hell yeah."

"What else do you think was expected of you?" the doctor asked as she continued to write on her pad.

"Not to get pregnant," Andria answered. "There was no chance of that happening because I wasn't even sexually active until I turned twenty-one. I lost my virginity to this white boy in college. A white boy! And believe me it was horrible even though the boy was gentle. It pained me for a whole week after."

"Andria, why do you blame yourself?" The doctor had paused from scribbling on her pad.

"Who else am I suppose to blame? God?"

"Don't blame anyone," the doctor answered.

"Doctor, you don't understand. I gave this guy everything, and it was not enough. Damn, doctor! what's wrong with wanting to be happy? What's wrong with wanting to have a family? "

"Nothing."

"Doctor, I hate dating. I hate being out there. Do you know what's out there? I doubt you do. You most likely have your 2.5 kids, the vacation house, and the social events. Look at me. I have nothing." Andria walked around the office, stopping briefly to look out the window. The sunrays hit a couple walking with a poodle. She wondered if she would ever get to that point again.

"Andria, why do you think you need a man to make you happy?"

"Doctor, don't even go there. I am as liberal as the next

person, but a woman has never interested me."

"I didn't mean it that way." For the first time the doctor started to laugh.

"You didn't." Andria joined in the laughter. She stopped for a second. "I know this is the nineties and everything so I had to say that."

She walked back to the window and saw half of the couple come back. It was the woman with the dog.

"It's better that way," she shouted through the window.

"Andria, what are you talking about," the doctor asked.

"Just giving advice, just giving advice," she repeated, feeling a little bit exhausted.

Andria stayed at the clinic for three days, and then the doctor gave her the okay to return home. The doctor watched her leave through the door and looked up to the sky for guidance. She liked Andria, and she knew there was a lot more they didn't cover in her sessions with her. She hoped Andria would come back to see her regularly.

Andria continued to go to the clinic to see the psychiatrist, and upon her release from the program, she continued to see the psychiatrist privately.

She had taken a three-month leave from her job and lived off her savings. She left her apartment and moved in with her mother, where she stayed for two months before finding another apartment. Her mother never dated or even considered going out with another man since her father died. She worked and sat home and watched TV. She did not go out and rarely would she visit the rest of her family. In essence, her mother had given up on life. Andria and different family members tried talking to her, but she didn't listen to them. Andria would come home sometimes and find her mother crying. She would hold her mother in her arms until the tears stopped. Her mother would keep repeating, "I am sorry, it is all my fault."

Andria had her own problems to deal with. She would sometimes have nightmares that caused her to wake up screaming. Her mother would come to the room, turn the light on, and stay with her until she fell asleep. The nightmares continued when Andria moved to her new apartment. Even though she had many different nightmares, one kept reoccurring.

In the nightmare, she was in a big room surrounded by family and friends. The room was purple and on the walls were various pictures of her. The pictures ranged from her as an infant through childhood and finally as an adult. Loud music blasted from speakers she couldn't see and everyone was having a great time—except her. The party was for her, hence the pictures and all her family and friends, but she still felt sad and lonely.

She wanted to get up and tell them that she wasn't having a good time, but she couldn't. She looked around to see what was holding her, and there was nothing keeping her from standing. She shouted at the top of her lungs to get the group's attention, but no words came from her mouth. She saw her best friend, Robin, next to her and tried to pull on her to get her attention, but she couldn't seem to get a hold of her. Her mother sat next to her in a big white wedding dress that flowed six feet behind her. She kept staring at Andria and shaking her head. Andria tried to ask her why she was dressed up like that, but again no words came out of her mouth. She reached to touch her mother's hand, but her hands remained by her side.

Suddenly, the room became very quiet and a man in a black robe turned around to look at her. It was Paul. She screamed at the top of her lungs, pointing at Paul in his robe, but her hands didn't move, nor did her mouth. After he finished giving the sermon, he took his right hand, closed both her eyes, and plunged her into total darkness. It was usually then that she woke up, frightened and trembling, in total darkness.

"Fucking white assholes! I pay her salary and she treats me like that!" the tall light-skinned black man shouted as he walked into the office.

"What happened, Mr. Roundtree?" Rashaun asked as he motioned the man to a black couch, one of two facing his desk.

"Look at you, like if you ain't shit," Mr. Roundtree dropped his six-foot-five-inch frame onto the couch.

Rashaun did not necessarily like the people he worked with, but he understood them. He was one of the few black lawyers in the firm of Oystein and Oystein, a father-and-son law firm that operated out of the sixtieth floor of the Faustin Building in Manhattan.

Mr. Roundtree, in his white silk suit and matching suede shoes, stood out among the sea of blue, gray, and black suits that were the trademarks of his business. He also walked soundlessly, on the tips of his toes, almost giving the impression he was floating. If Rashaun had not heard his loud baritone voice, he would not have heard him approaching.

"Suck my black dick," was the final comment he expressed for the white people in the office and the world.

"Mr. Roundtree," Rashaun said as he sat back in his tall black leather chair.

"Rashaun, why don't you open your own practice instead of working for those white motherfuckers?"

"Everything in time, Mr. Roundtree," Rashaun answered as he ignored the fact that Mr. Roundtree never addressed him by his last name. Mr. Roundtree never addressed anyone who worked for him by his or her last name. It would be showing them too much respect.

"Mr. Roundtree, what exactly happened on Friday, June 10, at 3:00 P.M.?"

"I already told that other lawyer. Ask him."

"Mr. Roundtree, Stevens already gave me the notes on your case, but I would like for you to tell me in your own words." Rashaun took his pen from his jacket pocket and arranged a pad on the desk.

"Why?"

"Mr. Roundtree, I want to give you the best defense possible, but I cannot do it without all the information. It's up to you. I am not going to argue with you." Rashaun put his pen down on the pad and leaned back.

"Alright, I'll tell you."

"Keep in mind that I am your lawyer and whatever you say to me will be kept in strict confidence."

Rashaun already knew the basics of the case: Mr. Roundtree was accused of killing a man who he said tried to shoot him. He was arrested and charged with murder. Due to his prior drug conviction, he was out on bail for one million dollars. He had paid the bail money in cash a week after his arrest. His trial was set for the following month.

Mr. Roundtree took off his shoes and lay back on the couch. Immediately the room was filled with a fresh pine scent from his socks.

"Rashaun, circumstances make me who I am. I was once like you, an honest, hardworking man."

"Go ahead," Rashaun said. Of course, he disagrees with lawyers being honest, but he had to leave that for another day. This was his client's time; therefore, he relinquished the stage.

Mr. Roundtree stood and started to speak, his hands accompanying this mouth "This motherfucker comes up to me and starts shouting, I am going to kill you! I am going to kill you, right in front of my wife and my two kids. Rashaun, I carry a gun, but I very rarely take it out of its holster. The only reason I carry it is for protection. You know, a man like me has many enemies. You know black people, they jealous of a brother. You got to know. You a lawyer and shit." Mr. Roundtree paused and turned around to look at Rashaun for confirmation.

"Go ahead," Rashaun said not wanting to get into a discussion with his client.

"All right, so I send my wife ahead with the kids because I had to take care of business. By now there is a group of people on the sidewalk looking at this guy ranting and raving at me. I told him I didn't even know him, and I didn't have any beef with him. If he got the fuck out of my face, I wouldn't have to kill him. He started taunting me, telling me to go for it. I say, 'Holmes, I don't want no trouble with you, so I'll walk away.' So I tried to walk away from him."

"You were just going to walk away?" Rashaun asked.

"Yeah, I would let one of my boys find out who the fuck he was and take care of him later. I have a rep. You just can't disrespect a brother like that but you also have to be smart."

"Would you like a drink?" Rashaun asked as he made a move to the phone.

"Nah, I'm okay. You know I don't drink or smoke. Alcohol deadens the brain and drugs make you stupid. I have to deal with reality with a clean mind. I can't afford to make mistakes; in my business that will get you kill."

"Mr. Roundtree, we are getting away from the point here." Rashaun had stopped scribbling on his pad.

"So he stepped in front of me, and I pushed him aside." Mr. Roundtree had gotten up off the couch and was gesturing with his left hand to show Rashaun how he pushed the man aside.

"As I'm pushing the motherfucker aside, I see him reaching to his back around the waist. Now you know what that meant, right. It was either he or I. Plain and simple. The brother was going to take me out. So I grabbed my nine from my waist and I waited for the motherfucker." Mr. Roundtree took a nine-millimeter gun from his waist, and he held it in his hand.

"Mr. Roundtree, please put the gun away."

"Don't worry, the safety is on." He now held his hand straight with his finger on the trigger and pointed the gun out the window. "So the brother comes around with a forty-five, and that's the last time his mother saw him. I ripped ten shots in the motherfucker's face. I ain't no street shooter. I go to the range every Saturday and practice. I got a permit for my gun too. It was then those cops from the van came and drew on me. So, I dropped the gun. These cops and them saw everything, I swear to God."

Rashaun waited for Mr. Roundtree to put the gun back in his waist before he spoke. Little bubbles of sweat had started to form on Mr. Roundtree's forehead and his eyebrows twitched. Rashaun had seen men with guns before, men who had no right having guns. It was his passage of youth on the streets to not fear the gun but be cautious of the person behind it. He would have to give his client a few minutes to calm down. Rashaun leaned back in his chair and inhaled deeply.

36

After Mr. Roundtree had left, Rashaun received two phone calls, one from his mother inviting him to dinner, and the other from George reminding him that it was Friday and they were hanging out that evening.

Andria wasn't frightened of going back into the social scene; she was terrified. For a year, she avoided the public, repeatedly turning down offers to movies, plays, and even a trip to the Bahamas. It was a part of society that she had started to dread; every part of it screamed hurt and pain.

Two months ago, Paul had called her to say he was sorry for what happened and he hoped she had forgiven him. She explained she had no ill feelings toward him and, although she had forgiven him, she hoped never to see his fucking face again. He said he understood her anger, but hoped one day they could be friends.

After months of prodding by her friends, Andria finally decided to go to the Sequin Club located on Flicker Street in Queens. It was a West Indian club that her friends Paula and Judy had frequented. Paula was a native of Trinidad, and Judy was from Barbados. They both informed Andria that it was a West Indian club where people from the same origin came to party. In regards to the dress attire, they both insisted that torn-up jeans and sneakers were not allowed in the club. Andria damned the world and argued with them on the topic of comfortable clothes for dancing. Their argument centered on the guilt syndrome. Stated plainly, if Andria could not go in, all three of them would have to go home, seeing that she was driving. Andria agreed to dress in the proper attire. She did not tell them that she had been to a few West Indian clubs before, and she knew what they were like.

Her general opinion on clubs was that they were like flea markets with everyone peddling their wares. Different approaches here and there, but they were about all the same. For the first time in her life, she was nervous about going out on the social scene.

In high school and college, going out and dating was a simple feat. She wasn't putting out in college, so she got very few second dates. After all, residential colleges were full of people breaking loose from Mommy and Daddy for the first time. The most important thing to these young people was to be able to fuck as much as possible, and that they did. The funniest part was seeing boyfriends and girlfriends coming up for the weekend and walking around the campus holding their partner's hands. By the time they reached home Sunday night, their girl or guy would be in their campus lover's room. Andria rarely dated in college except for the white guy she lost her virginity to.

It was very different now. She had about fifty percent of her life left to live, and the stakes had become much higher. Now when she looked at someone, she was thinking about the possibility of getting married. She wanted to know which man would make a good father and a provider. She wanted more than just the roll in the hay and the pretty face to look at. She wanted substance, substance she could hold on to. She had passed the age of twenty-five and all of a sudden she felt like she was running out of time. As she got dressed for the party, she wondered if Mr. Right would be at the club. She had paid her dues to society. It was about time she found some happiness.

The club was a big flesh market, just as she expected, a market with animals of every species looking for something they had or something they wanted. Everything in this place was overdone. The women had on too much makeup, the guys had on clothes they could not afford, the music was too loud, and the drinks had too much alcohol or soda depending on the bartender. There were about five people in the whole club with their natural hair. The lonely, the lost, the searchers, the unsatisfied, and the pretenders were all there. Their faces were plastered with the unreal; the twisted walk was exaggerated to bring out the most in every curve. The last time Andria was in a place like this she was twenty-four years old, it seemed like twenty years ago when in fact it was only seven. The place was different, and the color of the people's skin ranged from yellow to black.

A few years ago when she was into the fast life, Andria visited clubs like this one. She had a good time and even met someone one night, a twenty-five-year-old man named Chris. She was twenty-two at the time. It was to be the start of her decline. He said all the right things and did all the wrong things. He took her on a roller-coaster ride with his lashes hitting against her back as he urged her to go forward. Two months after she started seeing him, he told her of what he called a "minor detail." He was married, but he was in the process of filing for a divorce. He said that his wife was trying her best to hold on to him, and she was making the divorce difficult. He kept her at bay with that for about a year until one night she found him at another club with another woman. When she asked the woman if Chris was her husband, the woman turned around and slapped Chris in his face. That was the end of that relationship.

Andria walked into the club with Paula and Judy at around one o'clock am on Saturday morning. They had waited outside in the line for half an hour before they got inside. Since then, the line had gotten much longer, extending around the club. As they walked in, she could feel the eyes of the men undressing them, taking in every detail of their movement. She had never considered herself overly attractive. If she judged herself by the compliments she received from men and women, she would conclude that she looked real good. She always thought of looking good where men were concerned to mean three things. First, you look good enough to fuck on a regular basis with no solid commitment. Second, you look good enough to fuck and have one of their babies. Third, you look good enough to make love with for the rest of their lives. Andria had gone through the first two stages, and she was finally at the last stage.

As soon as they walked in, a tall, light-skinned brother came up to Judy and asked her to dance. Judy looked him up and down before taking his hand as they walked toward the dance floor. She turned back and gave Andria and Paula a wicked smile.

"Poor Steve," Paula said as she saw Judy fit herself in the brother's crotch.

Andria and Paula did not see Judy again until an hour later, burying her pelvis into the same brother's groin in the corner of the room. Andria wondered what Judy's husband, Steve, would say if he saw her pelvis rotation at that moment. She also knew that the pelvis grinding would not end there. Before the night was over, Judy would be in this guy's car with her legs spread apart, scraping the ceiling with her toes. The night would end with Judy awakening her husband as soon as she got home to tell him she loved him. It was something she always did after she had a hot night out. The next day, Steve

39

would swear to his friends that Judy would never mess around on him because he was the best fuck she ever had. Judy was the first woman who openly told Andria she had a train done on her. Andria didn't know what she was talking about. Judy said it was when a few guys, maybe more than five, fuck you one after the other. In her case, she had ten guys one after the other. She was on her back for about three hours. She told Andria the hardest part was seeing these brothers on campus the following day. They all hang out in a group. Andria wondered if she would see Judy and Steve on the *Jerry Springer Show* one day.

Andria also remembered Judy telling her about a close call she once had. It was right before Thanksgiving, and Judy always had her eye on this guy named Roger from work. There was a small get-together after work that day because it was a coworker's birthday. She had told Steve she would be home a little late. During the dinner at So-Shows restaurant in downtown Brooklyn, Judy said she felt the attraction between her and Roger was mutual.

Judy went home with Roger that evening, and they slept together. She didn't notice that the condom she saw Roger put on when they began wasn't there at the end. She felt it though when he emptied himself inside her. It hit her inside and cascaded back down. She started to drip immediately, but it felt good. He looked at her and smiled as if he had fooled her. She got her clothes together and headed out the door. On her way out, he told her to say hi to Steve. She told him go fuck himself. She got home at nine o'clock and her husband was waiting for her. As soon as she walked through the door, he grabbed her and tore her clothes off. He immediately went downtown and was amazed at how excited his wife was. She told him to stop, but he wasn't hearing her. He had waited since seven o'clock for his wife to come home, and he was feeling horny as hell. Judy told Andria she felt so bad after, that she couldn't look at her husband for days. She felt ashamed of herself for a while, but like most things, she got over it.

Andria did not understand Judy. She had a man most women would die for, yet she tried her best to destroy the relationship. Judy claimed she loved her husband and would do anything to keep him with her. She told Steve how much she loved him almost every second of the day. She even told the guys she had affairs with that she would never give up her husband for anything in the world. Andria tried talking to her repeatedly, but her words went in one ear and out the other. Andria warned her that one day her world would come crashing down, and she wouldn't be able to do anything about it.

"Look at that," Judy said as she hit Andria on the arm. "Isn't he gorgeous?" Andria felt the hit on the arm and turned around angrily. When she saw that it was her friend, she relaxed her posture. Andria followed the direction of Judy's eyes to settle on the same brother she was dancing with earlier. His face had a chiseled look, reminding her of a Drakkar commercial she was so fond of. He was heading toward them with two drinks in his hands.

"He's married too," Judy said, "I love it." She sounded like a schoolgirl who just got some candy and couldn't wait to dive into it.

"Judy, what about your husband?" Andria said, reminding Judy she had other commitments. She knew she was wasting her time, but she felt she had to try anyway.

"What about Steve?" Judy remarked, "I give him more than he could handle; just because a girl wants to get a little extra flavor now and then, what's wrong with that?"

Andria looked in her friend's eyes and knew that she had already made her mind up. If Steve had been at the party, Judy would have found an empty closet or a bathroom where she could fuck that man.

The brother gave Judy the drink and settled his eyes on Andria. Andria knew instantly that he wanted them both, and if the opportunity presented itself, he would take advantage of it. He was a player, not a player for now but one for life.

"I might not need a ride home after all," Judy said as she accepted the drink from the man whose eyes had found an interest in Andria.

Andria looked at him with disdain avoiding direct eye contact. He smiled at her, ignoring Judy for the moment.

Judy was easy. He knew that even before he asked her to dance. Andria was a challenge. He was sure Judy had a man at home. Andria was not in that class and he liked that. He was upset for asking Judy to dance. He should have waited and asked Andria. She was looking at him angrily, but that's because she didn't know him. He

41

estimated that she had only fucked about four to five men. In this game, he knew the players. Anyone who didn't wouldn't last long. Judy tugged at his arm, and he realized a bird in the hand was better than a rare one in the bush. He wished she would stop pulling on his jacket unless she was willing to buy him a new one. His wife had brought him that one.

Judy saw the interplay and tugged on his arm, telling him how she loved the song that was now thumping in their ears. It was an old song by Teddy Pendergrass in which love was promised for an eternity. As he walked away with Judy, he glanced back at Andria and smiled. Andria looked at him and shook her head.

"Another dog," Paula said, confirming Andria's thoughts. Paula concentrated on the music until she noticed Judy's newfound man's attention on Andria. From years of knowing Judy, Paula knew what her reaction would be. Andria was not into that shit. It took three months for Andria's last man to get some pussy. He sent her to the hospital two years later, but that was life. In this life, anyone could snap at anytime.

Paula herself felt like snapping a few times. God knew she had been through enough. For every good man out there, there were twenty with the stamp "dead end" on their foreheads. Paula felt she alone had found nineteen of them. The last man she had dated a few years ago turned out to be a drug addict. After giving up her apartment to move in with him, she found herself supporting a thirty-five-year-old man who'd lost his job and had resorted to selling everything in the house. In a matter of months, they didn't have a television or a VCR, when previously they had two of each. The final straw came when she came home tired from work and had found the sofa bed and love seat in the living room had vanished. Then she found her man on the kitchen floor shivering as he put the lighter to the glass stem.

The club had become very crowded, and Andria and Paula pushed their way toward the bar. As they went through the maze, hands came from all over, pulling on their hands, touching their butts and taking any quick feel afforded them by invisibility. She now remembered what she hated most about the club scene. One invisible hand tried to reach between her legs, but the person ended up with a painful memory. Andria had her keys in her hand, and she sent them down onto the hand with all the force she could muster. She heard the wince but didn't turn around or stop walking. She looked at her house keys and saw an inkling of blood on them. She took tissues from her bag and wiped it off. When they finally got to the bar, they had to wait for a space to slip in so the bartender could see their faces.

"It's on me," Judy said, as she was the lucky one to break through first.

"Excuse me, ladies, can I buy you all a drink" The man was sitting at the bar. From the look on his face, that position had been his for about twenty-five years the first time he was legal to drink. He had a long Jheri curls, a remnant of his glorious past. It seemed he was the only one who didn't know that it was years out of style. From the way he sat with his feet barely touching the floor, Paula estimated his height to be about five feet two inches.

"No thank you," Paula answered.

He immediately turned to Andria.

She looked at him, amazed that he wanted her answer too. "No thank you," she said as Paula signaled the bartender to come over.   At the bar, Paula ordered rum and Coke for herself and a ginger ale for Andria.

This time they didn't go back the same way they came. They walked to the edge of the dance floor and stood there sipping their drinks. There was a little more space at the edge so Andria finally was able to breathe.

"Much better," Paula said as she stretched her hand out in front of her. They had changed the music to reggae, and Andria started to move her hips to the beat. Even though Andria was born in America, her parents were from Jamaica, and between the ages of six and eighteen, she had traveled there at least once a year. She had stopped after her eighteenth birthday only to return there with Paul, two years earlier. They had a great time because she had plenty of family and friends there. She took Paul all over the country. Except for the first night, she was sick and couldn't go out so she told Paul to go to the beach and enjoy himself.

On his way down from the hotel room, Paul heard music coming from the ballroom. He went inside, and lo and behold, there was a party going on. He quickly went to the bar and ordered a drink. There he noticed this pretty girl watching him. He told the bartender to buy her whatever she was drinking. He took out his American dollars and paid the tab. Before he knew it, the girl was at his side.

"Foreign ah?" That was the only phrase he understood from her for the whole night. After about an hour of dancing and drinking, he led her down to the beach, and that night Paul came on the beach in Jamaica. When he got back to the room, he went straight to the shower and took a long one. After the shower, he got into bed with Andria. She asked him how was his first night in Jamaica. He said "Irie, man. Irie, man." She laughed and hugged him, and they fell asleep with the windows open and that beautiful Jamaican breeze flowing over their bodies.

"Can I have this dance?"

Andria looked up to see six feet two inches of very dark man staring at her. His eyes were glossy black, almost dazzling. They kept her drawn to him. It was as if he were looking deep down into her soul. It gave her a queasy feeling inside. She felt an immediate attraction to him, and she wasn't sure why. Yet, this was the nineties and anyone who played him or her would be played in the worst way. Well, at least that's what Paula told her.

She looked away from him and said, "No thank you." Her response was forced, and somehow her voice had been reduced by a couple of decibels.

"What happened? You don't dance or you just don't like this song?" He smiled, showing his perfect teeth.

"I do dance, but I just don't feel like it at the moment." She couldn't hold his stare. She wanted him to leave her alone, yet at the same time, she wanted him to stay.

Paula looked at her and smiled. She knew her friend was immediately attracted to that guy. She didn't know why though. When she looked at him, all she saw was darkness. She didn't like darkness. The light was her thing. If he wasn't two shades lighter than she was, he wasn't getting in.

Andria felt nervous and waited for his next move. She didn't know why, but she wanted him to say something else. The words that came after, she wasn't expecting. She had no response for them. Neither did they warrant a response.

"Thank you," he said and turned to leave. Two ladies approaching the bar hampered his exit. Their eyes traced every outline of his body. They smiled as he excused himself and headed in the direction of the railing separating the dance floor from the tables

44

that were elevated on the side.

"He seems nice," Paula said as she took a deep pull on her straw. "A bit too dark for me though, black and black make tar babies."

"He is the first one for the night who actually asked me to dance without playing tug-of-war with my arm," she said, taking another sip of her drink.

"So why didn't you dance with him?" Paula asked.

"I want to see what he does," Andria said, as her eyes became fixated on her recent suitor.

"Here we go again," Paula said. And they both looked at each other and started to laugh.

Rashaun walked back to where he was standing by George and Debra, who both knew what was coming next.

"I told you she wasn't going to dance with you," George said smiling. "You don't have any big gold chain around your neck or you not pulling out the one-hundred-dollar bills. I told you these women are trifling."

"She is sweet," Rashaun said as he retained his position on the side of George. George leaned against the wall and Debra leaned against him, her body rocking to the music erupting from the speakers.

"What's so nice about her?" Debra jumped into the conversation. "She looks like a wanna-be, wanna-be everything she is not."

"I doubt that very much, Debra. She doesn't look like that type of girl." Rashaun watched a woman dressed in a skintight red outfit parade herself in front of him. Every curve in her body was visible. He could have sworn that was the exact same outfit an ex-girlfriend of his used to wear to bed. These outfits only look good on a very select number of people in the world, and this girl happened to be one of them. Her body was made for this outfit. He gazed at her, admiring each well-placed curve. She looked at him and smiled, enjoying every bit of the touch less foreplay. Then she reached into her purse, took out a cigarette, and opened her full lips to accept her habit. Her hand went back into her bag, but before she could bring out a lighter, another hand appeared by her mouth with a low flame bellowing to the end of her cigarette. It was a short, pudgy, fat hand with a solid gold bracelet hanging loosely from it. She did not trace the hand that held the lighter to the person offering his favor; instead, she continued to stare at Rashaun. He did not like women who smoked. Granted he would fuck them, but he would not have a relationship. Cigarette smoking was a big turnoff for him. He had met women like her before; they preyed on the weakness of flesh.

"Do you want to dance?" His transfixion was broken by the female voice. He wondered who had the nerve. The girl he was looking at looked to the side of him. He didn't want to turn around and look. Always the fat or ugly ones summoned the nerve to ask a guy to dance. He turned slowly, letting his whole body go with the motion. Occasionally, he had no problem with charity. When he saw who it was he was shocked.

Andria finally had dealt deep within herself and got up the courage to ask him to dance. She chided herself for not telling him that she wasn't ready to dance before but maybe later. It was the standard line if there was interest; she had been out of the loop for too long. "You seen enough?" Andria had been watching him all the time, yet she didn't know why she said that.

"I don't think so, never enough of you." He took her hand and started to make his way onto the dance floor.

"Are you one of them?"

"Never one of them."

"Player?" She followed him unto the dance floor.

He was running and they were coming faster and faster. They were hungry, all ten of them. He could hear the clatter of their teeth. They seemed to be pulling him back by the sheer force of their willpower. He felt his legs pumping, pumping, as they never had before, yet he was not advancing. He let out a loud screeching wail that seemed to come from way inside of him. He had done nothing wrong; he did not even know them. What could they possible have against him? They were twenty feet away, and he could finally see the shiny metal. At the tip of each of their fingers were razor blades, glittering from the light, emitting from the middle of their palms. They said nothing as they drew closer. Suddenly, he realized why he couldn't run. He was curled up inside his mother's womb. As he made one last futile attempt to escape, an outside force penetrated his unconsciousness.

The ringing brought him out of his dream and into present-day reality. He pushed the top end of the blue silk sheets over his shoulders down to his waist. He picked up the phone with his wet sticky right hand. It felt cold and lifeless. "Hello?" The sweat from his face dripped down onto the black Sony cordless phone.

"Hello, Rashaun. Do you know who this is?" The soft female voice soothed his shattered nerves. He needed time to gather his thoughts and gain some kind of perspective.

"What?"

No, not again. He was tired of going through this guessing game. And this early morning was not the time for him to start the day with bullshit. He thought he recognized the voice, but he wasn't sure, and he wasn't in the mood to take a chance.

"Sorry, I don't recognize the voice, but how are you doing? You have my home number so it must be someone I want to talk to."

"I'm doing good."

Now he remembered the voice. It was Andria, the woman he met in the club about a week ago. "Andria, it took you long enough to call me."

She hesitated for a second, tapping her pen on the desk. "Excuse me."

"I was expecting a phone call a few days ago." He sat up on

the bed and glanced around the room, trying to decide what to do next. Maybe it wasn't going to be such a bad day after all.

"I didn't tell you I was going to call a few days ago. You said to call you the next day."

"So why didn't you?"

"I was busy, anyway it's none of your business."

"Okay, hold your horses." He could sense her getting irritated on the line. "Andria, I'd love to talk to you some more, but I have to get to work. Let me have your number, and I will call you later." He walked to the bathroom and looked in the mirror. "Boy, you look terrible"

"What did you say?" Andria barely heard what she thought he had muttered to himself.

"I was talking to myself."

"Is that a habit of yours? Tell me now so I know what to expect."

He laughed, happy that someone could make him laugh this early in the morning. He went back to the room and took off his blue silk pajamas. He neatly folded them on the bed that was barely disturbed even though he had slept on it for over seven hours.

"Nope. I only do it sometimes when I'm trying to get my thoughts together."

"Here is my phone number."

He ran to his desk and jotted down her home and job numbers. He went back into the bathroom, this time with a blue towel around his waist. The inside tiles above the tub were baby blue held together with white caulking. He squirted the body wash onto the spongy washcloth and turned the shower on. He stayed away from the water while he adjusted the cold and the hot to a warm mixture. He took the shampoo bottle and set it on the side of the tub, then took the extended shower spray he had recently brought and drenched his body. At that moment, he began to sing. As he sang, he wondered where Andria was and what she was doing.

Andria was at work. She had been in the office for about thirty minutes before making the call. She had tried calling him twice before, but each time she had gotten his answering machine. She didn't leave any messages. She did not know if he would even remember her. She spoke to her friends and mother about Rashaun before deciding to call again. She didn't know why she did that, but for some reason, she needed their consent. Paula maintained he was too black while Judy and Robin told her to give him a shot. Her mother was neutral, leaving the decision up to her. She then wrote his number in her things to do book and tried it. She called him at a time when she was sure he would be home.

Andria felt relieved after she finished speaking to Rashaun, like a burden had been lifted off her shoulders. She sat back in her chair for about ten minutes after the conversation, her mind blank as a foreign check. She did not look at the folder placed on her desk this morning by her supervisor. She already had an idea about what was in it. It was always the same. The city was full of children with problems.

When Andria finally opened the folder, she did not look at the case synopsis. Instead, the picture of a boy and the girl with smiles as bright as those in toothpaste commercials held her attention. They were of Indian heritage, most likely from Guyana, she assumed. She was also certain that the picture was not taken recently. If it were recently, she would not be seeing it now. No, these kids were in the system now, which meant somewhere along the line they got fucked.

Andria put the pictures aside and began to read about the kids' plight. The boy was eleven years old and his sister was nine. Both parents were dead and an uncle was killed around the same time. The kids had seen their father kill their mother and uncle after he had caught them in bed. The mother had pleaded with the father to let the children leave before he shot them, but he didn't. He shot them both right before their eyes. Usually the next of kin would have taken the kids, but they refused. The kids' relatives believed the children were cursed; therefore, they wanted no part of them. Recently, however, an uncle had petitioned the court for the kids, and it was Andria's job to make sure he could provide them with a fit home.

The kids also suffered from many psychological ailments. The boy had terrible nightmares in which the father turned the gun on him. He didn't like going to sleep because he was scared of the nightmares. This made him restless and irritated during the day, causing him to constantly fight with kids in school. The girl was constantly rubbing her vagina and making sexual comments to the kids in her school. Many times the teacher had to separate her from the rest of the class. The kids were receiving counseling three times a week to deal with their trauma. They had been in the system for a year, living with a foster mother in Queens.

Andria finished reading all the information, she made two phone calls. The first one was to the foster mother to make an appointment to see the children and the other to the uncle to have a meeting with him. She hoped the uncle would help the kids and bring back some sunshine into such young lives. She made a mental note to pray for the kids when she went to church on Sunday.

Rashaun hated suits. He felt like a stuffed rabbit in them. They limited his freedom, but he understood that in his profession, it was a necessity. He looked good in them too. He looked at his watch; it was 6:30 P.M. He extended his strides, making his leather bag swing as he walked. He promised the guys he'd meet them at the South Street Seaport at seven o'clock. He knew George would get there at six, just after he went home and changed his clothes. Before he got there, he also knew that George would have had two drinks. Then, of course, when he and Tyrone got there, George would insist that drinks were on them.

"Rashaun, over here."

He looked around among the sea of suits and found George the exception. George had on a collarless white shirt over a pair of black jeans. Rashaun pushed his way towards his friend who was sitting by the oval bar. His height and size limited the occasional retaliation from people who didn't want to be touched in a crowded area. Next to George were two empty seats. Rashaun took the third chair so that a seat separated him from George. Two white guys standing next to him with drinks in their hand growled at him.

"The same to your mother," Rashaun said as he turned the seat to face George.

"George, how did you manage to keep those seats?" Rashaun asked as he motioned for the bartender. He watched George finish almost a quarter of his drink in one gulp.

"With this, my man, NYPD," George said as he pulled out a fake police badge his cop friend had given to him.

"The usual?" Rashaun asked George as the bartender came over.

George lifted his glass and put it back down. "You know me, chief."

As Rashaun spoke to the bartender, George took the opportunity to screen the bar for the seventh time since he'd gotten there. First he looked to the left, and then slowly he twisted the seat around in a half circle, taking in all the people in that region.

"There goes the asshole," George said to Rashaun.

"Still chasing the pussy," Rashaun said as their eyes both converged on their friend Tyrone.

"Playing the quantity game again. I told him he had to chill. With seven women to one man, a brother should never have to chase a woman," George said as he took a sip of his drink.

Rashaun raised his drink to George, and they clicked their glasses. He had also brought a drink for Tyrone, which he put on the table in front of the empty chair.

"Tyrone will always be Tyrone," Rashaun said as he ingested the seven different rum flavors plus Coke that made up a Long Island Ice Tea.

"Here, guys, beeper number, cellular phone number, job number, and home number"

"What about Weight Watchers' number?" George remarked and reached over to high-five Rashaun. They both started to laugh.

"That's cold, guys, really cold," Tyrone said, shaking his head as he picked up his drink.

"Hey, Ty, that's where she'll be spending most of her time, so just throw away the rest of the numbers." George took another glance toward the girl Tyrone had been talking to. She held a large plate of French fries in her hand.

Tyrone followed his gaze. "She is a little bit heavy, isn't she?" he asked the question to no one in particular.

"Definitely not my type."

"We know, Rashaun. You like them tall and slim like your meager ass," George said as he turned around to pick up his quickly disappearing drink. He had thrown back two-and-three-quarter drinks and was a mile from a buzz.

"We know how you like them, George, short and thick."

"Check nine o'clock," Tyrone said as his eyes became fixated on a girl who had sat down at the bar. He quickly moved his chair back.

"Not bad at all," George said as he, too, started to watch the woman.

"I could work with that. Definitely workable," Rashaun agreed as he, too, gave her his attention. Tyrone was already out of his seat and moving toward the girl.

"There he goes," Rashaun said as he watched Tyrone. "He will be back soon," he then added as the woman they were giving all their attention to was joined by a big guy, at least six-five, more three hundred pounds.

Rashaun and George started to laugh as they saw Tyrone make his way back. Then suddenly he stopped and looked toward the opposite end of the bar. It was then that Rashaun and George saw what held Tyrone's fascination.

Andria had reluctantly agreed to meet Paula and Judy after work. They had also invited Robin, but she did not intend to fight through the maze of people at the South Street Seaport. She went there when she wasn't pregnant and that was bad enough. No, she wasn't about to go there with a big stomach. Judy and Paula had gotten there first because they left work early. Andria did not get there until 7:30 P.M. thanks to a coworker who wanted her to accompany her on a case visit.

"Andria, you have an admirer," Paula said as she saw Tyrone fixated on her friend. She didn't see Rashaun and George giving them an equal amount of attention.

Judy looked over at Tyrone, "Short but cute."

"Not interested," Andria said and turned away from Tyrone's gaze.

"There you go being picky again," Judy said as she returned Tyrone's gaze.

"Maybe he will buy us drinks or something. Short men love to please," Paula said as she looked down at her dwindling glass of wine. She took another sip and looked around the small table they were sharing. Judy's rum and Coke was half-empty, and Andria's ginger ale was almost gone.

"Why should three educated, working black women have to wait for some man to buy them a drink. Ladies, next round is on me," she said as she pulled her purse from the Coach briefcase she lifted from her shoulders.

"That's right, Andria. We could do it all for ourselves," Paula said as she knocked her glass on the bar. "Give me the money. I will go get it."

"Speak for yourselves, ladies. There is a lot a man could do for me." Judy had finally turned around and sat at the table. She had lost Tyrone as a short, fat white man stepped in her path.

"I can't believe it," Rashaun said. "Did you see who it was,

53

George?"

"Yeah, I saw her," George said as he turned sideways to face his friend. "There is something about that girl I don't like, but, brother, it's your world."

"George, you don't even know the girl."

"I know, but there is just something. Just be careful. My brother."

"I'm always careful."

"Not where your heart is concern. You fall hard." George took a deep gulp of his drink. "Remember your last girlfriend about six years ago? You still sleep with that videotape under your pillow."

"Did you see them?" Tyrone had joined them back at the bar.

"Tyrone, the one with the short hair is taken," George said as he watched Paula make her way to the bar.

"Damn, that's the one I wanted." Tyrone looked around the bar. "So you know whose controlling that? Maybe I can get in on the sneak tip."

"I don't think so, Tyrone you are already in the open."

"Not you, George." Tyrone looked exasperated, "You are a married man, yet you have more outside pussy than us single guys."

"Not me, Ty."

"It's the big man."

They both looked at Rashaun. He was looking over at Andria and her friends, trying to decide whether he should go over. He felt his friends' eyes upon him, so he turned back. "What, what?"

"Blacky, you controlling that?" Tyrone asked

"Don't look now, but Andria, do you see who's at the bar with Shorty?"

"You told me not to look, so how am I suppose to see who is at the bar?"

"It's that guy you met at the club."

"Rashaun?"

"Yeah, the tar baby."

"What guy?" Judy asked as her eyes swept the room. "You guys been holding out on me?"

"Don't worry, Judy, it was just one that you missed. After all, you can't fuck all the men, can you?"

"At least I'm getting some that has a pulse attached to it."

54

"Paula, where is he?" Andria asked as she searched the room.

"Look by the bar." Paula followed Andria's eyes. "No, not there, move to your right."

"Oh," Andria said and waved to Rashaun who had also been looking at her. He waved back.

"What bullshit is that, you guys waving like some school children?" George said as he watched the animation between Rashaun and Andria. "Go over there and talk to the girl."

"Nah, she's busy with her friends. I'll talk to her tonight."

"Well, Rashaun, seeing that you in there with what's her name?" Tyrone asked as he looked at Rashaun for the information.

"Andria," he answered.

"I'm going to see her friend. Thanks for the intro, Rashaun." Tyrone took his drink and headed toward Andria and her friends' table.

"Damn, he did it to us again. He was buying the next round."

"That short bastard."

Rashaun did not get home until ten o'clock that night. He took off his clothes, put his suit in a laundry bag, tied it up at both ends, and put the bag next to his front door. He made a mental note to take it to the cleaners the first thing in the morning. After that, he went straight to the shower with Andria on his mind. From the distance she had seemed properly dressed. She wore a tan sweater and a long black skirt. Well, he thought, it was long because he just saw a glimpse of it for a brief second when she tiptoed to wave at him. Her smile seemed vibrant and lively. He was still in the shower when the phone rang. He had the phoneon five rings before the answering machine picked up. After the third ring, he was out of the shower. He ran to the phone with his towel in his hands leaving a trail of water behind him and picked up the phone after the fourth ring.

"Hello?" Rashaun said as he dried himself with the towel.

"What's up, Blacky?" George asked. "Did you call her yet?"

"It's you."

"I guess that means you didn't call her yet."

The phone clicked signaling there was another call on the line.

"Hold on, George," Rashaun said and clicked the flash button to answer the incoming call.

"Hi," Andria said.

"Hold on, Andria. I have another call on the line." He clicked over the phone without hearing her say okay.

"George, I'll call you later."

"Hold up, Rashaun. I want you to remember what I told you."

"George, you told me so many things. What are you talking about?"

"Let me tell you again. This has been passed down by my father and my father's father."

"What are you talking about, how to treat a woman?"

"Yeah, like I said: Treat a woman like a queen, but always remember she is a bitch and what will a bitch do?"

"I remember, George, a bitch will sleep with your best friend, your brother, your sister, or your Doberman. She will take your money and laugh at you. She will make everyone else laugh at you, and if she is in danger, she will let your ass take the fall for her. Yeah, I remember that, George."

"And if you doubt that, just look at the videotape below your bed or remember your college days. Ain't shit changed."

"All right, George, the girl is waiting on the other line."

"See you later," George said and hung up the phone.

Rashaun clicked the phone back to Andria. "Did you have fun this evening?"

"Yeah, we did. How come you didn't come over?"

"I thought about it, but I didn't want to be intrusive."

They spoke for the next hour or so about the evening and their respective jobs. Rashaun asked Andria about Judy because she had given Tyrone her beeper number. Andria told him that Judy was married, but it was in name only. Rashaun told her it reminded him of someone he knew. At the end of the conversation, he had made a date with her for a dinner and a movie on Sunday. He would pick her up around seven, and they would head down to Brooklyn Heights.

The sun rose around five Sunday morning. Andria knew that because she was up at 4:30. She wanted to get up at 6:30, but some internal clock or a troubling or happy thought woke her up earlier. She tried to go back to sleep by staying in bed, tossing, but that didn't work, so she got up and turned on her radio. WBLS had just started its morning show. She liked listening to Hal Jackson on WBLS on

Sundays. It took her back to songs she had forgotten.

She didn't change from her long white T-shirt she had slept the night away in. Instead, she went straight to the kitchen, turned on the kettle, and put a peppermint herb tea bag in a white cup labeled to my best friend. She stood in the middle of the kitchen and tried to decide where to start. She was renting a one-bedroom apartment with a decent-size living room. Like most apartments, it was painted in an off-white semi gloss with the doors and cabinets deep brown in color. She went to the bathroom, took the dusting cloth from under the sink along with a variety of rags and spray can. She decided to start with her bedroom. She had three hours to clean before getting ready for eleven o'clock.

The bell rang three times before she went to it. She told him she would be right down. She grabbed her black shoes that match the long black fitted skirt and white blouse she was wearing. She took the small black bag, a gift from her mother on her twenty-third birthday and one last look in the mirror then headed to the door. The elevator was waiting for her when she emerged from her apartment.

"Looking good," Robin said to Andria as she stepped into the back of a green Toyota Camry.

"Late as usual," Robin's husband said to Andria as he put the car into drive.

"Good morning to you too," Andria replied sarcastically.

"You two better not start," Robin said in her peacemaker role.

Robin had invited Andria to her church on several occasions before, but she had always politely refused. Andria was an Anglican, and she was very active in her church. She had to admit the services were usually boring to the point of drowsiness, but that was the church she grew up in and her dedication was unwavering. But in all fairness to Robin, who had gone to church with Andria on two occasions and each time went to sleep five minutes into the service, she had to return the favor.

The church parking lot was filled with more than a hundred cars. It took Robin's husband about fifteen minutes to find a parking space. Robin had recently changed churches and she was very excited about this new church. She guaranteed Andria an uplifting experience that would make her feel alive, empowered, and exhilarated.

"Did you hear that?" Andria asked Robin. Andria had heard loud horns coming from the church.

"I told you it was different," Robin answered.

"I hope we find a seat because the service sometimes lasts a long time," Robin's husband added.

The door opened automatically as soon as they approached. As expected from the crowded parking lot, the church was filled to capacity. It was a big building, long and wide. Andria did not know it was that big from looking at it from the outside. No, the church showed that looks could be deceiving. The outside entrance gave the look of a tiny church with a powerful music system. As soon as Andria and company walked in, she saw eight horn players located on both sides of the church above the choir, and the live band that was raising the spirits of the living and the dead.

"Wow!" Andria exclaimed barely able to hear herself in the festivities.

"I hate to say I told you so," Robin said as she headed toward the front of the church. Andria and Robin's husband followed her lead. As she passed by, people rose from their pews offering her their seat. They finally stopped at the middle where three boys who looked to be between the ages of fifteen and eighteen were seated. The boys looked at Robin and her crew, then at their mother and father. The parents returned a look and the boys eagerly gave up their seats and headed to the back of the church. They looked a little bit too happy in their suits to be upset at having to give up their seats. As they walked to the back of the church, they had great big smiles on their faces, showing a freedom that only came from being in an unwanted situation.

"This is great, Robin. Don't have the baby too soon," Andria said as she rubbed her friend's stomach. She felt the baby kick immediately.

"Aren't they great?" Robin asked as they looked at the choir singing at the top of their voices. Their bodies shook with the rhythm of the band and their words seemed to demand all the attention from God. They were dressed in blue robes with a gold staff around their shoulders. Their size ranged from pencil thin to tipping the three hundred mark on a lenient scale.

"Unbelievable. This is great!" Andria clapped along with the rhythm that was moving her body. She was not alone in the enjoyment and sensation of the church. Robin and her husband, along with the rest of the congregation were singing praises to the

Almighty. At the end of the song, the church became quiet as a lamb, no pun intended. The preacher, a tall, skinny black man, approached the pulpit located on the elevated right side of the church. He opened the greetings by saying the usual pleasantries and acknowledging the choir. Even though his disposition was on the light side, he spoke with a deep baritone voice. Andria took the opportunity to scope the room for familiar faces. She turned her head slightly and glanced to the left then to the right. She noticed that Robin had drifted off to sleep, lifting her head frequently to deny that she was asleep. Andria smiled at her friend and continued her observation.

"No, it's not him," Andria said, talking to no one but herself.

"It's not who?" Robin asked as she realized there were more important things to observe in the world at this time.

"Rashaun," Andria answered.

"Who is Rashaun?" Robin's husband asked.

"He is this new guy Andria likes," Robin said and hoped that her husband would not inquire further.

"Here we go again," he said and returned his attention to the pastor.

"Look over there at the guy in the dark blue suit."

"Where?" Robin asked as she scanned the room.

"There."

Robin saw the man in the tall dark suit sitting next to a lady in her early sixties. She kept staring at him hoping he would turn and see her; she wanted to see his face. She wanted to see the man who had Andria yapping to her almost every night. She was rewarded when he turned and saw them staring at him. He smiled with intensely white teeth that seem to send a ray of light through to them.

"That smile," Andria said as she returned her own version of a happy day.

"He sure is dark.," Robin said as she checked out the side of Rashaun's face. "And boy, can he grin."

"We are going out this evening," Andria said, still smiling while trying to listen to the preacher. "He goes to church too." She seemed almost shocked and pleased.

Robin turned to Andria with a frown. "That doesn't mean anything. The church is full of wife beaters, liars, cheaters, prostitutes, lawyers, and politicians . . ."

"Okay, Robin, I get the picture. Now can we listen to the

service?" Andria asked, annoyed that her friend had put hope into perspective and in doing so, cut another straw from a dying woman.

The antique grandfather clock showed the time to be 5:30 P.M. Rashaun had told Andria he would pick her up at seven. He had spoken to her briefly after the service. She introduced him to her friend and her husband. Her friend looked him up and down, trying to read each thought that was in his head. He did not introduce her to his mother who had gone ahead to talk to some of her friends. When he did rejoin his mother, she gave him the third degree. "Who was that girl? Is that your girlfriend? Why didn't you introduce me? Is she married?" She went on and on. He told her when he met the woman he planned to marry, she would be the first to know.

She hated first dates. It was like auditioning for a part in a movie. Even though she felt she knew Rashaun from talking to him on the phone, tonight was the real test. She had tried so hard to postpone that part of her life. Now she wasn't sure what she was going to do. Robin had called and told her to dress simple, nothing provocative but a little bit sexy. Judy had spoken to her earlier that morning, and her advice was to show as much skin as possible. Andria settled for a long fitted green skirt, a white blouse, and a black jacket. It was 6:45 P.M. when she sat in front of the TV, her head feeling light from nervousness.

As he prepared for his date, old memories filled Rashaun's head. He was taking Andria to a small restaurant in Brooklyn Heights. He found out about the restaurant from an accountant, Tawanda Davis, he had dated only once. He had met Tawanda through a mutual friend who insisted she would be perfect for him. He told him she didn't have any kids and had a good job with a decent income. He met her at the restaurant after work. When he got there, she was having a small glass of wine. They ate and talked about their jobs and other frivolous things. The food was great and the service was excellent. He made himself a promise to return there. At the end of the evening, she offered to drop him home, since he hadn't driven. When they got to his place, she invited herself in for a late-night drink. He went to bed with her that night and promised himself never to sleep with her again. She was a woman of the nineties who believed there wasn't a lubricating gel in the world she couldn't use. She told him she was saving her real juices for when she got married. Fucking her was like fucking a bottle of Vaseline. He barely got his dick hard that night. After he faked cumming, he asked her why she put so much stuff in there. She said she wanted to preserve her natural pussy juices until marriage.

He pressed the black button on the electronic clothes hanger he had installed two years ago. First the suits came—black, gray, pinstriped blue, pinstriped gray—there were approximately twenty. Next came the blazers. He had ten of those, some European cuts, African and Asian designed. He chose a dark blue European designed blazer. He pressed the bottom button and the pants came forward. He chose a pair of black pants made of rayon and cotton that he had bought a year ago at a Manhattan boutique. He and his co-worker had gone in there during an extended lunch break. The first thing the salesman, twisting as he walked, asked him was what was his forte. Rashaun told him to "sit down and we will call you when we need you." The salesman thought they were very rude so with a twist and a turn, he went to forte` another customer. He asked his friend what the hell was forte`. He added a black collarless fitted shirt to complete his outfit. An ex-girlfriend had bought it for him for his birthday, one of three women he actually had a committed relationship. He had gone out with her for two years until a job opportunity in Washington took her out of state; that was the end of their tryst. Neither of them believed in long-distance relationships. He completed his attire with a maroon Georgie Panni shoe with pointed tips. He spent the next half-hour shaping up his beard and combing his hair. He looked at himself once more in the mirror, sprayed on some Calvin Klein escape cologne, and headed to his car. It was 7:15 p.m.

Rashaun called Andria from his cellular phone, and she came downstairs to meet him. She didn't say anything about him being thirty minutes late, maybe because he immediately told her how lovely she looked. She returned the compliment, and they headed to downtown Brooklyn. On the way, they engaged in light conversation on the coincidence of accidentally running into each other twice during the week. She asked him if he went to church regularly and he said no. He was there that morning with his mother who was planning to disown him if he didn't go to church with her. She said she was also visiting as a favor to a friend, that she regularly attended a different church.

When they got to the restaurant, there were about twenty people dining, the majority were Caucasian with a sprinkling of black, Spanish, and Asian. The waitress who came to seat them was a white girl about five-feet-four, approximately twenty years old, wearing a white fluffy shirt with black spandex pants. She guided them through the maze of people to a table that was meant for four but availability made it sitting for two. She put two menus down in the middle of the table.

"Enjoy your din..." before she had finish saying *dinner* she was on her way to the front.

Rashaun pulled a chair back for Andria and she sat down, then he walked around to the seat opposite from her. Two mixed couples occupied the four-seat table next to them. There was the Chinese girl with her white boyfriend and a white girl with a black guy. The waitress returned about three minutes after they were seated. She asked them if they wanted any appetizers. They both said no, and she took the orders for their drinks while they perused the menu.

"This place is nice," Andria said as she scanned the menu.

"Do you drink anything stronger than ginger ale?" he said, looking at the drink the waitress had just set down in front of her.

"I'm not a drinker. Occasionally, I will have a glass of wine or some Alize`."

"Alize`, that's me," Rashaun said as he took a sip from his Long Island Ice Tea. "So what do you like to do for fun?"

"Let me see, bowling, ice hockey, polo, and a little bit of sex."

"Excuse me." He looked at her as if she had dropped a plate in a formal dining room filled with dignitaries.

"Got you there, didn't I?" She laughed. "No, I like movies, occasional dancing, and traveling."

"What movies have you seen lately?"

"Black Debbie does the hood."

"I see you are a comedian."

"Not really. I just hate first dates, so this is my attempt to break the ice."

"I see we have one thing in common. I deal with that by asking a lot of questions so the person talks about herself."

"Well, I personally don't like talking that much so that won't work. Rashaun, why don't you tell me about yourself."

"You sound like you are doing an interview," Rashaun said as his eyes swept the room. He noticed two white guys holding hands in the right corner next to the kitchen. He had no problem with the display of affection, but some things were better left to a different setting. He didn't hate gays. He just would rather not be around them. He quickly turned back to Andria who had begun to get irritated.

"Are you finished?" she said asked sarcastically.

"I always like to know what's around me. My cop friend taught me that. Only fools run to trouble, and if you aren't aware of the people around you, you will be a fool." He watched her as he spoke, taking in her subtleties and admiring her raw beauty. She was wearing makeup, but he knew if he woke up with her devoid of the paint on her face, she would still be beautiful.

"Why are you smiling?"

"You don't want to know or then again you just might. But now is not the time." He motioned for the waiter. "Can we have some water?"

After the waiter left, there was a dead silence at their table.

"Would you answer some questions for me?" Andria had broken the void. "Twenty questions, answer them any way you please."

"Shoot," he said. "I guess we will have to put it on hold. Here comes the waitress with our dinner."

"I would assume you don't eat and talk at the same time?"

"My mother always said it was bad table manners."

They ate in silence, each enjoying their food. Rashaun was the first to finish his dinner. He didn't say anything but instead finished his drink and started drinking the water, maintaining complete silence. He watched her eat. She ate slowly, taking time to chew her food completely. When she was finished, she wiped her mouth with a napkin and pushed her plate away. She drank about half a glass of water then sat back in her chair.

"Let's continue our conversation," Andria said as she gave Rashaun her complete attention. "Are you ready for the first question?"

"How many questions?" Rashaun asked. "And are you going to answer them also?"

"At what age did you lose your virginity and with whom?"

"I lost my virginity at seventeen, and I paid twenty to do that. You?"

"At twenty-two. My first college boyfriend, a white boy from Long Island."

"Twenty-two is kind of late to lose your virginity. Why so late?"

"Simple, I was saving myself for marriage."

"And what happened? You gave up on marriage?"

"Nope, I gave up on myself."

"Oops, next question."

"Where do you see yourself five years from now in terms of a relationship?"

"Is this a trick question?"

"No," she said. "Are you going to answer the question?"

"Yes. I never know where I see myself in terms of relationships. I could be involved in a serious relationship or even married. Or maybe I could be running scared as I have been doing the last few years. Learning more about women and wanting to get as far away as possible with the added information. What about you?"

"I see myself as being married with hopefully my first child."

They stayed at the restaurant for the next hour playing the question game. Andria and Rashaun were going in the same direction, yet they were miles apart. They were both contented with their professional lives, but their personal lives were lacking. Andria told Rashaun about her last relationship and the hurt it had caused her. Rashaun did not tell her about his ex-girlfriend and that videotape he kept under his bed. He didn't want to rehash painful memories at this moment. Whenever he thought about it, he became very angry and hurtful. He told her about his niece and his love for children. She asked him why he wasn't a father. He told her that maybe it wasn't in the cards that were dealt to him. She told him about her wish to have three kids and to live a settled life. He had given up on that because of the life he had lived. Condoms were secondary to him. He never went in without one. He had forgotten the natural feel of a woman. There were always Ramseys between him and a woman.

They both agreed the dinner was delicious. Rashaun promised to cook a meal for her. Andria did not reciprocate. Cooking was not one of her strong points. Most people ate her food with neither complaints nor praises. It was 10:30 when they left the restaurant. Rashaun suggested they go to a club. Andria wanted to go down to the South Street Seaport. They decided to compromise, first the South Street Seaport then the club.

The South Street Seaport was always crowded. As they walked two feet away from each other, they talked about their dreams. Rashaun wanted to open up his own practice in downtown Manhattan one day, and Andria wanted to own a chain of day-care centers.

Andria watched Rashaun as he walked. His shoulders were held high at all times. He did not slouch. His eyes darted around, observing everything around him. He seemed totally at ease with himself. She wondered if this was the start of a good thing or if the dates would dwindle to an occasional phone call.

Rashaun knew Andria was by his side, but he couldn't help but glance at her every now and then. She was very attractive, and she had a mind of her own. Too many women he had gone out with seemed to marvel at his every word. They were impressed by his law training which broke down everything to logic or bullshit. Successful lawyers in the black community were rare. Sometimes the women would even forget about how dark he was until they woke up next to him or saw his reflection in the mirror. Andria was different, and she said whatever was on her mind. Rashaun wondered how she was in bed. Would she be a pushover like so many of the other women he had gone out with? He hoped she wasn't too easy, but he'd had relationships with women whom he had gone to bed with him on the first night. One such woman, he even came close to marrying. This world sometimes was so confusing. Other women had rules. They wouldn't sleep with a man for the first two months or so, and those were the fake ones. Once you had them, you realized it wasn't worth it, a champagne cola would have been better.

Manhattan wasn't confusing at all; it was a beautiful place. Manhattan at night was when he felt most at home in the city. There was so much to do, so many places to go. The city leaped up at you as it begged for your complete attention. They left the pier at 1:00 a.m. In another city, they might be headed home, but in New York the nightlife was just stirring. They headed to the Pulse, a West Indian dance club. When they got there, there was a line of about twelve people at the door. Rashaun did not wait in line, but instead went directly to the front. Three tall bouncers guarded the door. Rashaun went to the one who was letting the people into the club. He greeted him with a complicated handshake and a shoulder-to-shoulder hug. He pulled the rope and let Rashaun and Andria into the club.

Inside, Rashaun scanned the room to see if he knew anyone. He noticed two guys standing next to each other wearing identical suits. Their undershirt and tie were the only things that separated them. The one with the white shirt and gold tie kept looking back at them, first at her then at him. First, a smile then a frown, his facial expressions spoke his words. Rashaun ignored him, the same way he ignored most annoying stupid people. When he was younger, he might have taken a different path. He might have asked the brother what the fuck he was looking at. And maybe he might have gone as far as punching him in the face. He was older, much more mature, and he hated himself for that. Sometimes he still thought about the street life, a life where nobody took any shit from anyone. He lived it in his teen years, and he saw many people die by the code of the street. Maybe the brother saw the look in his eyes because he turned in a different direction.

As usual, the place was crowded and the tongues were lying. They passed a brother in a bright blue suit talking to a pretty woman in an outfit similar to Andria's. Rashaun overheard him explaining the difficulties of being a lawyer. Rashaun had met the same guy before when he went to a parent meeting with one of his friends. This guy taught mathematics in grades six and seven at P.S. 217. Rashaun smiled and walked with Andria toward one of three tables overlooking the dance floor. There were so many pretty women there. He counted at least ten that were pleasing to the eye. He knew better than to ignore the beautiful one he had on his side. A guy walking in and seeing all these beautiful women would assume he was in for a good night, but he would be sadly mistaken. First, he would ask the first one to dance, then the second one only to be told "No, not right now, I just came off the floor" or "I am tired." Soon he would find out that looks could be very deceiving. He would go to the bathroom, look himself up and down, and maybe take a few sniffs under the armpit. He would come out again and go through the routine, and after a series of nos, he would settle down and realize the night was too long. Rashaun had been through this scene numerous times; maybe the faces and the place changed, but the routine remained the same. He refused to tell these women what he did, and he sure as hell never told them what he drove. He understood their game, and he played it with the winning card. He only asked the beautiful women to dance because only then would he not feel self-conscious. When an ugly girl turned you down, it feels as if the world has slapped you in the face. And he understood the ugly girl's game; to them, guys represented a pretty baby. He was dark skinned with course hair and that was not good enough for them. His features emphasized too much blackness. They might see themselves in his reflection, and someone running from himself didn't want a constant reminder.

Andria saw his eyes dissect the club with a reflective mood. She did not say anything. She had been in these clubs before, not this particular one, but others like it. She could pick out the married ones without the ring, and those who had the ring but were looking for a side order. She had heard the stories before from many a suitor. The lawyers, doctors, engineers, and executives were all there yet they weren't. It was acting at its best. She had gotten the beeper numbers and been instructed when to call. Oh yes and the kids in the background were always nephews. Until one of the kids shouted "Daddy, who you talking to? Is it Mommy?" It was a game, and sometimes when she played it, she got caught up, but most of the time she had her plan. With her plan, she never lost, but when she got emotional she got taken for a ride. A ride might be two weeks or two months, but she always had to get off.

"Do you want something to drink?" Rashaun leaned over close to Andria. Again, the slight trace of the Calvin Klein cologne Escape made her shiver.

"No, I'm okay," she said.

"I'll have one, be back in a minute." He headed toward the bar, his six-foot-three-inch frame moving steadily among the different shapes and sizes. She liked the way he walked, his head held high, shoulders straight, the look of confidence in every move.

A minute after he left, a man she glanced at on her way to the table approached and asked her to dance. She politely declined, reaffirming that she was there with someone. One minute later, another man invited her to the dance floor; again, she declined. He, however, did not give up so easily. He wanted to know why she did not want to dance with him and being there with someone did not seem a good enough reason. She finally told him that she did not want to dance with his sorry ass looking self. His insistence turned into anger after her last comment. He started to say something to her, but Rashaun came back to the table overshadowing them both. The man made his exit, cursing her under his breath.

"Having fun?" He smiled at her. He did not ask what had transpired between her and the man.

They started the reggae music about twenty minutes after they had arrived—a driving beat that needed fast action to keep up with the rhythm. This used to be his favorite music in college when his energy was relentless and the sweat on his face showed what kind of night he was having. Now he rarely partook in such exercises, preferring to leave his sweating for the gym.

She liked house music, but she did not intend to ask him to dance. She felt if he wanted to, he would ask her; therefore, she just kept her fingers pounding the table to the beat of the blaring music. He explained to her that she could go on the floor if she wanted to, but he just did not feel like dancing to that kind of music. She declined. A half an hour later, the music changed to the slow erotic reggae beat. He stood up and took her hand. She hesitated, his facial expression changed, he was disappointed. She smiled and walked to the dance floor with him trailing behind her with her hand to guide him.

The lyrics to the song were as hypnotic as the beat. At first they were apart with him giving her the respect, he thought she deserved. She admired the fact that he did not push up on her as so many men had done before. She liked dancing close, but she did not like to be glued to the person she was with. He liked the way her body swayed to the beat; she moved smoothly, letting the music take control. He was no slouch either, after all, dancing was one of his favorite hobbies, and he enjoyed to all kinds of music. She watched his movements. They complemented hers perfectly, and he seemed to know exactly what she would do before she did it. His body swayed to the same rhythm as hers. She turned around and slowly started to inch backward toward him. He met her halfway, first he pressed his chest against her back, followed by his pelvis, and then he took his hands and ran them straight down hers. Then they started to rock. Sometimes he would time her perfectly and move to her rhythm, other times he would move in a different direction only to meet his eager pelvis thrust. His penis had gotten erect, and she seemed to be teasing him even more as she felt him sliding up and down against her butt. He smiled knowing well that she knew exactly what she was doing. She must have made guys have plenty of accidents the way she was moving. He had made girls have accidents also, but he had never had one himself. He had too much self-control for that. It was a young people thing. With experience came control. She turned around, and with the beat of the music, he came up to her burying his right leg with his penis extending down the right leg of his pants between her legs. He held her close to him, and they seemed to be alone on the dance floor. She looked at him, daring him, and the music and their faces became their only reality. The dance floor was almost pitch black with only sporadic light interrupting the sensuality of the dancers. He went down lower almost feeling her split between her legs on his penis as he pulled her harder and closer toward him. She smiled and slowly disentangled herself from him. He, too, smiled and danced a little bit away from her.

The music changed to slow lovemaking music. Again, she hesitated, not sure whether to head to her seat or to continue dancing. He made the decision for her, taking her right hand and gently pulling her toward him. His hands clasped her waist and hers went around his neck. She held him tight toward her as she buried her head in his chest. The music seemed to have taken over their bodies, no need for words, and body movements satisfied their yearning. His lips parted, and he gave her a soft kiss on her neck. She flinched but held him closer.

He could feel himself pressing against her, trying for some opening in that red dress. This whole evening had turned her on totally. It wasn't just physical and mental; he had placed a thought in her head that he was something to desire. Nevertheless, control was the most important thing in the beginning of a relationship. Not too far or too fast. After the third song, she felt tremors running through her body, something she hadn't felt for years. She had not allowed herself to feel like that since the incident.

He had started to make love to her on the floor. He felt her response with every move of her body, and penetration would only complete the act. He wanted to be inside her more than he ever wanted anyone in his life. Somehow, his mind was equating her womanliness to be the last frontier, only when he got there would he be satisfied. He was almost grinding her down, trying to force that material apart. Then she pulled away. Denying him the impossible, bringing him back to a reality he wanted no part of. Stopping to show him that the music had changed and the Deejay had started playing Soca music, a much faster beat. Fuck everyone else. He never wanted to be like everyone else. Slowly the insistent sound of Soca music filled his ear. His clothes were damp; his mind was clogged. He took her hand in his and led her toward the table. They did not speak for about fifteen minutes after they sat down. She asked him if he wanted to leave. He went for their coats, and as he helped her with the coat, he encircled her once again and inhaled all of her.

Andria sat at her desk, looking at the room but not seeing it. The file on Tim and Petra lay open in front of her. She had an appointment with the children's uncle at eleven o'clock and it was now ten. She had gotten to work at 9:05, the first time she had ever been late, and since she arrived, she was unable to do anything. A smile lit up her face as the thoughts of the weekend flowed through her mind. Then suddenly the phone rang, destroying her train of thought.

"Hello, Andria speaking. Can I help you?" Her voice did not betray her feelings at that moment. She understood what it meant to be a professional, and she followed the code of conduct.

"So you couldn't call me and tell me how it went last night? I stayed up all night waiting for you." Robin lied; she had fallen asleep right after a *Martin* rerun.

"Robin, I came home too late, and I was tired so I went straight to bed. And stop pulling my leg, you did not stay up and wait for my call."

"So tell me how it went, and don't leave anything out."

"Robin, I am ashamed of myself."

"No, you didn't, not on the first date. Tell me you didn't, Andria."

Andria sat back in her chair smiling "Of course not. I may be hard up, but I don't do that."

"Ah." Robin let out a sigh of relief. She knew her friend, and she knew that if she had slept with Rashaun on the first date, she would hate herself. Andria was brought up with old time morals and breaking them wrecked havoc on her soul.

"So come on. Andria tell me all about it."

"Robin, I like him a whole lot. I don't know if you can actually fall in love with a person on the first date, but I believe I have. There is something about him that makes me feel warm inside."

"Andria, slow down. You don't want to set yourself up like that, do you? How does he feel?"

"To be honest, I think he feels the same way. It's like two souls searching for each other on a big island, and once they found each other, there is no need to continue. I have never felt like that before."

"Andria, I think you are jumping the gun here. You have been hurt very bad before, and I think you should take it slow this time."

"I have taken it slow before, and look what happened. This time I think I will go with the pulling in my chest." Andria tapped the pen on the file in front of her, making some tiny ink dots around Tim's name.

He had felt good with her last night. She was funny, bright, and she had character. As he walked toward the private investigation division of his firm, he couldn't help but smile at last night's memories. He didn't want to jump the gun, but she just might be worth keeping. The feelings she evoked were similar to those he had experienced a long time ago, and acting on those feelings had made him the person he was today. As he contemplated taking a stab at the thing that was developing between him and Andria, his body shook with the thought of loving again. They say that you know in life when you meet the one you consider a keeper, but what happens if you are mistaken. Again, he shuddered at the thought. Blackfunk was underneath his bed as testament to that.

She wanted him last night; he could see it in her eyes. Most guys try to judge a woman's feelings by their body action, but that could be very misleading. The eyes held the key to her feelings, and last night she fought her body and soul to get her feelings under control. Before he even attempted to kiss her, he had looked straight into her eyes and they gave him a picture of her soul. It was tormented, yet it reached out to him. The fact that they did not do anything was not only a testament of her willpower but also his sense of righteousness. He was not sure if he could give her what she wanted so he held back. He listened to her and realized she was very vulnerable. He knew by pushing her further, he might get what he wanted for the moment, but would have probably lost her for a lifetime. He didn't want to do that, the same way he wouldn't want anyone to do that to him. He knew what his friend George would say: "Fuck them all. They are all bitches." Nevertheless, he was not, George.

"Rashaun, you back again?" The man that was speaking was a big, tall black man, a leftover from the NFL or a New York City cop. The latter was true of Jim Lethal, the head of the PI department of the firm. Rashaun liked the big man, and from the look on the man's face, the respect and admiration was mutual.

"When are you going to get married and have a few kids? All that money you making you gonna leave to the government." He talked with a southern drawl even though he had spent thirty of his forty-five years in the Big Apple.

"Don't worry about me, Lethal. I will just adopt one of your twenty kids," Rashaun said as he smiled at his friend. Lethal gave Rashaun one of his big throaty southern laughs.

"Anyway, big-time lawyer, what can I do for you?" Lethal said as his mood changed to a more businesslike tone.

"I want you to get me all that you can on Mr. Roundtree. Here is his background information." Rashaun gave him a sheet of paper with a short bio of Mr. Roundtree, including his address, social security number, and telephone number.

"Isn't he the drug dealer who they said shot a man in cold blood on the street?"

"Come on, Lethal. You believe everything you read in the newspapers? If you do, then we all would have criminal records a mile long."

"Rashaun, you know I don't believe shit they say in the newspapers. With the mayor having the news media doing everything but wiping his ass after he shits, how can anyone believe what they read?"

"You got it."

"Rashaun, when are we going to have that second drink?"

"Nope, not me. I'm not going drinking with you again. I had to shell out five hundred dollars to clean a yellow cab the last time I went out drinking with you. And I can't thank you enough for taking me upstairs, even though it was your fault."

"You are a big man, Rashaun. I can't tell you when to stop. Besides you were hilarious." Once more Lethal laughed the only way a southerner could.

"I will talk to you later, Lethal," Rashaun said, refusing to rehash ugly memories.

"Be safe, my friend," Lethal said and immediately took the paper Rashaun had given him and went to his computer.

Rashaun went back to his desk and told his secretary he would be out for lunch until three. He looked at his watch; it was 1:30. He left the office and went outside to the busy midtown traffic. He hated Manhattan during rush hour, and rush hour in Manhattan started at 8:00 A.M. and didn't end until 6:30 P.M. He had arranged to meet his friend at an Italian restaurant about five minutes from his job. He wiggled, bumped, and jumped the crowd all the way to the restaurant like a running back breaking through the toughest defense in the NFL. When he finally got there, he was glad to see the lunch crowd making its exit.

He chose a booth that was surrounded by empty tables at the back of the restaurant. The waitress came to him immediately to bring water and to ask him if he was ready to order. He told her he was waiting for a friend. She walked into the restaurant about ten minutes after he had sat down. Immediately all attention was focused on her, like a hurricane passing through. Whether anyone wanted to on not, her presence was felt. She wore a maroon business suit with the skirt cut about six inches above the knee, giving the scavengers a perfect view of her well-shaped long legs. When she saw him, she immediately smiled as her walk accentuated every curve in her body. Rashaun watched her, shaking his head and smiling. He had met her his junior year in college, and after months of trying to go out with her, he had accepted her offer. It was the offer of the F word meaning let's be friends that made many people cringe when they heard it. From that acceptance, they had become the best of friends. George had fallen in love with her as soon as he met her, offering her a life of servitude as his queen.

She took a seat next to him in the booth and immediately daggers were thrown at him from every man in the restaurant who thought they had an impossible shot.

"Okay, Rashaun. Who is she and did you sleep with her already?" she asked, sitting down and picking up the menu.

"You are too beautiful to be so mean," he said as he motioned the waitress to come and take their order.

She immediately closed her menu and said, "You know what I want already, Rashaun, so go ahead and order."

74

He ordered for both of them and pinched her to make her aware of the waitress' total focus on her as he placed the order.

"Never wanted to and never will. My man is all I need, and when he can't do it anymore, I will do it for myself, too many damn sick people out here."

Rashaun knew she meant it, and he knew she had been faithful to her husband. They had recently celebrated their ten-year anniversary. She had gotten married to a white guy she fell in love with during her senior year of college. Rashaun was shocked at first because she was so pro black, but once he met the guy, he gave his approval. They bought a home in New Jersey and had two kids.

"So tell me, Rashaun, who is she?"

"How are your kids doing?" Rashaun asked not wishing to get into his personal life just yet.

"Rashaun, you asked me that over the phone, and I told you they were all right. Now stop stalling and get to the point. She must have something over you because you have never been so evasive."

"I don't know, Monique, but this woman has me thinking." He stopped to look around the room, not knowing or seeing what he was looking for." You know I have been a player for a very long time, and sometimes it's hard to stop doing something you have done all your life. But I want to give this girl a chance, and I don't know why."

"Well! Well! Well! Someone finally got to you. I wondered if I would ever see this day, but I am happy to see this in my lifetime." Rashaun inhaled deeply as he looked at his friend.

"How do you trust again when you have accumulated all this experience with all these women?"

"Sometimes experience is the worst teacher, especially *bad* experience. Rashaun, you have had some terrible experiences with women, but you also know some very good women, present company included, of course. Life is about giving people chances and taking chances yourself. Look at you. You are a perfect example of someone taking a chance."

He knew she was right but he still felt afraid. He had gone through a terrible time after Blackfunk, and he had promised himself never to go through that again.

"How long can you keep running, Rashaun? I have known you for a long time and I know the life you live is not really you. You

75

act like a player, but you aren't one. You have told me about sleeping with different women seven days straight, and you still weren't happy. I know you enjoy one-on-one relationships but you run away from them because you are scared of getting hurt. But as Bob Marley said in a reggae rhythm, "You running and you running away, but you can't run away from yourself."

"Since when did you start listening to reggae?"

"My husband has more reggae albums than you can ever dream of."

"You are right about me running . . .." Rashaun said as he watched the waitress approach with a bottle of wine in her hand.

"Excuse me, ma'am, the gentleman in the booth in the gray suit directly across from you sent this." She gave Monique the bottle of wine and a business card.

"Excuse me, Rashaun," Monique said as she took the bottle of wine and opened it. She took the business card, ripped it up, and dropped it into the wine bottle. She corked the wine bottle and gave it back to the waitress who was grinning from ear to ear. "Tell him I said shove it from the bottom up to the place where the sun never shines."

Rashaun listened at the interchange between the waitress and Monique and started to laugh. "You have not changed a bit, have you?" he said it as a question, but it was more of a statement.

"I hate people who have no respect. I could be talking to my husband, anyone. Anyway let's get back to your love life."

Monique never once looked over to see who had sent her the bottle of wine, but Rashaun did. He saw the man get up and leave as soon as the waitress brought the wine back to him. The waitress gave him the finger as he was leaving. He was sure she did not use the exact words Monique had told her. Monique never used the F word, she would use many different words to say the same thing.

"I don't know, Monique."

"Rashaun, you have to stop living your life like this. You have more to offer a woman than half these guys out here. I know if you decide to do the right thing, there will be no stopping you. There is a certain beauty in having a family that you might never experience because you are not giving yourself a chance. The funny thing about you is that you are always testing women."

"What do you mean?" he asked, a surprised tone in his voice.

"Let's see, every woman you go out with you try to sleep with on the first date. If you succeed in taking her to bed, you call her a hooker."

"But they are!" he exclaimed so loud that attention was reverted to his table.

"You don't know what these women are going through. They could have been celibate for twenty years, met you, and decided you were the one for them."

"Yeah right," he said.

"The others you think are just after your Benjamins, when in fact, they might just have met a brother who has something going for him. Most women want a guy who has a job and some kind of stability. What's wrong with that? Would you date a bum on the street? I don't think so. I am not saying that the girl you just met is right for you, maybe, maybe not. But you will never know until you give her a chance. What's the most she could do to you? Sleep around on you? So you find her cheating; you won't be the first and you won't be the last man that's happened to. So you leave her and you walk away. God knows you are good at that."

"Would you like some water? God knows you've been talking nonstop."

"Rashaun, I have water right in front of me. If I want to drink some, I will. Listen to me, Rashaun. Stop running." She drank some of the water. "Satisfied?" she asked.

They remained at the restaurant for about thirty more minutes before they went back to work. Monique hailed a cab and waved goodbye. Once more Rashaun started his journey back to the office. Traffic was a little bit lighter now because the lunch crowd was back at their respective desks. He had a meeting with one of the partners in the firm at four o'clock to update him on the progress of the case.

Rashaun met Andria a few more times for lunch and dinner. They did not go back to the club, but when time permitted, they took in the sights of the city and went to a few comedy clubs. He felt comfortable with her, so much so that he invited her to meet his mother. She politely declined that invitation, stating that it was not the appropriate time. He had never been like that with any other girl; there was no more urgency to get her to bed. They spent countless hours on the phone, talking about everything from politics to toenails. George, of course, thought Rashaun had lost his mind and told him so with very explicit language. Two months after they had met, Rashaun invited Andria to dinner at his place. She was always ribbing him about having no skills in the kitchen.

On Saturday morning, Rashaun went to the fish market and bought some medium-size snapper. Then went to the supermarket and bought chicken, vegetables, and a variety of seasonings. Andria had told him she didn't eat pork and very rarely ate beef. He also stopped by the liquor store and picked out a bottle of wine and, of course, a large bottle of Passion Alize'.

Saturday he asked his mother to come over and help him clean his place. When she left, he was amazed at how spotless it was. Of course, she had her remarks about the mirrors around his bed and the pictures in the room. She again gave him her usual lecture on the many diseases out there. She brought him a new tablecloth and changed the curtains in his bedroom. He chose five CDs from his vast collection of music. The first CD was Sade, *Love Deluxe* the second Beres Hammond, *Sweetness*, the third Toni Braxton, *Secrets* fourth Stevie Wonder, *Songs in the Key of Life* and the last one was K-C & Jojo, *Love Always*. He bought the scented candles with the special holders and rented *Rush Hour* with Chris Tucker and Jackie Chan. At four o'clock, he started cooking the chicken, rice, and vegetables. He had asked his mother to prepare the fish for him. After all, he was trying to prepare a romantic meal, not smell the whole house up with fresh fish. It was six o'clock when he actually finished preparing the food. His brother had brought the fish over around 5:45 P.M. One piece, of course was missing and his brother had a satisfied grin on his face.

At 7:25, Andria pulled up in a Lincoln Continental cab. Rashaun had just pulled back the drapes to check to see when she would arrive. She had called him about twenty minutes ago. She wore a long white fitted dress. The cab driver remained about two minutes, watching her walk up the stairs. She was beautiful, that's all there was to say. Once again, he felt like he wanted to lose himself inside of her; he wanted her to be his wife, lover, friend, and mother of his children. His list for her was long, and there was a lifetime in that somewhere.

He opened the door for her, not giving her the opportunity to ring the doorbell. She had to have seen the look on his face, pure uncontrollable lust. "Hello there." The emphasis was so great on *there* he sounded like a singer hitting a high note.

"Impressive," she said as she stepped in and saw the arrangements of food he had on the table.

He stood like a child beaming from ear to ear. He was nervous and happy at the same time. In the background, Sade sang her melody in a smooth controlled voice. He had done this countless times before, but never was he so nervous.

"Are you gong to show me your place, or do I have to take the tour by myself?" She stood there smiling at him.

"Sure," he said, taking her hand and leading her through his apartment. When he got to the bedroom, which was in darkness, he hesitated for a moment before he flipped the switch.

"Whoa, you have it all, don't you?" She kept going from the mirrors to the art on the walls. She left him standing at the door to bedroom.

"What are you, black Trump? Everything is so expensive," she said. "Are these things always so neat?"

"Nope, I'm not rich but I try to buy things that will last. I also try not to do too much work at home, so generally, they remain like this." He watched her walk around the room.

She hesitated at the top of the bed then suddenly jumped on top of it.

"Watch out!" he said as he saw her make the motion.

The waterbed almost threw her off with its sudden rippling effect.

"This, this, this is a waterbed," she garbled trying her best to get her bearing. When the bed finally stopped moving, she eased herself up onto her feet.

"Are you okay?" he asked with a big smile on his face.

"You definitely need to give me some time before we eat."

"Definitely," he agreed as she weaved herself toward the bedroom door. He walked with her to the living room and gently helped her onto the sofa.

"This is not a water sofa, is it?" she queried, smile lighting up her beautiful face. "How did you know I like Sade?" She swung her body to the beat.

"You told me. Remember?"

"No. Let's dance." She lifted her body off the chair.

Immediately he got excited. "I don't think so. Let's eat first." He took her hand and headed to the dining table.

"I have to give credit where credit is due." She took a napkin and wiped her mouth. "This was delicious."

"Well," he said, " I got skills like that."

"No. Rashaun, your mom had to have helped you cook."

"Nope, she didn't. She just taught me well. Honestly, I cooked everything except for the fish, and that was only because I didn't want to smell up the place."

"Honest?"

"I swear."

"I don't think that I can move."

"I guess my cooking was too good."

"Yes, it was. Can you come help me to my feet?" she asked trying her best to get up.

Rashaun came over and gave her a hand. "Have you seen *Rush Hour*?"

"No, I was dying to see it, but by the time me and my girlfriends made our minds up to go, it was out of the movie theatre."

"Well, I have the next best thing. I have the videotape. Do you want to watch it?"

"Sure."

Rashaun put the empty plates in the sink and covered the rest of the food. When he went into the living room, Andria had already sat down in front of the TV, her feet up on the sofa.

"I have been trying to operate this remote, but it doesn't seem to work."

Rashaun pressed a few buttons on the remote control, and the whole room became a movie theatre. Sound came from every corner of the room, and the big fifty-two-inch screen lit up the room as he dimmed the lights. As soon as he sat down, Andria came straight into his lap. She curled up next to him like a baby.

They watched the movie holding on to each other and laughing as the movie went on. Rashaun had seen the movie before, but that did not stop him from laughing. While the movie was going, Stevie Wonder's CD played low in the background. As the credits started to roll, the K-C and Jojo CD started to play.

"May I have this dance, ma'am?" Rashaun asked, getting up and bowing in front of Andria.

"Yes, you may, sir." Andria took his hand and stood up. She picked up her glass of Alize and took a sip. She held it in one hand as she slipped the other around his neck. She brought her body to rest against his. He took his glass of Alize and finished drinking it, then put his hands around her body, letting them go over her perfectly shaped ass before settling on her waist.

"Bad boy." She giggled as she took his hand and put it back on her butt.

It was then he knew he was going to have a problem. Big Johnny, who had been standing straight all night, was now lying dormant as a sleeping volcano. Rashaun held her tight, and as they danced, he kissed her on the neck. She did the same to him. Still Johnny was dreaming. Rashaun took her lips in his and a blissful union was formed. He took her by the hand and they headed to the bedroom. He flipped the light switch off and touched the night lamp. He stood her up in front the bed and took off her clothes. The outline of her clothes did not lie. Standing in front of him was one of the most beautiful bodies he had ever seen. He took his eyes off her one-second too long and looked at Johnny. Johnny boy was dead to the world. Rashaun kissed Andria, starting with her forehead and working his way down. Her whole body responded to every touch of his lips. He gently laid her down on his bed, and she started to giggle as she got used to the rocking of the waterbed. He took his hands, turned her over, and viewed a black man's dream. Slowly he pulled the G string off. When he was finished, he took his right hand and touched Johnny. Johnny was the only guy fast asleep at the party.

"Excuse me," he said to her and headed to the bathroom.

He stood in the mirror and then slowly started touching himself, something he had done countless times before and Johnny always responded. He went through his routine, but Johnny did not respond. He spoke softly and kindly to Johnny but to no avail. He apologized to Johnny for asking him to get up to fuck this ugly girl he met at a club once. He promised Johnny the best treatment allotted to a king. He asked God to let Johnny rise and take control. He asked God and Johnny to forgive him for all the wrong things he had done, but please let Johnny rise. He stayed in the bathroom for about ten minutes then he went back in the room.

"What's wrong?" she asked.

"I wish I knew," he said.

"Come here," she said.

He came into her arms like a newborn baby. She laid him down on the bed then she started to kiss him. She started from his eyebrow and worked her way down; his body leaping to her every touch. Everything was standing except Johnny. Johnny was in a stupor. Somehow, the brain was not getting the signal downtown. She did her best as her body yearned for satisfaction. She wanted him more than she ever wanted a man before. After she had finished with him, she lay next to him. There was an awkward silence between them. She took his head and rested it on her ample chest. He felt so damn comfortable. He did not know when he fell asleep, but they both did. He woke up a 2:00 A.M, almost as if he had forgotten something. It was then that he saw the flagpole protruding straight up from the sheets. He felt it was rock steady. He reached into one of his side drawers and pulled out a condom. There was a marking of large on it. He looked at the condom, and then he looked at this dick. He definitely needed an extra-large, but he would somehow make that do. He woke her up with soft kisses all over her body. She automatically looked down between his legs and when she saw how big he was, her eyes opened wide.

"Do you want to kill me?" she asked as she hugged him, letting her body relax for what was about to come.

"No, beautiful. I just want to love you. Love you in a way to set an example so that any man after me will fail in your eyes. This is just the start, there is a lot more where that came from."

"Remember, no holding back." She opened herself to love and death.

They were sitting in Russel's car because Andria needed him to accompany her into the building. Russel was short and broad like an NFL football player. He looked at his watch, and she looked out at the boy playing in the streets. Andria was nervous. This was her first time here. He had offered to come along with her when she asked for a companion. He liked her the first time she set foot in the office a month ago. He wondered if he had made a mistake coming with her. Their conversation on the way was brief, too brief and too impersonal for his liking. He wanted to get a feel for her, but she didn't leave any openings. He had been with this job for more than five years, but he had just transferred to this unit. Like most jobs, there were good and bad times. But it was an honest paycheck. Not like what most of his friends did.

Andria looked across at him. He was a big man yet she understood he was a gentleman. Most of the women in the office wanted him, but Andria wasn't interested. Even though he was big, she was not afraid of him. She knew he would not hurt her even though he had told her coworkers he liked her. She wondered how he had gotten so broad; his chest extended endlessly across. She might have been interested a few years ago but not now, she was contented with Rashaun. Rashaun was the only man on her mind these days. She did not hear from him for the day yet, therefore, she made a mental note to call him when she got back.

The apartment building they were looking at was in one of the most crime-ridden areas in Brooklyn. Gunshots after nine o'clock were bedtime stories to most of the people who lived there. Even the cops refused to patrol the area after ten, and their captain at the precinct understood. At the same time, crime had gone down in most parts of the borough; the mayor touted his horn every chance he got. He gave credit to the only person he believed deserved credit and that was himself, of course.

Andria wasn't giving anyone credit for the situation she was in now. She had plenty of eggs every month that she wanted to use one day. She had finally met a man she was sure would be a good father. "Ready?" she asked Russel.

"Ready as I will ever be." He took the keys out of the ignition and opened the car door. Andria followed his lead, and they both headed up the long black-and-white staircase to the apartment building. Russel's wide body shielded her from the wind and any other flying objects.

When they got into the building, they automatically went to the elevator, hoped, and prayed it would be working. Of course, it wasn't. Andria wondered if there were any working elevators in the projects.

"I knew it, I knew it—they never work. What floor are we going to again?" His voice was starting to get a menacing tone to it.

"Ninth," Andria replied.

The steps were short and wide. There was foot tracing in the cement to show the preferred side the tenants in the building took. The other entrance was on the opposite end, and there was a closed door on top of it with a barely legible sign readingexit. Andria and Russel did not have any trouble deciding which exercise route to take. And to reinforce their decision, a guy with a hooded jacket, and a woman who seemed to have had better days, opened the door, making their way to the entrance. On their way out, they watched Andria and Russel with an eye for detail and inspection. Andria and Russel headed up the stairs following the path the tenants had made for them.

At the top of the stairs, Andria pulled out her paper and double-checked the address she had looked at four times before. The doors on the ninth floor were all of a rustic silver look. They were doors that should have been primed and painted. Each had a minimum of three locks. Andria went from one door to the next, squinting to make out the numbers. Some of the lettering on the doors seemed to have been etched out on purpose, others had simply fallen off. They found a 9A and a 9B, but no lettering on the third door. Andria knocked on that door. There was some shuffling on the inside before a deep voice asked who it was. With the sound of the voice came the barking of dogs, from at least three apartments on the floor. Andria·stated her name and stepped back from the peephole so that the occupants of 9C could see her and her companion. Finally, the locks on the door started to turn.

"You can never be too careful," said the fat lady with a checkered dress that ended two inches from the floor. Her face, like the apartment she lived in, seemed old and battle tested. Yet, she moved around with a strength and vitality of a young woman.

Andria immediately appraised the room with the eye of her profession. She looked at the rug she stepped on as she walked in and counted how many shoes were in the hallway. She and her companion followed their host to the living room. The hallway was long and narrow, barely fitting her companion's broad shoulders. The living room was the opposite. Andria noted that it was almost twice the size of hers. In the living room, there were two long couches and a love seat. Both couches faced the twenty-five-inch TV that sat on top of the big floor-model set that of course, wasn't working. Andria and Russel took the seat that was extended to them by their host.

"How are you and the kids doing, Ms. Dobson?" Andria asked.

"Everybody is doing fine. I haven't been able to get the kids in school yet, but you already know that."

"Where are the kids?"

"I think they are in the back room watching TV. Do you want to see them?"

"Definitely."

"Tim, Petra, come here," she called out to the kids.

The kids came out in procession, Tim in front and Petra behind. They stopped at the entrance to the living room, which was located on the left side of the couch in which Andria and her coworker were sitting.

"Say good morning, kids," Ms Dobson said in a stern but controlled voice.

In unison, they turned to Andria and Russel, and said "Good morning."

"Good morning, Tim. Good morning, Petra," Andria said, "Come over here and let me take a look at you two."
They looked at Ms. Dobson and did not move until she bowed her head slightly.

"How you guys doing?" Andria asked as she inspected the kids from head to foot.

"Okay," Tim said, and Petra nodded in agreement.

Andria spoke to the kids for the next twenty minutes, touching them as she spoke. She looked for signs of abuse by their reaction to her touches. She made mental notes to be transferred to their folders later on. When she was finished, she thanked Ms. Dobson and made her way to the door. She waited as Ms. Dobson went through her unlocking procedure. She unlocked it in a few seconds, and then stepped back for Andria and Russel to leave. As soon as the door was shut, she heard the locks slamming back in place. They headed down the stairs, not even attempting to go to the elevators. On the stairs, Andria and Russel encountered the same guy and girl they saw when they entered the building. They stood opposite from each other, staring at Andria and Russel. Russel did not stop; instead, he put his right hand under his coat and motioned Andria to go forward.

"Keep an eye on the girl and don't stop no matter what happens," he said. "If anything starts, just run and don't look back."

Andria inhaled deeply and started her movement toward the obstruction in her path. She kept her eyes on the girl as she walked by. The girl and the guy looked at her coworker. Andria stepped between them, her body shaking. Russel followed, his broad shoulder brushing against the guy as he walked by. The guy looked at him, but when Russel looked back, he looked away. Andria and Russel headed down the stairs, their stalkers behind them. It wasn't until they were out the building that Russel took his hand out of his pocket.

"What do you have in your coat?"

"Nothing," he said. "Nothing for you to worry your pretty head about."

Mr. Roundtree was worried, very worried. He got to Rashaun's office exactly at 10:00 A.M. He was wearing a maroon rayon suit with matching suede shoes. As usual, he glided into the room, sat down, and immediately began to tap his feet. He greeted Rashaun but that was all he said. He looked at Rashaun a few times and waited for him to say something. Rashaun did not say anything. He knew why Mr. Roundtree was nervous. The New York daily newspaper had run a story on him. Mr. Roundtree had two children and the piece in the paper was less than flattering.

"Did you see that shit they printed on me?" His eyes were red with anger. "They're not going to get away with this, are they?"

Rashaun answered both questions by answering the second.

"There isn't anything we could do to stop the press. They did their investigation, and they printed what they believed their readers wanted to read. Whether it is positive or negative, it is irrelevant."

"Rashaun, I have two children and a wife. They all have to live in this world with me. I love my family, and I would do anything to protect them. My wife could deal with this I think, but how about my children? They have to go to school every day and hear ribbings about their father being a drug dealer and murderer. It's not fair. A child should not have to deal with this."

"I agree with you, Mr. Roundtree, but my hands are tied where that is concerned. The best you can do is file a suit for defamation of character after your trial. But I read the article and ninety-nine percent of what they said was true. You do have an extensive criminal record dating back to your teenage years."

"I know about my record. You don't have to remind me."

"Mr. Roundtree, I think we should concentrate on the case. Your winning or losing will be the thing that makes a difference in your life. Forget about all those other nonsense."

"I just want this whole thing to be over with. I want my life back."

"Certain things you and I have no control of. What we do in that case is inhale deeply and move on. This is what I am asking you to do today, Mr. Roundtree. Today you are the story for the scared white people. Tomorrow there will be someone else. The important thing here is that you keep away from trouble the best way you can. Be very careful because if anything else happens, you will be thrown to the wolves."

"Rashaun, I understand what you are saying, and I know you are telling me the right thing. But sometimes I get so angry. I feel like lashing out at anything in my path."

"That's exactly what they want, and that's exactly what you shouldn't do."

Rashaun watched Mr. Roundtree. He had calmed down considerably since he had come into the office. He continued speaking with him for the next twenty minutes until his client was calm enough to go back home. After Mr. Roundtree left, Rashaun made two phone calls. He called his friend who worked at a beer distribution store in Manhattan and reminded him of the beer he had ordered. He called his mother to ask her how she was doing and reminded her that he would stop by later. This weekend he was having the boys over to watch the fight.

The guys started to arrive around nine. The first one to walk through the door was Tyrone. When he walked through the door, Rashaun looked at him then his hands. Tyrone understood what the look meant; yet, he ignored it.

"I shouldn't even be letting you in," Rashaun said as he stepped back from the door.

"None of the other boys here yet?" Tyrone asked as he headed to the refrigerator. "You don't mind if I start, do you?" he asked Rashaun as he took a Heineken out and popped the cap with his teeth.

"Tyrone, I do have openers," Rashaun said as he saw Tyrone make his way to the couch.

"That's all right, man. By the way, where's the food?"

"You . . ." Rashaun didn't finished answering him when the doorbell rang.

He walked to the door shaking his head. He kept saying to himself *that broke, cheap motherfucker.* By 10:30 all the guys had arrived and were sitting in the living room talking about their favorite pasttime.

"As a rule, you should know all women are bitches," Tyrone said as he gulped down his Heineken. It was his fourth for the night.

88

Most of the other guys were still on number two. "Therefore, you got to treat them like bitches."

"Nah man, you're wrong, Tyrone," Jerome said as he leaned back into the chair and a Wise potato chip disappeared in his mouth.

"Check this out, right." Tyrone stood up and waved his left hand as he talked. "You guys, you remember Lisa, right?"

There was a collective "uh-huh" that came from the six men, some sitting on the sofa, others on the floor in front of a large fifty-two- inch RCA projection TV.

"Yeah, Tyrone. What happened to that bitch?" The voice was hoarse and rough, coming from the only Jamaican in the group. His name was Pedro. How did a Jamaican brother get a name like Pedro? Well that's one of more than a million stories left in Jamaica.

"You remember I used to treat her real good, right," Tyrone said "Man, I took her everywhere she wanted to go, bought her everything she wanted. I was spending crazy time with her." He stopped to take another gulp of the Heineken. "You know what that bitch did?" He was silent for a few minutes waiting for the others to urge him on.

"What did she do, man?" Rashaun answered his cry. Actually, Rashaun already knew what happened because Tyrone had called him crying on the phone the night he found out. Of course, Rashaun knew Tyrone would leave the crying part out.

"You guys remember Terrence, right?" He again paused to get a reaction.

"Yeah," they all said in unison.

"Man, while I was treating that girl like a lady, homeboy was fucking the shit out of her, I mean that literally too."

"You know I don't fuck no ass, and I don't eat no pussy."

"Me neither, man. That shit is nasty." That voice came from the accountant in the group. He was a tall light-skinned brother named Lance. He had the look that Christopher Williams had in the film *New Jack City*.

"Shut the fuck up, nigger. You don't have to eat pussy. Those bitches be giving you the pussy just because you winked at them," George said, angrily because he didn't get pussy that easily.

"Fucking player hater," the light skinned brother said.

"Go ahead, Tyrone," George said ignoring the remark. "Pretty motherfucker."

"You know what she told me when I confronted her?"

"No man, what did the bitch tell you?" It was the pretty motherfucker again.

"She told me she loved me and all that shit, but I didn't do what she wanted me to. As if she was trying to console me, she said they use a condom every time."

"You believe that shit, Tyrone?" Rashaun had gotten up to get another beer. "Women don't ever insist on using a condom." He took the Heineken out of the refrigerator and popped the top with a can opener he had on his key chain. "The bitch is lying. Anyone want another brew?"

"Man, I hope you kicked that girl's ass." It was the pretty motherfucker again. "I don't take shit from women."

"Damn right, I kicked her ass. I nearly killed the bitch."

Rashaun knew better. Tyrone had called him that same night, crying like a baby and talking about how much he loved Lisa. They had broken up for a week after that, but Lisa kept calling and saying she was sorry, asking him to forgive her. He told her he never wanted to see her again. A month after the incident, Tyrone was back with Lisa. Two weeks later, they broke up; he couldn't get over the image of Terrence fucking Lisa in the ass. From that day, he had sworn never to mess with only one woman again. He had adopted the policy of many of his friends, which was, if a man treated a woman like a dog, she would act like a puppy. Presently, he had seven women he was treating like dogs, two of them married with kids.

"You didn't go back with that bitch, did you?" Pedro asked as he moved a Red Stripe beer from his right hand to his left. His father had told him that he should never drink from the left hand only faggots did that.

"Hell no. You crazy, man? Never, never!" Tyrone lied as his voice rose in anger and false pretense.

"You saw that punch," Rashaun said as he saw the white boxer stagger on his feet. It was the second of two undercard matches before the main event.

"Who the fuck wants to watch prerequisites, man? Turn that shit. We'll wait for the main event," George said.

The main event was a fight between Julio Cesar Chavez and Pernell Whitaker. The first undercard bout had finished about twenty minutes before; two Mexican fighters had beaten up on each other until a manager had thrown in the towel. Now, a white boy was getting his ass kicked by Terry Norris.

"Yo, Lance, what happened to that married chick whose husband lived in Virginia?" It was Jerome inquiring this time. "I heard she moved south to be with him."

"Yeah, she lives with her husband now, but I am still fucking her."

"How the fuck you do that?" Peter the oldest virgin in New York City, had finally spoken. That was soon going to change. He had a girl in church, and they were going to be married in a month. Lance, the best man in Peter's wedding, had planned the surprise bachelor party.

"That bitch called me about three months after she moved down there and told me to come on down." It sounded like one of the TV game shows. "She said she had told her husband about me."

"That bitch crazy." Tyrone had finally woke up from the slump he had fallen into after his magnificent storytelling.

"Nah, nothing like that, man. She told her husband I was a very close cousin from New York City."

"Very close, huh?" Rashaun had made his mind up—if he ever got married, none of his wife's male relatives would be coming to stay with him.

"Yo, the first time I went, I was really nervous and shit, but home girl was cool. She acted like I was really her cousin." He too stopped for effect. He loved attention.

"Check this out, I slept in the guest room that night, and the next morning she told her husband that she was taking me around town in the morning."

"She took you around town alright." It was Tyrone again.

"Yo, that next day I think we fucked all day. My dick got sore and her pussy was all red." They looked at him trying to picture themselves in his place, that pretty motherfucker.

"It was pure Blackfunk ah. You hated that woman for what she was doing, therefore, you took it all out on her pussy and in the man's house too. You see, that's why I'm not letting any niggers stay in my house, nope! Not with my fucking woman around. I'm not going to give a nigger a bed to come fuck my woman. Because I'm sorry, but if I come home, and I meet a nigger fucking my woman, they will be digging two graves and neither will be mine. After I'm finished, I am going to call that black lawyer, sorry, Rashaun, not you. The one that got OJ off." Tyrone said his piece and looked around the room to welcome challenges.

"Cochran," Rashaun said.

"You know all about Blackfunk don't you, Rashaun?" George asked.

"Yeah, I have firsthand experience with that. Once your woman has had some Blackfunk, there is no way you could do anything to her with your dick. You are fucked after she was fucked."

"What the fuck is Blackfunk?" Pedro asked.

"Check this out. When her husband came home she went straight to bed. She told him that she had eaten something that didn't agree with her," Lance said, ignoring Pedro's question in his eagerness to finish his story.

"More like drank, inhaled, swallowed through all the holes in her body, some meant for input, others for output only," Jerome said. They all burst out laughing.

"They all are bitches," George said, putting his two cents in.

"Man, when you going down again, maybe she could tell her husband I'm a long-lost cousin from Indiana." Jerome tried his best Bob Knight Indiana accent.

"What the fuck is Blackfunk?" This time Pedro stood and waved the Red Stripe beer around. "Someone better tell me or I'm going to crack a bottle on someone's head."

"Sit back down, Pedro. Let me explain what Blackfunk is," Rashaun said as he took the remote and lowered the volume on the TV.

"You are the perfect person for that, Rashaun," George said as he covered his mouth to muffle his laughter.

"Fuck you, George!" Rashaun said.

"Let the blood cloth man go on nah," Pedro said as he flung his right hands out in the direction of George.

"Finally, the Jamaican come out in you," Jerome said. "Anyway go on, Rashaun."

"Pedro, Blackfunk is what you might call acceptable rape. Even though it is consensual sex, it is a very vicious kind of sex. The man doing it is trying his best to hurt the woman. He is angry with her for something she might or might not have done. He might even be angry with another person, but that person is connected to the woman in some way. Therefore, if he can't get to the person he is angry with, he would try to hurt the nearest person." Rashaun stopped for a few seconds and took another swig of beer. The people around him kept their eyes focused on him. Once more, he was a litigating attorney. "But not everyone could actually commit Blackfunk because you have to have the tools and the necessary strength. If you have a small dick, there is no way you could perform Blackfunk. You could try your best, but the woman would just be laughing at you."

"What do you mean by small?" Peter asked. He was the one most affected by the comment.

"Don't worry about it, Peter. No one will ever accuse you of Blackfunk. You safe." George watched Peter squirm in his seat. "You have to be more than five inches erect."

"Damn, Peter, your dick ain't reach five inches?" Pedro asked.

"Let Rashaun continue, man," Peter said, trying to change the subject.

"Blackfunk started way back in the slavery days when the white woman, would come to the black man. She would not go to the house slave but the field slave. You see the house slave might try to make love to the woman he is taking care of, in no way would he try to hurt her. His mentality is of a docile nature, the opposite of the field nigger. The field nigger would be so angry at that white woman, he would try to kill her with his dick. The black slave would take out his rage and anger at the white man through his woman. Imagine you getting a chance to hurt your enemy, the enemy you hated so much that if you got a chance you would kill him. There will be no repercussions to the slave, because if the white woman goes back to her husband and tells him she fucked the slave, the white man would kill the slave but then the white woman would be discarded as used clothing. It would be the end of her life in high society, so it would be stupid of her to tell her white man. He would make sure she never forgot him and that she would be in pain for weeks to come. When the white woman went back with her husband or mate, she would be hurting because of what the black man inflicted on her. Her pussy would be all torn up and useless to a man for some time. The black man inflicting Blackfunk also had to deal with a lot of pain. His dick would hurt him for days. You see, after a man has committed Blackfunk, he is totally wasted. The woman's vagina, butt, or both would be cut bruised or plain out painful for days. She or he would most likely be unable to perform for at least a week. If anal sex were also performed, the woman would be unable to walk or sit properly for maybe a couple of days. You see, when she sits she would have to sit to one side so as not to experience the full pain. In Blackfunk, it is useless to use a condom because it is usually ripped apart during the process. At the end of Blackfunk, the man's fluid can be projected yards in front of him. Imagine that hitting a woman's vaginal walls that have been bruised during the course of Blackfunk. At the end of that release, a small child can push a two-hundred-and-fifty-pound man and he will fall. The man would also be totally drained of fluid. He would need a lot of fluid intake for the next few days to be replenished. If he or she has any diseases, they are usually transferred during the act."

"You guys are bullshitting me, aren't you?" Pedro asked.

"Please, Pedro, you Jamaicans are known for Blackfunk," Lance said.

"What?"

"That is true, Pedro," Rashaun said. "Why do you think a lot of European and American women go to Jamaica? It's sure not for the reggae music. And the Jamaican man knows he is being used so he tries his best to leave his mark. He wants her to think about him for the rest of her life. He knows when the woman goes home that she is most likely going back to her man, whether it be her husband or boyfriend. There is a certain rage there the man feels to that woman. The same is true of a man after he gets out of prison. When a man is released from prison after serving an eight-year term, he is not thinking about making love to a woman. He is thinking of destroying the pussy. There is so much anger and pain, it doesn't make a difference that the woman he is hurting is his wife who stood by him the whole time he was in prison. Some men who really love their women actually go and see prostitutes before going home to their wives because they know their capability to inflict pain at that time. The same is true of a man who finds out his woman has been having dessert on the side. What do you think the man wants to do to his wife? Do you think he would want to make love to her if he were hurt by the affair? No, he is going to want to inflict pain on her. He will concentrate on her destruction, especially the part he perceives was responsible, even though he might be trying to salvage the

94

relationship."

"Tell him how a woman feels when she has experienced Blackfunk," Lance said.

"You see, different women have different reactions to Blackfunk. Some think it might have been the best sex they ever had. Why do you think some women have people in prison for pen pals?"

"You bullshitting me! You mean . . ." Pedro started.

"Of course. You didn't think it was all about a good deed. They know most of those guys belong there, but they also know once their man is released, he will be awesome because of the anger and pain. So they wait patiently for that one night when his anger and pain will be transferred to his dick. Some people believe that Mike Tyson was conceived during Blackfunk."

"How do you know so much about it, Rashaun? Did you have a case involving Blackfunk?" Pedro asked.

"Rashaun, do you want me to answer that?" George asked smiling.

"Shut the fuck up, George." Rashaun looked at George angrily. He knew his friend was fucking with him.

"Yeah, Rashaun, tell us about it," Tyrone said eager to hear some gossip.

"I guess it would have to be another time because the main event is about to start." Rashaun grinned as they turned to the TV screen.

"Oh, one more thing. Tyson was said to be a product of Blackfunk," George said barely able to contain his own laughter.

"Shut the fuck up, George," Rashaun said. "Tyson."

FUNK 12

The women convened at Andria's apartment for Judy's baby shower did not have Blackfunk on their minds, except maybe for Judy. Judy had experienced Blackfunk, and she couldn't wait to experience it again. They were professional black women who had achieved a certain amount of success in their lives but were lacking in certain areas. The host of this event was a beautiful black woman getting very close to thirty with a nice figure but no kids, no wedding ring, and she was now beginning to get over her deep hatred toward men. Her hatred was born of negative experiences with the opposite sex, however, her latest relationship was doing wonders in re-establishing some kind of trust in the male of the species.

The oldest of the group was Hilda. She had two kids and a husband, and she was one of the most respected women on her job. Hilda had one problem: Lately she had been getting tired of that same old loving three hundred and sixty-five days of the year. Infidelity, however, was out of the question for her; she was from the old school, a school that taught her no matter how bad the situation got, one should never break that vow. Therefore, her sentence was to take the humping and dumping, which is what she called making love to her husband, and fantasize about different men. Only once in her lifetime had Hilda actually cheated on someone she was committed to. It was at her wedding shower, just before her marriage sentence. The stripper that Carla, her best friend, had invited was called Big John. At first he came in and he did his thing with all the girls in the room humping and jumping all over the place, paying no attention to Hilda. Hilda had begun to wonder who invited this jerk and decided maybe socks created the bulge in his briefs. Before she could ask her friends if her speculations were correct, the stripper turned to her. Then all of a sudden the lights went out and Hilda found herself being carried away. When he did put her down and clicked the light on, she was in Carla's bedroom. The bulge in his pants prove to be the real thing. He started his gyrations, and as he moved, his penis began to get larger and larger. Barry White was singing about practicing what you preach. Hilda felt uneasy, and her body was tingling all over. There was a candle on each night table stand with matches right next

96

to them. Before he turned down the lights, she saw a big banner in the room. It read, enjoy it, Hilda. it's all for you! He brought the wine, and she clasped the bottle in her hand. He started to dance a slow swaying hypnotic dance that made the earlier tingles spread throughout her body. She sipped the wine, and before she was finished drinking it, he beckoned her to join him and she did. And they did. And she was very happy that night because Big John lived up to his name and more. There was only one thing that Hilda didn't know about and that was the camcorder in the closet recording the event. There was a beautiful wedding the following week.

Paula was a great person. Though lacking in beauty, she had a warm personality. Dates, however, came very seldom for her, and when they did, they usually included tinted car windows. They never stayed the night even though they said she was the best. She had started to seriously consider the options of lesbianism. It seemed to be the in thing these days. There was one problem she had with it—she didn't know how the fuck a pair of tits and an artificial dick could give a person a good night's sleep.

At least Sharon was satisfied with her part-time lover. He was never there on weekends and special holidays, but she was fucked properly and her rent was always paid without any money coming from her pocket. She told her friends she was only twenty-five, and she needed this kind of relationship while she attended college. She told them the same thing when she was in high school when the affair started. Sharon had never told them about that one time when she had gone over her boundaries. It was a secret between two women that created an eternal bond between them. It was an act between two women she believed, God, in his majestic ways, would never approve of. It happened after work. Why it happened she did not know.

Her girlfriend Samantha was the only other person who knew her secret. Samantha had been married for more than ten years now. She got married at the tender age of twenty. There was always talk on the job about Samantha's strangeness, but to Sharon, Samantha was always cool.

Samantha was the one who mentioned that Mr. Fox, their boss, had left his office open. All the other workers had left a half hour earlier. Only Sharon and Samantha were left. The door that represented uncharted territory for most of her coworkers was now for the taking. Sharon felt like a little girl about to break her mommy's rules. She stood in front the door petrified, but Samantha insisted they go in. Once they were in, Samantha asked Sharon to lock the door, which she quickly did. Mr. Fox's office was like someone's living room; it had everything. There was a brown couch in the left corner of the office, with two end tables on each end. Each on table had a vase with fresh flowers on it. Opposite the couch was a stereo system and a bar containing all different types of alcohol.

Samantha went to the alcohol and almost knowingly pulled out the glasses from behind the bar. Sharon asked her if the glasses were clean, and Samantha staked her life on it. Sharon turned the stereo on, and immediately, the Sade CD *Love Deluxe* started to play. Then the women started to talk and the alcohol started to disappear. Sharon found herself getting a little tipsy, but she didn't worry because Samantha was there to hold her. But, Samantha did not just hold her. She started to dance the slow music with her, and those forbidden feelings came over Sharon. She started to say no, but Samantha had her breast in her mouth, doing things to it no man had ever done. Instead, she gave Sharon her other breast so that they both could have the same feeling.

When Samantha had finished with her breasts, Sharon opened her legs to let the juices run down. Then she felt Samantha's tongue, and she decided she would blame it on the alcohol. "Fuck it," she said to herself. "I am not here with a woman eating my pussy. Fuck it, I'm drunk and I don't know what is happening. Fuck. Who will ever know?"

She took Samantha's head and buried it hard between her legs. Soon her world exploded. When Sharon got home that evening, she went straight to the shower and let the water hit her and wash the feeling off her body. When she looked between her legs, she couldn't believe it. Blood was pouring down the drain. Her period had started. She wondered how long it had started. Then it dawned on her that what she felt coming down her legs weren't juices but . . . When she went to work that Monday, Samantha had blood-red lipstick on. When Sharon passed by her desk and said, "bitch." Samantha licked her tongue over her lips and said, "blood sisters." Sharon never said a word to Samantha after that. Every time she thought about it, she always reasoned that she was drunk and Samantha had taken advantage of her. It was funny though, after the incident, Mr. Fox always looked at Sharon with this knowing smile. There were now rumors in the office that Mr. Fox was banging Samantha. Maybe there were always rumors, but only now did Sharon hear them.

Last, but not least, there was Judy. She was well deserving of center stage with her stomach protruding ahead of her. She had finally gotten pregnant after she and Steve have been trying for more than three years. Actually, she had been trying with Steve and at least six other men who had come in and out of her life. She wasn't sure who had hit the target, but she hoped it was Steve; all the other guys looked totally different from Steve. Her prayers at night usually included a line praying for the child to be Steve's. Her gynecologist warned her about the stress she'd been putting on the baby. She told Judy she should be very happy to have a wonderful husband and a baby on the way. Judy did not confide in her gynecologist. The only person who knew the baby might not be Steve's was Andria. If you asked anyone in the room if they would be surprised if the baby was not Steve's, they would've honestly said no.

The room was filled with many different colored balloons; there were baby pictures and drawings on the wall. Andria had spent more than two hundred dollars on the decorations and the food for the party. There were also more gifts than there were people. There were gifts from Judy's coworkers and family, and from Steve's friends and family. There were about fifteen money envelopes in a pink pouch to the right side of the gifts. Her best friend Robin had called to say she would be late. Andria expected at least eight more people; many of them accompanied by their young kids. In the background, soft romantic reggae music soothed the senses of the people in the room.

Judy had retained her position on the lone armchair in the room. The rest of the women, excluding Andria, were seated on the sofa and loveseat. Andria was in the kitchen getting the fruit punch that Hilda had brought with her. It was a punch made with different fruits and a combination of natural juices and ginger ale—alcohol free. Andria made the rounds, handing the drinks out to her guests. After Sharon received hers, she headed to the liquor cabinet, drinking a quarter of the punch on her way. When she came back, her punch cup was filled again. She nestled herself back into the couch, bringing up her knees to her stomach while her feet rested one on top of the other.

"So, Judy, what name did you guys choose for the baby?" Sharon asked as she sipped lightly on her drink. She did not wait for Judy's answer. "Kashanna, Lawana, or Keisha for a girl, or Shaka, Tupac, or Kareem for a boy?"

"Sharon, stop," Hilda said, trying her best to contain her laughter.

"No, Sharon. We did not pick any of those names for the child. Actually Steve picked the name if it is a boy and I chose the name if it's a girl." Judy again tried to get comfortable in the chair; lately it seemed that only her bed was comfortable.

"So what are the names?" Sharon insisted.

"Steve chose Michael if it's a boy and I chose Samantha if it's a girl." She finally seemed to have found a spot on the chair. She was slumped to the right side with her feet crossed on the footstool.

"Samantha? Why choose an ugly name like that?" Sharon looked visibly upset by that name.

"Tell us, Sharon. When are you going to have a child?" Hilda smirked.

"When sheep fly," Paula answered for her.

I don't see any dropping from you either," Sharon remarked, turning to meet Paula's gaze.

"You two better not start anything now," Andria stepped in to clear the air of tension.

"So, Hilda, how is your old man? Can he still get it up?" Judy smiled mischievously.

"No, you did not go there. I can't believe you went there," Hilda replied.

"Uh, that hurt," Sharon added, and all of them started to laugh. Their laughter drowned out the voice of Beres Hammond.

Sharon was the first to stop laughing, and she reverted her attention to Paula. "What you laughing for, Paula? You don't get any anyway."

The words hit Paula like a dagger somewhere in her chest. For a minute, she looked sad, almost tearful.

"But at least I'm not stealing mine on the side and waiting in vain for another woman's lover." She recovered nicely and watched as Sharon took a gulp of her drink.

100

"I told you two to stop it." Andria again tried to end the banter.

"Well, Andria, why don't you tell us about this new man you've been seeing lately? After all, it's been how long?" Hilda dropped the question not waiting for an answer to the latter part but the former.

"Yes, Andria, tell us about your big-time lawyer. What's his name again, Rashaun is it? I heard he is black like soot from hell." Sharon had to somehow get into the conversation.

"Did you have him take an AIDS test?" Hilda asked, trying to find out if Andria had slept with him.

"Why don't you guys relax with the thousand questions?" Judy said.

"Yeah, it's none of your business," Paula said. "Leave the girl alone."

"Damn, Paula, no wonder you becoming an expert at masturbation," Sharon retorted as she dismissed Paula with her right hand.

"Rashaun is a nice guy. As for where our relationship is going, I don't know," Andria answered, ignoring most of the questions.

"That's it?" Hilda inquired.

Andria did not have to continue because the doorbell rang to save her from the third degree. Robin and her husband had arrived with their son. Robin's son immediately went to Andria with his arms open. He began to tell her what his recent acquisition was, and he asked her when was she coming to their house. Robin's husband took one look inside the room and quickly said bye to his wife and child. He wanted no part of whatever was going on.

FUNK 13

The boardroom was located at the end of the floor they rented from Donald Trump. It was a big room with a large table in the middle of the floor. When Rashaun walked in, there were already five people seated at the table, shuffling papers in front of them as if playing a card game. He briefly acknowledged them and took his seat opposite them. The firm held these meetings three times a year to report any substantial changes in it's operating procedures or to introduce what employees called "important hires." He had gotten e-mails from the partners to inform him they had recently hired two lawyers from a competing firm. They would be working in the real estate department so their interaction with Rashaun would be very limited.

He picked up a glass of water and took a long sip. There were glasses of water in front of each of the chairs surrounding the long oval table. A second after he put the glass down, a young white woman in a white apron came out from a seamless door in the office and refilled his glass. He looked at her strangely as she disappeared among the wood paneling in the office. This time he took a tiny sip and looked around for the lady, but she didn't return.

He looked at the clock located above the three large chairs at the top of the table. The time was 10:45 A.M. In the next few minutes, every chair would be occupied, and there would be an assortment of snacks, including fruits, bagels, muffins, and croissants. Rashaun took out the report the detective had left for him earlier that morning and began to read. The detective had gotten the police report of the shooting, including the names and addresses of witnesses. He had interviewed the witnesses and had given a short synopsis of what they said at the end of the interview. He had also given his opinion on whether they would make good witnesses. Out of the six, he had listed four as potential witnesses for the defense and two as hostile. Rashaun jotted down his own notes on the capabilities of the witnesses. The detective also found three other witnesses who weren't in the police report and that the Feds were keeping video surveillance of Mr. Roundtree and his operation.

At five minutes before eleven, Rashaun closed the folder and watched as the partners walked into the room; all the careless whispers and useless mutterings came to a halt. The head of the firm, an old white man with a full head of gray hair, took the middle seat and said good morning. He had started the law firm about thirty years ago in New Jersey and was a graduate of Harvard law school. Recently he had donated two million dollars to Harvard to aid in the research and development of a cure for diabetes. Everyone in the law firm knew him, not from talking to him, but from his picture that was in every office on the floor. The picture was taken ten years ago, and it showed a strong-willed, middle-aged man with a charming smile. There were many rumors going around about that smile and the millions of dollars he had at his disposal. His interest in women would rival President Clinton; as long as they were eighteen, there was no problem. Unlike Clinton, he preferred the skinny model type with blond hair.

Rashaun watched the man who had this multimillion-dollar law firm and wondered if he would ever command such power. He knew his skin color would be a hindrance, but he believed in his ability to be the best he could. Damn, he sounded like an army commercial, but he believed hard work would pay off in the end. He looked at his watch. Four hours from now, he was meeting with Andria at her job. He couldn't wait to see her. All these white faces made him feel like a black ghost. They had made plans to go to the movies in Manhattan.

"It better be important, Judy, for you to call me to meet with you at 11:30," Andria said as she pulled her chair and sat down opposite Judy.

"I met someone today," Judy said, twirling her straw in the glass of cranberry juice.

"Infection again?" Andria asked looking at the drink and then her friend.

"Did you hear what I said?" Judy asked.

"Yeah, I heard. So what? You meet someone every day."

"I think you know him."

"What you mean you think I know him?" Andria asked, sitting upright in the chair.

"It's your ex, Paul."

"You can have him. You two will make a perfect couple. You

both believe in fucking people over."

"Are you angry, Andria? You must be. I think that is the only time I've heard you curse."

"I'm not angry. I guess that name just rubs me the wrong way. Judy, are you asking my approval to sleep with Paul?"

"Not really. I already slept with him. I just don't want anything to mess up our friendship."

"You already slept with him? When did you meet him?"

"It was a one-hour stand, but it was a good stand."

"I bet it was."

"Oh, I forgot you knew how Paul is. How did you give that up?"

"I realize there is more to life than humping and pumping."

"I haven't found anything better."

"I know, Judy, and I pity you."

"Okay, Andria."

"If you don't mind, I won't stay and order. I definitely lost my appetite."

"So we are okay, no love lost."

"See you, Judy, and take care of your baby."

Andria walked out the door as dormant thoughts and sleeping feelings awoke to tremors inside her body. Instead of jumping into a cab and heading back to work, she started to walk to nowhere. She had thought that her feelings for Paul were dead, but Judy had proven her wrong.

"You didn't like the movie?" Rashaun asked as he changed into his blue silk pajamas.

"Do you always sleep in pajamas?" Andria asked as she went into the closet and pulled out one of his shirts. She put it on with only her panties underneath.

"You have a problem with my sleeping garments now?" he asked.

"No, all I asked was do you always sleep in your pajamas. Don't you ever just sleep in your briefs or naked?"

"No."

"Are you getting angry with me, Rashaun?"

He looked at her but didn't say anything.

"Andria, you have been in this fucked-up mood from the time I picked you up to go to the movies. I don't know what is going on

104

and I will not try to assume anything. I have been asking you what's wrong from that time, and you keep telling me nothing. Then fine, I am going to bed." With that, he slipped smoothly under the covers.

"That's it. You get piss and go to sleep. I don't have to stay here tonight if you don't want me to." She slipped into bed next to him. She hugged him as she always did, expecting him to do the same as he always did, but he didn't. She pulled her arm away and went all the way to the end of the king-size bed. He seemed miles away. Her thoughts about Paul had jumbled her thoughts about Rashaun. Should she tell him what happened that morning and what made her feel so awful? She looked at him and wondered if he would understand.

"Paul, I want to talk to you." She put her hand over her mouth. "No, I mean Rashaun I want to talk to you."

"What?" he said and sat up in the bed. He clenched his teeth, as his eyes had turned red with anger. "Did you fuck him?" He turned and held her two arms tightly by her side.

"What? What are you talking about?"

"Just tell me what's on your mind," he said, letting go of her arm and relaxing his contorted mouth.

"Judy went out with Paul."

"Your married friend?"

"Yes."

"Rashaun, where did that anger come from? You were ready to kill me, and I didn't even tell you what happened."

"No, baby, I wouldn't hurt you. Bad memories had resurfaced, and I lost it for a minute."

"Uh huh," she mumbled.

"So that's what put you in a bad mood this evening?"

"Yes."

"Baby, memories don't live like people do. They always stay with you."

"Isn't that a record?"

"I think so." They looked at each other and began to laugh. It was a shared laughter between two people who were finding themselves in each other.

Rashaun and George got to the bachelor party around ten. At that time, there were only about five other men there. The only one Rashaun and George recognized was Tyrone, who found his comfort, a forty-ounce bottle of Heineken was nestled between his legs.

"What's up, Tyrone?" Rashaun said as he extended his hands. As he did so, he brought his right shoulder to meet Tyrone's as they kept their hands together bonding black man's solidarity. George gave Tyrone the same greeting. Tyrone introduced Rashaun and George to the rest of the guys, and they all did the same salute while keeping their left hand with their drink intact.

"So where is the main man?" Rashaun asked Tyrone.

"Lance went to get him," Tyrone answered.

"When does the pussy get here?" George asked. As he made his way back from the liquor table located in the far right-hand corner of the room, he handed Rashaun a cold Heineken and held a mixed drink that was filled to the top.

"Three pussies, George. Lance hired three bitches to take care of business tonight," Tyrone corrected George.

"What you got in there, George?" Rashaun asked, peering into George's drink.

"All the motherfucking hard liquor on that table, a little of this, a little of that, my own fucking imitation of a Long Island Iced Tea. You wanna try it?" He pushed the drink to Rashaun's face.

"Nah, man. I'm cool with this Heiny," Rashaun answered.

"Where the poissy at?" The voice was loud and deep. The person it came from was a big seven-footer named Lloyd. He tipped the scale at three hundred and forty pounds.

"There goes that crazy non-English speaking motherfucker," George said, as he looked in the direction of the rapidly advancing big man. "Can't someone tell him the word is *pussy* not *poissy*?"

"Why don't you tell him, George," Rashaun said as Lloyd went to the liquor table. "You better do it now because you know what liquor does to some people."

"Nah, it's cool with me," George said as he fought the effect of the alcohol on his thoughts.

"Nigger is nasty though. Fucking nigger will eat any pussy."

Tyrone said as he gulped down the rest of the beer and headed to the bathroom.

"I will bet you twenty bucks that Peter won't fuck the girl." Rashaun pulled out twenty dollars from his wallet and showed George. It was the rites of passage for the groom and his best man to fuck the women at the bachelor party.

"Yo, man, after Lance finishes talking to Peter, Peter will jump all over the first pussy he sees. Lance is no joke where pussy is concerned," George said, wondering what the fuck he had put into the drink.

"Yeah, right."

"Okay, man, I guess money comes easy to you. I'll take the bet."

When Lance walked in with Pete, there were about twenty men in the room with professions ranging from doctor to sanitation worker. Peter kept clasping and unclasping his hands.

"Look at the nigger. He is ready to jump," George said as he drank the last bit of his concoction and headed to the bar to improve on his bartending skills. Rashaun's beer was barely past the midway point. Lance turned up the stereo and Bounty Killa sang about his sexual prowess. The wait was now on, as the doorbell became the center of attention. Every time the bell rung, everyone would look and see who came in. If they knew the person, they would go and greet. The others would just mutter under their breath and turn back to their companions.

At 12:15 A.M., the somewhat intoxicated group was finally rewarded. The ladies who walked into the small apartment that evening were a sight to behold. The first one was a tall light-skinned woman with a booming bosom and tight spandex pants that imprinted her fat womanhood. As she walked in, her ample ass sashayed from side to side as she tempted the intoxicated group. Tyrone's tongue was out of his mouth as he reacted to her provocative movements. She walked over to him, took her finger, passed it between her legs, and touched his tongue with it. The second woman was shorter than the first and also a little bit on the dark side. Her body, however, was a replica of the first. She, too, did her walk around the room in a suggestive manner. The third one was chubby, to say the least, but her lips were big, fat, and juicy.

"You guys ready for us?" the first one asked.

"Yeah!" the group shouted in unison.

"Not yet, guys. We have to get ourselves ready first." With that said, she beckoned her two friends to her. They each tongue-kissed her then began to undress her. The short one worked on her spandex and the taller one took off her top. Lance brought a gray blanket out and threw it on the floor next to the girls. The one who had taken her friend's spandex off took the blanket and spread it on the floor next to the other two. The other one guided her friend down to the floor onto the blanket. Once the tall one was on the ground, the other two continued their assault on her. They sucked her breasts and dived between her legs, alternating each other's position. Plenty of "oh shit" exclamations went off all around the room. When the tall one finally stood up, not only was she ready but so was every man in the room.

The loud shrill of the whistle sent a shiver down the spines of the excited men and women in the room.

"Men, it's time for the smell test," Lance said as he took the whistle out of his mouth. As if on cue, most of the men started making a line around the room. The women took their clothes completely off.

Their friends pulled some of the men who didn't know what was going on into place. Peter, sweat showing visibly on his forehead, was at the front of the line. The first woman came to Peter and spread her legs. Peter looked around the room and all the guys looked at him. He took his middle finger and inserted it in the woman's vagina. She moved on to the next man in line. The second girl moved to Peter. He did the same, and she went on to the next man in line. The third one did the same. After he was finished, he smelled the three fingers on his right hand. All the men in the group smelled their fingers.

"Okay, guys, let the main man choose," Lance hugged Peter as if he were a little child. Peter whispered something in Lance's ear.

"Gentlemen, Lord Peter has made his choice." Lance took Peter by the hand and brought him to the first woman who had walked in. Peter trembled like a leaf in a hurricane. Lance kept whispering in his ear. Lance chose the second one. The third one was left to entertain the rest of the men while Peter and Lance disappeared into the same bedroom.

When Lloyd saw that Peter and Lance had chosen, he shot out of the corner of the room and grabbed the remaining girl who was about to begin her solo dance. George was about to touch her tits when Lloyd made his presence known.

"Motherfucker!" George turned around to say something, but upon seeing Lloyd, reason came into his intoxicated self. Rashaun leaned against a beam in the corner of the room.

"Go, Lloyd. Go Lloyd," the men were shouting. Lloyd and the woman were in the middle of the room, his face buried between her legs. Lance had vanished with the other girl. When Lloyd took his face out and stood, he flexed his big muscles for all the guys in the room to see.

"Come on, big man, give it to me. Please, big man, give it to me!" she coaxed.

Lloyd began to undress. The men formed a tight circle around him. The short ones tried to push their way to the front. Then Lloyd dropped his pants.

"Damn," was the only word uttered from all the men in the room.

"Lloyd is king!" George shouted above the crowd. "Crown him now for being more than fifteen inches."

Rashaun looked at Lloyd's dick and had to agree Lloyd *was* king.

"Let the man with a bigger dick show it now or forever hide his dick!" Lloyd shook his dick around for everyone to see.

George attempted to unzip his pants. Rashaun looked at him. George stopped and they both began to laugh.

"That's all you got, big man," the woman on the floor said to Lloyd. All of a sudden, Sprint could have dropped a pin in America, and you could have heard it in Jamaica.

"I guess I will have to take this one up my ass." She turned around and pushed her ass in the air. "Come on, big man, let me see what you can do."

Lloyd slid on his extra-large condom. He took some beer and poured it on the lubricated condom. The bachelor party was in full swing.

Rashaun dropped the incoherently muttering George home at two o'clock. He had to practically carry him up the stairs. Rashaun deposited him in the guestroom with the help of some direction by George's wife.

"He smells awful," she said.

"It was a long night."

"What do you guys do at those bachelor parties anyway?" she asked.

Rashaun said, "Nothing much," and headed to his car.

"Joanne." He stopped, turned around and headed back to Joanne. He took twenty dollars from his wallet and gave it to her.

"What's this for?" she asked.

"Give it to George. He'll know." He turned back again and headed to his car.

"I am in love with Rashaun but . . ." Andria's voice reflected her confusion.

"You don't have to tell me how you feel, Andria. I can see it in your face, the 'but' I don't understand."

"Is it that obvious?" She started to blush. "I can't believe it's been over a year since I started to see him. He is so good, Robin, I am afraid something bad will happen anytime."

"Would you stop that, Andria? You know there are some good men out there. Not all of them are like Paul."

"Speaking of Paul, did I tell you Judy was seeing him?" She went to pick up the baby who was beginning to frown. "She came to ask me permission after she went to bed with him."

"That damn hooker. How old is her child? Two months?" She gave Andria the bottle.

"About that." Andria held the child in her arms while Robin adjusted the bib under the baby's chin.

"Did you tell Rashaun about it?"

"Yeah."

"Andria, sometimes you are a little bit too honest for your own good."

"I don't know. I had mix feelings about it, so I spoke to him about it."

"No, sister, no! You don't talk to men about these things."

She watched Andria put Rainbow on her shoulder to burp her. She was Robin's second child, and she was only a few months old.

"I don't know. I felt funny about not telling him. I have told him almost everything about myself." She lifted the bottle up so the baby could continue her assault on it.

"Andria, do you still have feelings for Paul?" Robin asked as she made herself comfortable on the couch next to Andria.

"I would be lying if I tell you I don't. I guess we had some good times together with the bad times."

"I don't like the way this is sounding. It seems to me that you are still thinking of seeing him."

"I did not say that, Robin. I just said that we had some good times."

"You did not forget that he was the one who put you in the hospital."

"Robin, you don't forget someone you loved for such a long time. You move on but memories will always be there. It doesn't mean I want to get back with him." The baby was closing her eyes periodically. Robin took her from Andria, went into the room, and placed her in the crib. She came back and sat down next to Andria. Andria tried her best to avoid Robin's questioning look.

"Andria, don't do that to yourself. Paul is not worth it." She stressed *worth*. "You know why he is messing with Judy, don't you?"

"What do you mean?"

"Andria, he is using Judy to get to you. Paul does not care for Judy. He wants to get back in your circle, and the hooker Judy is an easy way in. He thinks he knows the button to push on you no matter who you are involved with. He has the ego that tells him that if he can get to talk to you, he could convince you to go back with him."

"Robin, I don't know if I can handle seeing him."

"What is there to handle? You just look at him like the dirt bag he has always been and move on."

"I was with this guy for a long time. He knows a lot about me."

"So what? People have been married for more than ten years; they break up and still see their exes. You just have to keep reminding yourself why you're not with him and be thankful you have a wonderful man, because, girlfriend, I don't think Rashaun will put up with any bullshit."

"I know he won't, and I don't think he will have to."

"Andria, please don't be a fool like all these other black

111

women who have a good man and give him up for shit. Life is too short for that. "I don't believe you. One minute you are telling me how you are in love with Rashaun, the next minute you are telling me how you're thinking of going out with Paul."

"Robin, all I told you was Judy was seeing Paul. I never said anything about making a date to see him."

"Andria, let's just suppose here. Suppose you go out with him, and you have a good time. He gives you all these bullshit lies about how much he has changed. Next minute you're caught up in his lies and one thing leads to another. The next thing you know you end up in bed with him; you guys have a great time. But you know what? Ain't shit changed. Paul will still be the same fucked-up shit he was before, and now you will be on a guilt trip. Because, Andria, you are not a player. You never were and you never will be."

"Are you finished now, Robin?" Andria asked shaking her head. "Can I be excused now?"

"I know that you are mad at me, Andria, but that's okay. I don't care if you stay mad at me as long as you don't go out there and act stupid. Because that is exactly what you will be doing."

"Robin, I am not mad at you. I just think you should have a little more trust and faith in me. Anyway, I have to leave now. I told Rashaun that I'd be home at nine tonight. He's supposed to come over." She kissed Robin on the cheek, went into the baby's room, and kissed her on the forehead. She said good-bye to Robin and left.

"You know what's wrong with you, Rashaun?" George asked as he bit into a chicken roti. "Can't you see?" George took the chicken bone out of the roti and pointed at Rashaun with it. "It's plain and simple. You are pussy-whipped. Yep, she took that pussy, and she whipped you with it good."

Rashaun took a deep pull on his carrot juice. He had barely touched his shrimp roti. He had bitten into it but that was it. He did not know exactly what wasn't right about it, but he knew it didn't taste right. He was mad at himself for trying something different. He usually got the chicken or the goat roti. But no, this evening he felt like something different. Now he had to look at George eat his roti and talk shit.

"George, have you ever seen me get pussy-whipped?"

Rashaun asked in defense of the ultimate insult. "There isn't a pussy born or a woman with a pussy that can whip me."

"Whip, whip, whip." George took his free right hand and imitated someone being whipped.

Rashaun could not help but laugh at George's antics. "As I was saying, George. I think she is very special, and I am crazy about her."

"So that means you've not going to be fucking all those other girls anymore?"

"I told you, man, I don't do that anymore."

"So can I get the black book?"

"George, you are a married man."

"Rashaun, I look at it like this: there is a surplus of beautiful black women. Do you know that black women outnumber black men three to one?" He paused, not waiting for an answer, but to sip on his sorrel drink. "Now if I choose to settle down with one woman then one guy is left with five women. The other factor you have to understand is the criminal element in our society. Most of our black brothers are in prison and, of course, you have the sick ones who don't want women. Now those are the batty boys, and if they go with another batty boy, you know what that leaves? Now, can we afford to leave our sisters in the hands of the white man? I dare say not. It would be a tremendous disservice to our beautiful black sisters."

"Well, why don't you explain that to your wife?" Rashaun asked drinking the last of his juice.

"Well, that takes us to another point. You cannot tell women the truth all the time. My wife will never understand this reasoning mainly because of the infiltration of the women's movement on the minds of our sisters. In Africa we were allowed to have as many women as we could afford. Before a woman understood that a man must have a domain, but now they believe in a domain of only one. Black women do not understand that it is in our nature to roam the pastures. Our African ancestors have always been like that and the fact that most of us have been compromised with white blood should not change us. You see, me and you are two of the last virile men remaining, therefore, we cannot contain ourselves with only one woman."

"George, as usual, I have never heard so much bullshit in my life. Your history lessons and everything else seem to be taken way out of context. Arguing with you is a waste of time; therefore, I will not get into it. And the answer to your question about my black book is no. I have burned it because I need not have comfort in the fact that I could call anyone anytime. If this relationship doesn't work out, I am sure I would be able to have another woman tomorrow if I wanted one." He motioned the waitress over to their table and George accepted the check.

"You know what your problem is, Rashaun?" George continued as they headed out to the car. "You believe in that love thing, and that will hurt you. You don't realize that a pussy only loves a dick. And believe me, dicks comes in all shapes and sizes."

"Yours being a little bit below normal size."

"Funny, funny, ignore the wisdom I am imparting on you."George sat down in the car and released the club from his steering wheel. His wife's 1994 Maxima came to life with a turn of the key.

"Blacky, let me take you home and show you something."

"George, are you turning on me? What are you AC/DC now? That's all cool with me, but there is no need to show me. I'll take your word for it."

"Blacky, shut the fuck up and get in the car."

Rashaun slid into the passenger seat and George put the car into gear. The ride to George's house was short, a little less than ten minutes.

"Blacky, this is for your own protection," George said as he led Rashaun up the stairs.

"Please, George, I have been to your house so many times. What's in here I haven't seen? All of a sudden, you have secrets in your house. You're not a mass murderer, are you?"

"You think I'm bullshitting, don't you? Blacky, I have known you more than ten years now. I should've told you about it but I didn't. Maybe if I had, you would not have gotten so fucked up when that shit happened to you."

"What are you talking about?"

"You're one of those people who falls, and when you fall, you fall hard. The jails and the graves are full of people like you. You see, you are never prepared for what happens, and when it does happen, you are fucked. You don't love often, but when you do, you give it your all. You do not hold on to any bit of yourself, therefore

114

when you lose a love, everything comes tumbling down. The only lesson my father taught me was that all women are bitches and whores until proven otherwise."

"George, like I said before, what the fuck you talking about?"

"Men like you are sitting ducks for women. I am not saying that Andria is anything like that but you never know. I want you to protect yourself, Blacky. I will give you the eyes to see things before they happen."

Rashaun followed George past the bedroom up to the attic. George pushed the door open to the attic, and they both stepped in one at a time. The attic smelled like stale chicken cook-up, a specialty of the Grenadian people.

"Damn, George, when was the last time you been up here?"

"Sometime last month." He quickly went and opened up the small windows that barely took the scent out.

There was a ton of clothes, old lamps, blinds, drapes and other household items. In the right-hand corner of the room, there was a big chest with a massive padlock on it. George reached over one of the boards that were strewn across the room and pulled something that seemed to be glued to it. Rashaun looked in George's hand, and he saw a single key.

"What I'm about to show you is between me and you. Nobody else knows I have these things, and because I trust you with my life, I have no problem showing you them."

"George, what the fuck is this?"

After George opened the chest, Rashaun picked up a small electronic device no larger than a small button. There were five similar buttons in a small plastic bag.

"Those are transmitters."

George picked one from Rashaun and took a white phone he had in the box. He opened the receiver end of the phone, put the device in, and closed the phone.

"George, what do you need this shit for? Are you FBI or something? Don't tell me you are a secret agent working deep cover."

"Rashaun, this isn't any bullshit. You got to protect yourself."

George took up a small radio with a tape recorder attached to it and fiddled with it.

"This will record everything that is said into this phone. The tape is continuous for forty-eight hours."

Rashaun picked up a big electronic binocular and tried to adjust it by pressing a red button. George took it from him. He reached on the side and flipped a switch. The red button lit up. This will see a mouse from half a mile away, and you press the red button and it will take a picture for you.

"What do you do with these things?"

"I have a wife, don't I? You think I'm stupid? You think I will let anyone laugh at me behind my back? You think I'm gonna end up dead from some kind of disease just because I didn't protect myself? I know what I do, Rashaun, and I am human. Taking a day or two to protect yourself isn't bad. I am one of those people that if shit is happening I want to know."

"But you are . . ."

"Rashaun, this is here for you anytime you want it. I could show you how to use all of it. Don't let what happened to you before happen again. I saw what it did to you. It made you become something you weren't. Protect yourself, my brother. It's better you find out on your own instead of getting the surprise of your life."

"George, I'm home," The voice came from George's wife.

"I'm up here with Rashaun, hon. I'll be down later."

"Hi, Rashaun, did you guys have something to eat?"

Rashaun said hi to George's wife, and they both said they had eaten something earlier even though Rashaun did not complete his meal. The little he had eaten was beginning to play havoc with his stomach.

"George, won't your wife come up here and see this?"

"Nope, she will not come up here. She hates this room."

"George, I thought I knew everything about you, but I guess I was wrong."

"Rashaun, the offer still stands. Whenever you want it, it will be waiting for you."

"Nah, George, this isn't my style. I can't live like that."

"It's better than dying of ignorance. I love my wife and my child, and I will do anything to protect them."

Rashaun looked at George, and he believed his friend, at least part of it.

Andria pulled the tote umbrella with all the strength remaining in her; she had given up on sheltering herself from the rain. Damn, she was upset with herself for leaving home without breakfast. Andria had a one-on-one meeting with her manager at eleven, and like most meetings, she was not looking forward to it. It was her second meeting with her manager, Mrs. Rostein, in the past two weeks.

Mrs. Rostein's eyebrows twitched as she spoke, and the words came out like venom from an attacking rattlesnake. Andria recoiled at every syllable as her mind searched for an opening for her own remarks. It wasn't going to be easy. The words were penetrating. There were tears locked up somewhere inside of her, and someone was trying to turn the key, but she wouldn't give her the satisfaction. She had cried enough tears after Paul had left, and she had promised herself not to cry in front of anyone again. Yet her face was a picture of her insides with hurt written on it.

Mrs. Rostein was enjoying the pain she was inflicting on Andria. She loved to see her employees break down in front of her. She lashed out again, this time raising her voice to make sure all the workers heard her. Lessons had to be taught, and she was in the midst of instructing an important one.

"You disobeyed a direct order." Her pencil in her right hand shot out across the desk. If she were closer, it would have pierced Andria's chest.

"But, Mrs. Rostein, I . . ."

"There are no excuses, and I do not care for your reasons for doing what you did." She inhaled deeply and silenced Andria by shaking her pencil before she started again. "I am going to write you up in my file, and if this ever happens again, you are out of here." Her chest heaved again, and she started to write on a white pad she had in front of her.

Andria sat slumped in a small brown chair in the office. Mrs. Rostein's chair was big and black, and she felt six inches being put on her otherwise five-foot-two-inch frame whenever she sat in it. She never stood to emphasize a point when she was in her office; it would defeat the purpose.

On the wall above her chair was a picture of a child being held by its parents, the caption read, keep the family together overshadowing her big mahogany desk. There were no other pictures in the room, and the only other piece of furniture was a small coffee table with a brewer that made the worst coffee in the whole of Brooklyn.

Andria felt small sitting in the office. She had known immediately why she was called in as soon as she arrived. No one ever got called into Mrs. Rostein office on a congratulatory note. No one even liked being congratulated by Mrs. Rostein. She was a bitter sixty-two-year-old woman who thought life should have offered her more than what she had received so far. Andria knew that and so did everyone who encountered Mrs. Rostein, the forgotten Jewish princess. Andria watched her, hoping that she never became like that when she grew older. She heard stories about Mrs. Rostein; she was once married to a very rich man. He left her for a Spanish maid, and he was currently in Spain speaking the language with his new wife. He had hated Spanish-speaking people when he lived with Mrs. Rostein. She also thought he hated Marie—little did she know. Mr. Rostein did not divorce her so she kept his last name, hoping he would get tired of salsa, but that was fifteen years ago.

Andria did not think that gave her the right to talk to her this way. Andria would have told her so, but the rent was due every month. So instead, she said "yes" repeatedly and meant, "fuck you" repeatedly. After Mrs. Rostein was finished, she dismissed Andria with a backward wave of her hand. Andria muttered "bitch" under her breath and exited the foul-smelling room. On her way down the hall, she heard whispers coming from the different dividers and to them she said "bitches" under her breath, especially to the faggot who had just transferred from Manhattan.

"Got a copy of the cassette," Jim Lethal said as he waved the videocassette at Rashaun.

"I'm not even going to ask how you got it. I'm just glad you did," Rashaun said as he walked into the room.

"Your boy is innocent," Lethal said as he stood. His massive frame seemed to overshadow Rashaun.

"Don't tell me you don't have a TV and VCR in here," Rashaun said, his eyes scanning the room.

118

"That's why we have an audio and video room. Let's go," Lethal said as he threw his jacket over his shoulder and opened the door for Rashaun.

They walked down the long hallway until they came to a door that read N105 audio and video room. authorized entry only. Lethal took his keys out of his pocket and opened the door. Only four people had keys to the room—the building manager, two of the partners, and of course, Lethal. If anyone in the firm needed to use the room, they had to sign the keys out with the building manager, and most people in the firm agreed that he was an asshole.

Inside the room was some of the most sophisticated equipment Rashaun had ever seen. George would love to explore this room. There were four televisions with VCRs on the bottom, and each had a computer keyboard attached to it. There were six computers with eyepieces and some other gadgets Rashaun did not recognize.

"The last time I was here, the place did not have all this equipment."

"I heard the old man put up half a mil to upgrade this place," Lethal said as he switched on a TV and VCR. He took the keyboard and pressed a few buttons. He snatched up a pair of headphones and gave a set to Rashaun. Rashaun slipped on the headphones and immediately knew he couldn't buy them at any electronic store he knew about. The Sony TV screen was white then Rashaun saw Mr. Roundtree gliding down a familiar street. Mr. Roundtree had on a purple suit and was walking with his wife. Rashaun had met Mr. Roundtreee's wife before. She was a beautiful woman; her complexion almost the same as Rashaun's. Mr. Roundtree was talking to her when the man came in front of them and pulled out a gun.

"You pussy cloth must die for what you did!" The voice came loud through the headphones and Rashaun motioned to Lethal to turn the volume down. Rashaun saw the man pull his gun and point it at Mr. Roundtree. Mr. Roundtree then pulled out his gun out, and there was a loud popping sound.

"Look at this," Lethal said as he again punched some numbers and letters on the keyboard.

Rashaun watched as Lethal rewound the tape, then put it in slow motion. He zoomed in on the trigger hand of the man who had accosted Mr. Roundtree. He saw the man pull on the trigger three times before Mr. Roundtree took his gun out and shot him. That was the piece of evidence that would lead to an acquittal. Once the judge saw that, there would be no trial for murder. The gun possession charge would have to be worked on.

"Why did they even try to take the man to court?" he asked Lethal. "This is a clear case of self-defense; even a baby could see that."

"Babies won't be able to get hold of this tape. If we didn't get this tape, anything could have happened." Lethal rewound the tape and played it one more time in slow motion.

"Do you have copies?" Rashaun asked him.

"Yep, I already made three copies. I have yours in my office."

Rashaun thanked him and made his way back to his office. When he got there, he called Mr. Roundtree and told him the good news. He said he would come right over. He made four more phone calls, one to the district attorney's office, another to check the judge's schedule, one to his boss, and the last one to his mom. His boss wanted to schedule a meeting with him to go over the latest development. His mom wanted to know if he was stopping by for dinner that evening. He called his secretary and together they prepared for the dismissal appeal.

He did not reach Andria's house until seven that night. He had called Andria when he was leaving to tell her he was on his way, and he asked her if she needed anything. She was in the process of making dinner so she told him not to buy any snacks before he got home, especially that Snickers bar he likes to buy. When he got home, she stood naked next to the table filled with food.

"What do you want to eat?" Andria asked smiling.

The sweet smell of barbecue chicken filled the air. Yet he knew if he even went a step closer to Andria, it would be all over, and for him to get to the food, he had to get closer to Andria. A woman's fragrance was the most erotic thing to him.

"Call it, " he said as the penny went spinning in the air only to fall about two inches away from Andria. She glanced at it and started to smile.

"Heads!"

"What is it?" he asked maintaining his distance.

"Come see for yourself," she said, beckoning him over with her index finger.

"You are not right," he said, smiling. His mouth was watering, yet his dick was hard. He was hungry and horny. If he ate first, he could always fuck later, and if he fucked first, he could always eat later. Choices, choices. Who said life was easy?

"I promised my sister I would sponsor the birthday party for Sheila. Do you think we should have it at my place or at McDonald's or one of these other kids' places?"

"Definitely McDonald's or Chuck E. Cheese. Your apartment is not suitable for a kids' birthday party."

"What do you mean by that?"

"An adult movie yes, but nothing else."

"Okay, I got the picture"

"Are you inviting George?"

"Come on, Andria. When have I had anything without inviting George? I know you don't particularly like him, but you do get along well with his wife."

"How did he end up with her anyway? She is such a nice woman."

"Love is a funny thing. Sometimes it has no rhyme or reason."

"Does he mess around on her?"

"Andria, we went over that already. I told you I will not discuss my friend's love life with you."

"If he does, I hope she catches him and dumps his ass. I have felt the pain of a cheating boyfriend and it's hell."

"Andria, just suppose you find me in bed with another woman are you going to dump me?"

"I will kill you then dump you. Rashaun, I told you I am not going through this shit again."

"You mean even though you love me so much, you would still dump me? Even though you know I love you and it wouldn't mean a thing."

"Excuse me, what is this all of a sudden? Do you have plans? Rashaun, tell me right now so I can step off." Her voice had changed and she looked to be on the verge of tears. "Rashaun, I need to know what's going on. Tell me, what kind of man are you?"

Rashaun smiled trying his best to ease the tension that had filled the air. He came over to Andria and held her hands.

"I told you before that I would not cheat on you. It is not in my nature. I could never make love to someone else then come back and make love to you. I have never cheated on any of the women I have cared for, and I care for you more than I care for any other woman. I told you before, it will take me a lifetime to please you and it will." She had started to relax, and he felt the tension leaving her body.

"I love you, you know. Sometimes I think I love you more than I love myself, and that is very scary. Sometimes I wake up at night and you are gone, and I start shaking. Then I look and you are fast asleep next to me. Then once again, I am peaceful and I could go to sleep one more time. Rashaun, I don't ever want to lose you."

"Then don't," he said.

"What?" she asked, looking up at his smiling face. "Be smart, and you are not going to get any more."

"I guess you won't be getting none either." She untangled herself from him and went into the bedroom.

"Let's see who wants it the most." She came back in a red teddy.

He acted as if he didn't see her even though Johnny boy was at full salute.

"Hey honey. Can you pass me the remote?" he said as he settled back on the couch. "I heard *Alley Mcbeal* was going to be good tonight."

She picked the remote up from off the table and threw it down in front of the TV. She came and stood right in front of him. He bent to pick up the remote, and all he could see were her long, shapely legs. She unsnapped the hook that held the teddy between her crotch.

He started to bark.

"I don't trust any man. They all think with their dicks," Paula said as she paced in the living room.

"Paula, how long have you been going with Kevin?" Andria asked, trying to get some idea of what was going on. Paula had called her and said she wanted to come over and talk.

"Two months," she said without turning to look at Andria.

"Does that make a difference?"

"No, I just wanted to know who and what happened, seeing that this is the second time you are telling me anything about this guy."

"Andria, why couldn't he tell me what was going on?"

"What's going on, Paula? You still haven't told me anything."

"Andria, the fucking bastard is married. M-A-R-R-I-E-D," she said, spelling out the word for Andria. "He said if he had told me, I wouldn't want to see him," she said, getting angrier and increasing the speed of her pacing. "He said he and his wife don't even sleep in the same bed, like that makes a difference. Andria, all I want is for a man to be honest with me. Tell me the truth. I'm big enough to handle it." She had finally stopped pacing and dropped down on a chair at the dining table.

"Andria, I'm decent looking, aren't I? I have a good job with the post office. I can cook, clean, and I don't have any children. Ah!" She paused, took a deep breath then continued. "Andria, all the men I meet seem to have something wrong with them. The statistics on black men only tell half the story. Fine, there are those black men who are gay, in prison, or married, but the statistics don't tell you about all the other worthless guys around. No wonder we're left with women fighting for the few good black men around and some others jumping the racial barrier."

"I know what you mean, girl, but you have to be patient."

"It's easy for you to say. You got yourself a lawyer friend who seems to be every woman's dream. Your nights are not lonely, and the TV is not your only companion no more."

"But I have been where you are so I know how it feels," Andria said a little upset that her friend forgot all the times she told her about the different guys she had met.

"I need to go shopping. I need to go and buy a nice sexy negligee and call him over to get his opinion of it. And when I see him drooling with his tongue outside, I will tell him to get the fuck out and I never want to see his ugly fucking face again."

"You go, girl!" Andria said as she started to laugh. "But make sure it doesn't backfire."

"Paula came by today," Andria said.

"And what man was she upset with today?" Rashaun asked as

he took a seat next to Andria.

"What do you mean by that?"

"It's the broken-record complex, the same old shit over and over."

"Well, if those black men out there treated women with respect and learned to appreciate them, maybe the record wouldn't always be broken."

"Yeah, it's that all-men-are-dog shit again."

"Aren't they?"

"Yes, Andria, I am tired of you saying how men are dogs, and how much black women have to go through. Tell me, if men are dogs who are they being dogs with and how many bitches are out there? I'm tired of that shit about a good man is hard to find. What happens when you women find a good man who treats you really good? What do you do?" He did not wait for Andria's rebuttal before he continued. "Let me tell you what you do. You go around and tell all your friends about how you have a sucker. You have him wrapped around your middle finger, and he doesn't want to let go. He is a sucker who jumps when he is called. Yeah, you go around and tell your girlfriends how you have a man that's toilet trained. You women don't appreciate shit. No wonder all these guys are running around treating you women like that. You know what the prevailing opinion on the treatment of women is?" This time he waited for an answer.

"No, Rashaun, but I'm sure you are going to tell me," she said, more annoyed than angry, and it showed in her tone. All she'd said when she came over was that her girlfriend had stopped by, and he jumped all over her. Now she had to listen to this shit.

"They say you treat a woman like a bitch and she acts like a puppy. And if you treat her like a queen, she acts like a bitch." He went to the refrigerator and poured himself a glass of juice. He didn't offer her any.

"Aren't you going to get me some?" she asked surprised at his action.

"I'm sorry, dear. Would you like some juice?" he asked sarcastically.

"Oh, it's going to be like that now, hah." She started to smile.

"And some cheese and crackers to go with it." They both started to laugh.

He gave her the juice he had poured for himself and went

back to get a glass for himself.

She looked at him and realized how lucky she was. He was the most honest man she had ever known, a little bit obnoxious and egotistical sometimes, but he stood behind his principles. Her man had a backbone.

She understood that men were very puzzled these days. In a world where everything was becoming so unisex, one sometimes forgot which sex they are. The roles of men and women were not defined anymore; there is only that gray area. She hated the gray area; there was no right or wrong, or male and female anymore. And the gray area hurt the black man the most; he wasn't prepared for that gray area. He was the subject of ridicule in his home, in the workplace, and on social occasions. He was no longer the head of the family and, therefore, was not looked upon as such. In most households where he was present, he was not the main breadwinner. Society had made his wife surpass him; therefore, he was just a figurehead.

Try telling a black woman who made twice the money as her man what to do with her money. His children notice that, therefore, they looked to their mother for guidance and support. He has lost his place, it had made him frustrated and angry, and as a result, he does things just to prove that he was still a man.

One of the few things he seemed to be successful at was getting a woman in bed with him. It was one of his few remaining sanctions where he was still looked upon as king. Sometimes he purposely did the opposite of what his woman told him, spending his money unwisely just to prove it was his, and he could do whatever he wanted with it. He was constantly disagreeing with his woman just to keep his manhood.

The feminist movement has pushed the black man even farther into the back of the bus while allowing his woman to come inches forward. Of course, having a black woman in a certain position satisfied all the affirmative-action requirements in the world. What could anyone say about hiring a black woman? The minority quota is satisfied both ways, a female/minority.

Andria understood that, but she did not intend to be someone's wiping cloth. She wasn't going to be the one who is abused because of someone's frustration with his or her environment. She

125

saw the weakness in so many of their eyes, and it made her feel sick. She was very happy that she had met Rashaun because she did not know how to build up that lost self-confidence. She didn't want to dedicate the rest of her life to bringing up a man who had fallen so low.

Rashaun didn't need anything, and he kept reminding her of that, sometimes a little bit too much. He always told her that he wanted her, but he did not need her. She was not this crutch to keep him from falling. Instead, she was there with him to enhance his happiness. He once told her she could not make him happy, but she sure could make him unhappy. He also said that anytime she made him unhappy, she would have to leave because he didn't need anyone in his life making him unhappy. He could do that himself. He always made sure women knew that whatever relationship they had included an open-door policy. Either person was welcome to leave at anytime. He thought it was that easy. Of course, he didn't know everything.

"You can go in now, Mr. Jones," said the middle-aged white-haired lady sitting at the desk to the right side of Mr. Jacob's office. Rashaun got off the soft leather chair and headed to the heavy oak door of the office. Mr. Jacob was one of the partners in the firm and also Rashaun's direct supervisor. He had called Rashaun and scheduled a meeting with him at 2:30. Rashaun was in Mr. Jacob's office at 2:15. He had an idea of what the meeting was about, but he wasn't going to second-guess his boss. He had told Andria about the meeting, and she had mentioned maybe it was about a raise for his excellent work with Mr. Roundtree's case. Rashaun did not believe that there would be any congratulatory speeches.

"Come in, Rashaun, have a seat," Mr. Jacob said as Rashaun walked into the office.

"Thank you," Rashaun replied as he sat down on a soft antique leather chair. It was one of two identical chairs facing Mr. Jacob's desk.

"Would you like a drink, Rashaun?" Mr. Jacob asked as he went behind the small bar located in the left corner of the room. As he stepped behind the bar, the lights came on and lit up the whole bar. There was the smallest ice-making fridge Rashaun had ever seen and a large selection of wines, vodka, brandy, champagne, and all sorts of alcohol.

"I think I will have me a small one. My wife would be very upset with me if she saw me now, but you only live once, right, Rashaun?"

Rashaun did not answer. Mr. Jacob took the drink and walked back to his desk.

"Rashaun, you are one of the best criminal lawyers we have, and I am very happy you are on our team."

"Thank you, sir."

"But sometimes you are a little bit too honest."

"Excuse me, sir?"

"I received your message about Mr. Roundtree's case, and I am very glad you found the videocassette that's going to clear him, but there was no need to inform him at that moment."

"Excuse me, sir?"

127

"Rashaun, the firm gets paid by the hour, and your quick handling of the case has deprived the firm of additional revenue, revenue that would have gone toward making our firm better. I am not asking you to charge our clients erroneously, but only to think about the company that pays your salary."

Rashaun looked at his boss and started to calculate the cost of the man's wardrobe. The office, bar and drinks, pens, papers, and the entire knickknacks. They all were essential in the presentation of an image. Every client who walked into the office paid for that image. Clients like Mr. Roundtree took care of all the homes, cottages, expensive cars, and even mistresses. The more it cost for the expensive gifts, the more the company charged for its services.

"Will that be all, sir?" Rashaun said and got up to leave.

His boss hesitated for a second but didn't say anything.

"Yes," he said in a dry flat tone as he took up his drink and swung his chair toward the window. He was facing the opposite direction when Rashaun walked out.

Andria looked at the house from her position at the entrance to the gate. It stood apart from all the others on the block; it was a two-story house with bright red bricks. The windows were large, and the edges were painted white. Andria rang the bell located right above the lock for the gate. A voice came from a speaker next to the bell.

"Come in, Ms. Jackson," she said and Andria pushed the gate in when she heard it buzz. She walked up the tarred pathway past a two-car garage with a black Lexus parked in one of the half-opened garages. She barely touched the first steps when the French doors opened and Mrs. Persaud welcomed her in. Andria followed Mrs. Persaud down a short hallway into a large living room. The living room was twice the size of her apartment. There were three white antique couches, all of them spotless. Andria was amazed at the space in the room. On one side of the room was the most beautiful cabinet she had ever seen. Andria walked up to it and inspected it.

"Beautiful, isn't it?" Mrs. Persaud asked joining Andria in front of the cabinet.

"I have never seen anything like this before," Andria said as her eyes scanned the different carvings in the wood.

"It is all handmade, every carving was selected by me and my husband. We choose the wood and every detail was meticulously prepared by my husband."

"How much did this cost?" Andria asked.

"I don't want to be rude, Ms. Jackson, but the cost of this cabinet could feed a small country."

"I believe you," Andria said as Mrs. Persaud escorted her to the medium of the three couches.

"Would you like something to drink? My husband will be down shortly. He is in his office finishing some last-minute details."

"No, thank you."

"Andria, can I call you Andria?"

"I would prefer you do, Mrs. Persaud," Andria said. "You have a lovely home.

"Thank you, Andria, we have been fortunate in life," Mrs. Persaud said, "but sometimes you are fortunate in one thing but unfortunate in another."

"I know how that goes," Andria said.

"We have spent a lot of money trying to have children, but sometimes when it's not meant to be, it just won't happen." She made a heavy sigh and leaned on the top of the couch Andria was sitting on. "I am forty-five now, Andria my time is gone"

"There is always hope," Andria said, not knowing what else to say.

"Maybe you can help me." She turned to look Andria in her eyes.

"What my wife is trying to say is that she would like your help in adopting Tim and Petra."

Andria did not see him walk in, but she had felt his presence in the room. He came around the couch and sat opposite Andria.

"I don't see that as being a problem," Andria said as she returned his stare.

"Again, I thank you for letting us see the kids. I know it was against your agency's policies."

"That's okay, I understood your situation," Andria said. If he only knew the thrashing, she had to endure from her boss. Her ears were still ringing from the verbal assault she received.

"Ms. Jackson, I don't think we will have a problem adopting the kids, but what we need to do is to take them away for a short while. We know your agency's policy on that matter; there is no way they will let us take the kids away. We also need a witness in the ceremony. We are willing to pay for your airfare and accommodations. We need for you to be there."

"What are you talking about?" Andria asked searching his face for answers.

"Before we can bring the kids into our home, we have to expel the evil spirits from their bodies. The way their parents died was very evil, and for that, the kids will be cursed. This is not only for our benefit, but also for theirs."

"The kids have already received serious counseling, and I'm sure they are okay now. Their foster parent has not made any statements to the contrary."

"Counseling, that is an American thing. We deal with our problems a different way. Until these kids have gone through the ceremony, evil will follow them and whomever they come in contact with."

Andria looked at him and for the third time that afternoon she didn't have any words.

"I don't know what to say, Mr. Persaud, because I don't really know what ceremony you are talking about," Andria said, feeling very uneasy.

"Ms. Jackson, did you notice that none of the kids' family visits them?"

"Yes, but I think it is because they are in the system."

"No, that's not it. These kids have been cursed by their parents act, and before they could come back into the family, they have to be purified."

"What happened to Tim and Petra's parents was terrible, but it happens to families every day and they survive."

"Hence all the killing and horrible acts that gets recycled day after day. No, Ms. Jackson, we already took the risk to see the kids. Now give us the chance to save them and ourselves. We are also willing to pay for you and a companion to come with us to Grenada to see the cleansing. Only with that cleansing, can we accept the kids into our home and back into the family. These kids need to play with their cousins and get the support that our family brings."

"What are you asking me to do?"

"I'm asking you to be an observer and a witness."

"Why can't you take someone else?"

"You have been elected their guardian and that makes you a

witness.

"Ms. Jackson, all I am asking you to do is think about it. If we were going to do anything harmful to the kids, we would not have invited you. Please take some time to think about it. Thank you."

Andria did not know when he left the room. The next thing she heard was his wife's voice, soft and gentle. Andria looked at Mrs. Persaud, and she knew she had to do something. She had never felt the need to help someone so desperately in her life.

"Rashaun, I don't know anything about that cleansing stuff." Rashaun's limited experience with cleansing entailed his mother coming over and sprinkling holy water in the corners of his apartment.

"Andria, I have never heard of anyone being hurt by a cleansing, and like the man said, if he was doing something that would hurt the kids, they wouldn't have invited you."

"And you have no problems going with me, do you?"

"When were they planning to leave?"

"I think as soon as they get custody of the kids. That's supposed to happen next week."

"Well, I have already been to the judge earlier this week and the case, except for some formalities, is over. I have a meeting with Mr. Roundtree on Monday, and we could leave anytime after that."

"Rashaun, I'm scared."

Rashaun got off the couch and went to Andria. He circled her waist with his hands, and he held her tightly against him. He felt her body tense, and then she relaxed in his arms. He kissed her on the back of her head.

"It's okay. Everything will be all right."

Rashaun had spoken to his boss, then his secretary earlier in the morning. He made a few phone calls to tell his friends he was going away for a week. He had mentioned it to George when he saw him earlier. George had asked him if he could come along. He had heard how the Grenadian women went crazy over guys from the States. George also wanted to know why Andria was going along. He believed that would limit the fun to be had in the sun. Rashaun told him that it wasn't that kind of trip. George thought he was stupid to bring fish to the fish market.

Andria called Rashaun earlier that morning to tell him they could leave either Friday or Saturday. Rashaun told her it was better if they left on Saturday. She agreed because it gave her more time to make arrangements for the rest of her cases. His secretary buzzed him at three to inform him that Mr. Roundtree was waiting to see him.

"Thank you again for taking the time to handle my case," Mr. Roundtree said as he stretched his right hand out to Rashaun.

"You are welcome," Rashaun said, shaking Mr. Roundtree's hand.

"As a show of my appreciation, I have brought something for you, but please open it after I leave. I am a little self-conscious." Rashaun looked at Mr. Roundtreee's purple suit and smiled inward. He wondered how Mr. Roundtree could say he was self-conscious with a purple suit.

"I understand, but you didn't have to give me a gift."

"I always show my appreciation when someone does something good for me. In this world where people are only after what they can get, I really appreciate your kindness. I also know you could have delayed the showing of the tape and gotten more money from me for the defense, but you didn't and for that I'm thankful. Hopefully, I won't have to use you again, but I will definitely remember you."

He again thanked Rashaun and handed him a Macy's bag with a gift-wrapped box in it. He turned and walked out of the office. Rashaun sat back in his chair and looked at the Macy's bag on his desk. He wanted to open it, yet he wasn't sure if he should. He went and locked the door to his office. He pulled the shades down over the windows and went back to his desk. He took the box out of the bag and weighed it in his hands. It didn't feel particularly heavy. He took scissors from his desk and started to cut the wrapping off the box. He opened it to find two boxes, a black one and a white one. He opened the white one first. In it he saw nothing but hundred dollar bills. He estimated it to be about five thousand dollars. Rashaun had gotten monetary gifts before but never so much cash. He eagerly opened the second box, which was the heavier of the two. The glint of the silver metal was the first thing that caught his eye. Maybe he should close the box right now, but he hadn't felt one in years. He didn't take it out, but instead he reached for the note that was above it.

This is a gift of life, not death. It has never been used, and hopefully you will never have any reason to use it. But, if you do, you would be the only one to use it. I took the number off it to protect you. Please accept it because you saved my life. With sincere appreciation, Mr. Roundtree.

Rashaun looked at the door to his office and saw that the latch on the back was turned up. Only then did he lift the gun out of the box. On the side, he found the sixteen-shell clip and slid it in. He took the safety off the gun and pointed it straight ahead. He sprung his chair around aiming the gun at different parts of his office. He wondered if he would ever have the need to use a weapon again. It had been so long since he held a gun in his hands. The last time he did, someone got hurt. It was the only time he had put down his fist and picked up a weapon.

A weapon was not good enough to use on Paula for messing up her schedule. Andria stood in front the store on Flatbush Avenue, tapping her right foot on the pavement.

"What's up, Shorty? You waiting for me?" A boy no more than sixteen said as he rode by on his bike. She ignored him the same way she had ignored the guy in the Lexus who promised her roses.

"What?" She felt someone tap her on the shoulder.

"Damn Andria, why are you so tense?" Paula said as she looked into Andria's angry eyes.

"Come wait here for half an hour, and tell me how you would feel," Andria replied. "I think I got hit on by every man on Flatbush Avenue, and I didn't like how some of these women were watching me either."

"Okay, Andria. I'm sorry for making you wait," Paula asked a big smile on her face.

"I'm glad somebody is happy. Are you going to tell me why you had me come here when you know I'm trying to get ready for my trip?"

"I met someone."

"And?" Andria said, looking ahead to the lady in the bright colored dress entering the store.

"He is young."

"Like I said before, and?"

"Really young."

Andria stopped walking and turned around to face her friend.

"How young are we talking about here?"

"But he is very mature for his age."

"That young, huh. Are we talking early kindergarten here or a high school diploma?"

"Andria, please."

"Tell me, does he have a job at least or does he need his working papers from school?"

"Andria, you know my history with men so please don't make fun of me."

"Are you that serious? What have you done with that guy?"

"Did I sleep with him is what you are asking?"

"I'm not asking anything. You said you wanted to talk to me before I left. Here I am, but all you have told me is that you have met someone and he is young. As far as I'm concerned, there is nothing wrong with seeing a younger man."

"He's eighteen."

"Eighteen! What did you do? Ask his mother if he could come out and play?"

"Andria!"

"I'm sorry, but when you said he was young I thought you were talking about early twenties or something."

"You don't approve?"

"It's not whether I approve or disapprove. I personally would not date a guy so young. He doesn't have anything to offer me."

"And what have all these older men I have dated offered me? They didn't offer me shit. Not a damn thing! Andria, you know my history. You know where I've been. What's so wrong if this guy is giving me what I want?"

"You mean boy, " Andria muttered under her breath.

"What did you say?"

"What do you want from me, Paula? I can't tell you what to do. You are a grown woman."

"I wasn't asking you to tell me what to do. I don't know what I wanted from you. I just wanted to tell someone, and you are one of my closest friends."

"I'm sorry, Paula, I guess I don't deal with different too well. I guess if he is good for you and it works, then go for it."

"I guess."

"Mama never told me there were going to be days like this."

"Maybe she did, but we just weren't listening."

"Come, Paula, I have to go to this store and get some things for the trip."

If there was someone who loved his mother more than Rashaun, he didn't know who it was. She had always been there for him, and he made a promise to himself that he would do the same for her. She was getting older and she didn't have that commanding presence she had when he was a kid, but she was still Mommy, one of the strongest black women he had ever met. She set the plate of food in front of him and then went to get him some juice. He did not dare tell her he could pour his own juice. It was the way she did things. It was the way she brought him up. Rashaun never touched the pot until Mom shared the food.

"So you're going to Grenada for a week? Boy, you remember anything about the West Indies?"

"Mom, I did go back in the early eighties."

"You know how many times your sisters and brothers been back to Barbados? I bet you don't."

"Mom, I'm not like my sisters and brothers. You should know that. I'm not going back to the Islands every year to see the same thing over and over. I have been to Barbados twice. That's enough. Half of the people I grew up with are up here so who am I going to hang out with. I don't even like carnival, so forget about Cropover."

"Boy, I don't know what to say to you."

"Mom, all I asked is if you know anything about cleansing." Rashaun's mother pulled out the chair next to him and sat. It was one of the few times he had seen his mother sitting. His memories growing up with his mother were of constant movement. She was either walking around doing chores or running to work. Even now, whenever he came to the house, his mother was still on her feet. Her face was not as smooth and sharp as it used to be, but it was still strong.

"Boy, are you thinking of getting a cleansing?"

"No, Mom, it's not for me."

"Who is doing the cleansing?"

"A woman in Grenada."

"There is only one woman in Grenada qualified to do a cleansing, and she is very expensive."

"Well, the people have a lot of money so I guess she will be doing it."

"Good."

"Mom, does this thing really work?"

"Why don't you try it and see? God knows you need a cleansing."

"Very funny, Mom."

"Do you see me laughing? I think I will suggest that to Andria when I speak to her. You are still with Andria, aren't you?"

"Yes, Mommy dearest. I'm still with Andria."

His mother got up off the chair and pushed it back in.

"I'm tired. I'm going to lie down. Make sure you wash all the dishes before you leave."

"Love you, dear."

"Yeah, yeah," she said and disappeared from the kitchen.

Rashaun held on to Andria'sds as the plane took off, but he wasn't sure if it was for her benefit or his. He hated flying. His heart always skipped a bit at takeoff and landing. He looked into her face and saw a tight restricted smile on those beautiful lips. He leaned over and kissed her.

"What's that for?" Andria asked him finally relaxing as the plane started to climb farther away from land.

"Because you look so cute trembling and nervous as the plane took off."

"Well, I did feel an extra squeeze in my hands as the plane took off. Don't tell me that a big, strong man like you, is afraid of a little flying.

"Me? Scared of flying?" He pointed to himself.

The plane trembled as it passed through a little turbulence. Again he squeezed her hand.

"You want something to drink? You look a little pale. You are not going to throw up or anything like that."

"Ha ha," he said relaxed as the pilot turned off the seat belt sign. The flight attendant, a beautiful Jamaican hostess, came with their snacks and soda. She smiled at Rashaun as Andria looked on.

"What was that big smile about?" Andria said as the hostess finished and headed down the aisle.

"Insecurity is an ugly thing," Rashaun said smiling.

"You could have her if you want. I don't care."

"You are so beautiful when you're angry," he said as he took her hand and pinched her cheek.

"Ah ha, here comes a man."

Rashaun watched as a tall light-skin black man walked down the aisle. Andria pushed out her tongue and licked her lips. Rashaun kept smiling. The man looked at Andria and continued to walk past them, not once acknowledging her attempt at seduction. He went to sit next to a white man in a brightly colored shirt.

"He's got to be gay," Andria said and slumped back in her seat.

"You're right, baby. Anyone who could pass up this fine black woman got to be a fruit."

"But the least he could've done was smile."

"Baby, you are too much."

She pulled him to her and kissed him long and passionately.

"Have you ever done it in a plane?" Rashaun asked when she released his tongue.

"Nope and today is not going to be the first time."

"Just asking."

As Andria leaned back to get comfortable, a short young boy passed by and winked at her.

"You see and you weren't even trying."

"Rashaun, he was only sixteen, maybe seventeen at most."

"Seventeen is legal."

"Rashaun, you would go with a seventeen year old girl?" she asked, her eyes rolling up at him.

"Andria, people do different things in different times of their life. Sometimes not everything is logical. Things a person does when he is at certain points in his life, he might not do in other times."

"Rashaun, you are rambling and that means you are bullshitting. In other words, you would have a relationship with a woman half your age. Maybe my question should be, whether you slept with a teenager before."

"Andria, we both agreed we would not talk about our pasts so let's cut this right now."

"I guess I got my answer."

"Whatever," he said.

The last thing she remembered was turning around to go to sleep. She felt Rashaun reach over and put his arms around her. At first she struggled to get away, but when he released her, she pulled his arms back around her. They nestled their heads together as the sky became their companion, for now.

"Yes, you do have to walk to the terminal," Rashaun said as they got their onboard luggage together. When the airhostess opened the door, Rashaun smelled the sweetness in the air. It was a fresh scent that flowed through the plane, welcoming the passengers to the isle of spice. He followed Andria toward the exit. The full scent of this little island hit him when he stood in the doorway of the plane. It was a scent he was unaccustomed to in the hustle and bustle of New

York City.

It was like a woman's fragrance without the added chemicals. Instead, the plants and the flowers mixed with the sea in the distance had combined to create a very refreshing scent. He felt like he was being lulled to sleep just by standing there for a second or two. Andria pulled on his arm to remind him to continue his progress. She, too, was enjoying the beauty of an untouched island. Grenada was one of the few remaining islands untouched by technology and the evils of the industrialized civilization.

"This is beautiful but hot," she said as she put her arms up to stretch. At the same time, a cool breeze hit her body and took her only complaint away. "Rashaun, you gave this up to come to New York," she said as she looked at him, her eyes reflecting the sunrays.

"Andria, you are forgetting that I am from Barbados not Grenada. Grenada is a much more mountainous country. I came over here when I was very young, but I can't remember much about the country . . .."

"Rashaun, take my picture here."

"In the back of the airport?"

"Why not?" She took the camera off her shoulder and handed it to him.

He arched his back and snapped her picture. She put the handbags down and threw her hands in the air.

Once again, he took her picture.

"Now you."

"Andria, we did not clear customs yet. Can this wait?"

She pushed her mouth out and started to walk to the terminal. He felt good. He needed this time off from work and New York. He hadn't taken someone he actually cared about on vacation in a long time. He took women on vacation often, but he didn't really care for them the way he felt about Andria. Many times when he went on vacation with his friends, all they did was meet women and party, but looking at Andria in that short skirt strutting down to the terminal made him very pleased with this vacation.

"Wow this feels good," Andria said as she walked out of the shower, naked except for a thong that disappeared between her well-shaped butt.

"Looks good too," Rashaun said as his vivid imagination lifted him off the couch and into . . .

"Rashaun, I know that look," she said, giving him a wicked smile.

"Where is the camera? Now I feel like taking pictures. Just stay right there."

"Rashaun, don't even think about it."

He got out of the wicker chair and made his way toward the room. On the way, he reached out and smacked Andria on the butt.

"Stay right there," he said and walked on.

"I intend to, for a long time."

In the middle of the room was a king-size bed made up with sheets that had the nutmeg embroidery on it. In the corners of the room were small flowers giving off a nice fresh scent. There was a loveseat at the far right corner of the room and a chair with a desk and a cordless telephone opposite from it. On top of the desk was a menu with all the food, wine, and drinks available with the touch of a button on the phone. On the sides of the bed were two night tables with lamps made from the country's coconut fruit. Rashaun touched the bristle coming from the lamp and the light came on. He went immediately to the right drawer because he knew that was where Andria would put his clothes. Sure enough, the drawer was packed neatly with his undergarments. He began to take his clothes off; halfway through the process, he heard music coming from the living room, calypso music, a popular Soca song from one of Grenada's most popular singers, Inspector. Rashaun started to whine as he continued to change his clothes and hastened off into the shower. The warm water beat down on his skin almost as if it were trying to pierce his blackness. He tried to adjust it, but the lowest level still gave him a sting, and he realized it wasn't the water pressure but the water itself that was heavy.

He emerged from the room to find Andria had moved out to the patio. She stood there with a small halter top and that damn thong on. There were no words to describe her so he did what came naturally to a man—he went to his woman.

She could feel him behind her. She had ordered two drinks when Rashaun was in the shower and hers lay half-empty on a small table. She did not know if it was the drinks, but her body was wet in anticipation. She wanted him then and there; she wanted to feel all of him in her. Her body shivered when he came up behind her and kissed her on the neck, a soft brush-like kiss that started behind her right ear and ended at her shoulder. He continued with his kisses moving from the left to the right; then his magic tongue painted pictures of butterflies on her neck. He reached down just above her navel and pulled her halter top off from the back, then slowly flicked his thumbs over her nipples. With his tongue, he continued to trace the hollows of her back, over the butt he had admired so much earlier, working his way all the way to her ankles. Then he moved to the left side and moved up from her ankles.

She felt him against her, hard and powerful. He had engulfed her body as well as her soul. As his tongue traced her body, she felt his penis against her butt, hard and unbending. She wanted him to be inside of her. She loved that black man, the way she loved the child she never had. She loved him the way God intended a woman to love a man. She would love him today and forever.

"I love you," she whispered, not sure if he had heard her.

"Don't say anything," he said as he continued kissing her.

This time his tongue raced the inside of her thighs. She held tight to the railing for support, as her knees had become weak. He nudged her legs apart, giving himself total access from the back.

He followed his finger with his tongue, pulling the thong to the right side of her butt cheek. His tongue kissed the line that was previously hidden by the string. She smelled clean and sweet, and as his tongue traced the lips of her vagina, he felt the tremors in her body. He continued to flick his tongue in and out, swirling his thumb over the nubbin that held the key to paradise. As her body shook, she could no longer hold herself back and climaxed with a force that reverberated along Rashaun's tongue into his penis. Like the night that surrounded them, she disappeared in those big beautiful black arms, which cradled her as she collapsed.

Rashaun watched her asleep in his arms and realized he was a very lucky man, blessed with one of God's most beautiful creations. He kissed her on the forehead and looked up at the stars hovering above this beautiful island. He felt at peace with Andria, a feeling a woman had not given him in years, too many to count. He did not know when he had fallen asleep but was awaken by Andria trailing his body with kisses. He tried to reach up and touch her, but she pushed his hands easily and continued kissing him. Her soft, wet lips ran over his skin with feathery touches. His torso arched up to her demanding mouth. Her tongue darted in and around his navel and then down to his scrotum. She continued doing that as his penis stood twitching at the sky. Slowly her tongue traced the full length of his rock hard penis.

"Damn, damn," he groaned as his toes curled into unnatural positions. When she engulfed him in her mouth, he felt like the world was about to explode. Then she stopped.

He looked at her.

She looked at him and smiled. She reached for him with her right hand to help him up. When he stood, there was a distance of about nine and a half inches between them. She turned around and bent down, touching her toes and exposing him to what he had craved all evening.

He looked up at the sky and thanked the Lord for an angel like Andria. When he entered her "whatever" was sweet in this world, he had. Whatever felt the best in the world he was with it. Whatever was nice, cozy, and warm, he had just found. He could feel his heart ticking and hear the fishes a half-mile away communicating. And as he started to go back and forth inside of her, for the first time, he saw the Macy's day fireworks explode in Grenada.

"Don't leave me," he murmured to her.

"Never," she replied.

The knock on the door was not loud but persistent. He took Andria's hand and moved it from around his neck. At first he thought he was dreaming, but the knock continued as his eyes became accustomed to the brightly lit room. He sat up on the bed and searched for his robe. Unlike Andria, he had his underwear on. That was part of his nature. He never went to sleep without his underwear. On the chair on the side of the room, he saw his silk robe and hurried to it. It was obvious the person at the door had no problem knocking; it actually seemed like they were enjoying it. Rashaun went into the bathroom, washed his face and quickly brushed his teeth. When at last he opened the door, a small Indian man in colorful shorts and a bright yellow shirt stood looking at him.

"Good morning," the little man said, immediately breaking the silence.

"Good morning, sir," Rashaun said, recognizing the Indian man for the first time. Andria had briefly described him.

"My name is Mr. Persaud." He put his right hand out for Rashaun to shake it. "Are you enjoying your stay in Grenada?"

"Yes, we are enjoying every minute of it, but I'm sorry Andria is not available at the moment. Do you want to leave a message for her?"

"Please tell her that we are leaving tomorrow. The truck will be parked in front of the lobby at five in the morning. Please pack clothing for at least two days, just in case we have to stay longer. You are coming also, aren't you?" He looked at Rashaun with a penetrating gaze that demanded an immediate response.

"Yes, I will be going with Andria," Rashaun replied, surprised that the man would ask such a question.

"I will see you tomorrow then." He turned to walk down the hallway.

Rashaun closed the door and went back to see if Andria had awoken. It was twelve, midday, when they left the hotel to tour the island.

The guide awaiting them in the lobby was a tall dark man whose face appeared tanned by the relentless rays of the sun. He met Rashaun and Andria next to the phone in the vestibule as arranged by the bellboy. Dressed in white shorts and a blue shirt, he looked to be in his early forties.

"Good evening, sir, madam," he said as he stretched his hand out to greet Rashaun. He gave Rashaun a firm handshake and bowed his head politely in Andria's direction. "Have you been to the island before?" he asked.

"Yeah, I was here when I was very young. Don't remember much."

"Well, much has changed, yet many things remain the same. I like to believe that our island remains untouched by industrialization unlike many of the other Caribbean islands. Many of our old ways are still the same, and modernization has not poisoned our water and polluted the air."

Rashaun thought he sounded more like a scholar than a tour guide. Even though he spoke with a Grenadian accent, his words were polished and smooth.

"Have you always lived on the island?" Andria asked as they stepped into the open-back jeep. The jeep was painted gray with a black stripe going around it.

"Well, I was born in Grenada but educated in London where I worked for a short period before returning home. I realized there wasn't enough money in the world to keep me away from the splendor and the beauty of my homeland."

They blew past a car on the road, and Andria grabbed onto the side of the jeep, certain there was going to be an accident.

"Do you guys always drive this fast on these narrow roads?" she asked as another car came too close for her comfort.

"I think we should go to the market first," Rashaun said as he tried to adjust his legs in the confines of the jeep. Behind him Andria had gotten hold of the two passengers handles on both sides and as the jeep bounced, so did she.

"I've heard that Grenada has a lot of history. The only thing I know about the island is our invasion in 1982." Andria said.

"1983, " the man corrected. "Let me give you a brief history lesson on Grenada. "Our recorded history began in 1498, noticed I said recorded. I believed our history started a long time before so-call Christopher Columbus landed on our island. The English tried to set up tobacco plantations, but the raids by the Carib Indians were too much for them to handle. In 1650, Governor Du Parquet bought Grenada from the Caribs for a few hatchets, some glass beads, and couple of bottles of grog."

"Cheap price for a country," Andria said.

Rashaun turned back to see her with a beautiful naughty smile on her face.

"As I was saying," the driver continued.

"Excuse me, I didn't get your name," Andria said.

"Albert James the third," he said with a little irritation.

Rashaun looked back at Andria, who rolled her eyes. They were about to go around one of the many curves in the road when the jeep stopped and pulled up closer to the grass.

"Is there a problem?" Rashaun asked, wondering if Andria's clowning was going to get them stranded in God knew where in Grenada.

"No problem, man, just waiting for the truck to pass."

"What truck?" Andria asked.

Before Albert answered, a midsize truck carrying bananas flew by them, shaking their vehicle as it passed.

"Wow," Andria exclaimed.

"Now we proceed," Albert said and slipped the jeep into gear. "Within a year, the French were weary of skirmishes with the Caribs and sent a contingent of soldiers to sort the locals out. The Caribs were routed at Sauteurs Bay, but rather than submit to the colonists, the survivors—men, women, and children—jumped to their deaths from the precipitous coastal cliffs."

"Why did they have to take the kids?" Andria asked.

The jeep slowed down as the streets suddenly became very crowded. There were people walking all over the place, daring the drivers to hit them. On the corner, a group of kids danced to Soca music blasting from a boom box.

"This must be it," Andria said, her voice cracking with excitement.

"No, we are not in the market yet," Albert answered, "but we are very close."

"These roads have more curves than the Interboro" Andria said.

"What?" Albert asked.

"The Interboro is a highway in Brooklyn that has a lot of curves," Rashaun said.

"I think we should park here," Albert said to no one in particular.

Albert rode up on the sidewalk and parked behind a car that was called a Daihatsu.

Andria was the first one out of the jeep followed by Rashaun. She waited for Rashaun, and then when he came out she slipped her hand in his. Rashaun was not much for holding hands but submitted gracefully. It was a different country, therefore, his rules were different. Rashaun and Andria stood on a sidewalk barely wide enough to hold one, waiting for Albert to secure his things in the jeep.

The walk to the market was a short one. Albert continued to supply them with more of Grenada's history.

"The smell! It is so fresh and clean," Andria said as they walked into the market.

"Wait till you get to the back of the market," Albert said.

There were vendors all over the place, some with only brown string bags spread on the ground to keep their products from the asphalt. The people in their colorful attire sold almost anything and everything. Fruits and vegetables seemed to be the major produce. The vendors with produce were situated in the middle of the market while the vendors selling cooked food had their stalls on the side. These people sold fried fish, roti, roast corn, cake, bread, and blood pudding, a delicacy that consisted of pig intestines stuffed with bread soaked in pig's blood. Albert asked Andria if she wanted to try it, and she countered by asking him if he was an escaped mental patient. Rashaun bought them some roast corn, which they ate as they moved through the market. Andria also brought some fish and bakes, a flat bread to eat later at the hotel. They had waited patiently as Andria picked the fish out and watched the lady fry it in a big black frying pan. She then put a sauce with plenty of onions on top of it. Albert then challenged them that if they ever ate sweeter fish than this he would move to whatever country they brought it from.

"I am starving," Rashaun said as he threw the cornhusk in a big garbage container.

"I know just the place for you guys to get something to fill your stomach," Albert said and increased his pace. He stopped in front of a roped-off section of the market. Inside there were about five small tables with two chairs for each table. Three of the tables were occupied, two with white couples and one with two black men who seemed out of place in this setting. Rashaun and Andria followed Albert as he squeezed through a small opening in the rope. He motioned them to sit down and went to the back where a large lady in a black apron was talking to a tall skinny middle-aged-looking man. He spoke to her for about fifteen seconds, and she followed him to Rashaun and Andria's table. Albert pulled a chair from the other table and turned it around so the back of the chair was facing the table.

"This is Mrs. Paul. She owns the best restaurant in Grenada," Albert said as Mrs. Paul's face lit up with a smile that covered the marketplace.

"Nice to meet you," Rashaun said as he stretched his hand out to be engulfed by the big fat hand of Mrs. Paul. Andria murmured her greetings, as her hand was also lost in Mrs. Paul's big grip.

"Pauly, what we have today?" Albert asked.

"Well, today, boy, we got crab-and-chicken soup, steam down with manicoo, and stew chicken or beef with rice and peas and provision. We got calaloo and okra on the side, and to wash it down; we have cola, sorrel, and ginger beer."

"What did she say?" Andria asked.

"I think if you want to eat a traditional Grenadian meal, you should start with the steam down with Manicoo. Manicoo is a meat only found in Grenada and steam down is our way of preparing certain vegetables and things you will not find anyplace else," Albert said as he rocked his chair back with a toothpick sticking out of his mouth.

"I say when in Rome, we do like the Romans do. What can't kill you will only fatten you. Steam down for me," Rashaun said.

Everyone turned to look at Andria. Andria looked at Rashaun.

"Girl, you got to try it. If you don't like it, you don't have to eat it. My husband is a great cook but not everyone likes what he cooks. I promise if you don't like it, I'll give you stew chicken with rice and peas. You ate that before, haven't you?" Mrs. Paul asked.

Andria shook her head in agreement.

"What you guys drinking?" Mrs. Paul asked.

"A large glass of sorrel for me, Pauly," Albert answered.

"I will have ginger beer and a glass of water," Rashaun said.

"I will have the sorrel," Andria said, remembering the time she had sorrel at a friend's Christmas party. The sorrel was sweet and delicious. Her friend informed her after she had drunk it that she had put little rum in it.

"Do you put rum in the sorrel?" Andria asked Mrs. Paul.

"No, sweetheart, the sorrel is just pure sweetness. Now if you want some rum in it, I will be glad to put some for no extra charge."

"No! No! I had it once and there was rum in it so I was only checking."

"It must have been at a private party around Christmastime," Mrs. Paul said.

"Yes, it was."

"Well, I will go and put the order in now," Mrs. Paul said and went over to her husband who was leaning on the entrance door to the kitchen.

"Well, I guess you don't want the chicken with peas and rice anymore," Mrs. Paul said a while after looking down at Andria as she took her fork and tried to scrape the last piece of breadfruit with calaloo off her plate. Rashaun and Albert laughed as they watched the concentrated look on Andria's face.

"This is the best meal I have ever had," Andria said, as she took a white napkin and wiped the oil off her mouth.

This was the quietest Rashaun had ever seen Andria during dinner. He had tried to talk to her while they ate, but after the third "un-huh," he had given up. Andria had not spoken a word until now.

"Mrs. Paul, I have to have the recipe," Andria said looking up at Mrs. Paul with a pleading look in her eyes.

"There is no recipe for steam down. Everybody cooks it differently. Half the time my husband don't know what he going to put in it until he start cooking."

"Please, Mrs. Paul, just give me the main ingredients and tell me what goes in." Andria was not ready to give up.

"Okay, I will write it down for you, but remember you might not be able to get the fresh stuff in the States. I know you guys get everything from the Chinese man, but they don't be fresh. I will give you guys a bowl of soup to go with. Don't worry, it's on me," she said as she headed back to her husband who had resumed his position against the doorframe.

"Pauly has a big heart, and I think she's taken a liking to you, Andria," Albert said.

"I think you are right, Albert. But it is time for us to leave. We have a full day ahead of us tomorrow," Rashaun said.

Albert motioned to Mrs. Paul to bring the check. She brought it over and gave it to Rashaun. Rashaun looked at it and was surprised that the food cost so little. She left the check on the table and told them she would be right back. She came back with a paper bag that looked weighted.

"This is for you." She gave it to Andria.

"Thank you very much," Andria said.

"There is some black cake and plain cake in there," Mrs. Paul said and took the money that Rashaun had left. "Will be back with the change"

"No, it's for you." Rashaun said.

"Thank you very much," she said.

The ride to the hotel was uneventful. Andria kept talking about the food and how nice Mrs. Paul was. She was already making plans to return to the restaurant very soon. Rashaun reminded her that their time here was short and there was a purpose to the trip. Andria told him to relax and, as the Grenadians would say, "take it easy." Albert smiled as he listened to the exchange between Rashaun and Andria.

Rashaun looked at his watch and shook his head. It was much too early in the morning to be jerked all over the place. He kept his eye on the driver who seemed too busy watching Andria and not the road. He kept smiling at Andria, whose attention was on the surrounding area. In the passenger seat, Mr. Persaud sat staring straight ahead. He was the first one in the jeep after they had made their greetings earlier. Andria had hugged and kissed Tim and Petra who seemed to be enjoying the vacation. It was the happiest she had ever seen them. They seemed to love their aunt, and there was obvious respect and admiration for their uncle.

The second jeep was about two lengths behind the white jeep; that jeep held Mrs. Persaud and the kids. Mrs. Persaud was in the front seat and the two kids were buckled down in the back. The twist and turns in the road made it difficult to sit without sliding. Andria took great interest in bumping into Rashaun even when the jeep wasn't swerving. Mr. Persaud had said that the ride was going to be about an hour and a half. They were going from St. Georges through Grenville and up Grang Etang. The drivers knew how to get there but were not allowed to enter the gate.

Twenty minutes into the ride, it started to rainsuddenly and heavyly. They had just left the town when it started. As they drove through, Rashaun noticed the small rivers of brown water flowing on the side of the road. The driver put the wipers on high, yet he had to peer through the glass to see in front of him. He drove the jeep the same way as if it wasn't raining at all maintaining his speed. Rashaun's heart pounded as if expecting his demise on the small island. Andria looked for Mr. Persaud to say something before she opened her mouth. Then as fast as the rain had come, it stopped. Once more, the sky was cloudless. Andria and Rashaun breathed a sigh of relief.

As they drove through the country, they had to stop to let a man with a donkey pass and then a little boy with about six goats. The driver shouted something to both the boy and the man on the donkey. Neither Andria nor Rashaun understood what he said, but the reactions of both people were the same. They both stuck their middle finger up at him and shouted something that the engine noise drowned out.

"We have to go up that hill?" Andria asked as she looked up at the steepest hill she had ever seen in her life. It seemed to stretch for miles until the human eyes couldn't see anymore.

"Take it easy," the driver said. "We go up the hill all the time."

"Rashaun, wake me when we reach the top," Andria said as she leaned her head on his shoulders and closed her eyes.

The driver looked through his rearview mirror and smiled. Mr. Persaud eased himself in the seat. Rashaun hoped he hadn't farted.

"This is a steep hill," Rashaun said.

"Un-huh," Mr. Persaud agreed.

"Don't worry be happy, don't worry be happy," The driver started to sing the only American song he actually liked. Rashaun hated that song, and he had had enough of the driver.

"If we go up, it means we have to come down," Andria said as she straightened with this sudden revelation.

"Relax, baby, everything will be all right," Rashaun said, trying to console her by putting his hands around her shoulder and pulling her back to him.

The driver gunned the motor and continued to sing "Don't Worry, be Happy." It was the only words he could remember from the song. Rashaun looked out the window as they started their ascent into the mountain. The air was cool and misty as the truck climbed steadily. The driver changed gears frequently as the Japanese technology was put to a test. Once, Rashaun actually felt the truck stop once and start to roll back. He looked at the driver, who kept smiling as if it was funny. Rashaun knew then he hated the driver, but he also understood his life was in his hands. Rashaun turned and stared at the tall trees that stretched up to the sky. The wet dew on the smaller leaves fell to the ground as the truck passed on the narrow road, the road that was barely large enough for one vehicle. Rashaun saw tracks where the bigger trucks had passed earlier, breaking the branches off the trees that had grown over the road.

Andria had fallen asleep, and the snoring that was coming from the front belonged to Mr. Persaud. The driver had changed his tune; he was in a reggae mode now. He was totally destroying Bob Marley's song "Kaya." Rashaun shook his head, wondering what it would take to get him to shut up. He considered paying him, but he didn't like him so that was not an option. Rashaun gritted his teeth and tried to drown out the noise coming from the two men in the front. He looked ahead to see the flat top that meant the end of the upward flight. He had to give it to the driver. He knew the terrain very well. He looked behind to see the other truck was also close to completing its flight. The mist had made it impossible for him to see the faces in the truck.

"Want to stop and look down, man?" the driver asked Rashaun.

"No, just keep driving. How much longer?"

"Nah, not too long."

"All right."

"I heard they have a lot of money in America, you rich?" the driver asked Rashaun.

"No, I'm not rich," Rashaun answered.

"But you going to give me a good tip?"

"I am not the one who hired you. Mr. Persaud did," Rashaun said, wishing he would shut up.

"Those coolie man cheap, me tell you," the driver responded.

At the same time, Mr. Persaud opened his eyes.

"We cheap, ah?" Mr. Persaud said to the driver.

"Me naw talking 'bout you," the driver said.

"You want to hear some music, sir?" he asked Mr. Persaud.

Rashaun sat back and smiled as the driver turned on the radio without waiting for an answer from Mr. Persaud. Bob Marley's "No Woman No Cry" filled the jeep. Rashaun started to move his head to the rhythm, while Andria slept on his shoulder, oblivious to the men in the truck. The driver kept his eyes and head straight ahead. The rain started to fall without warning, coming down fast and heavy. The driver put his lights on and continued to drive. Rashaun looked at his watch and wondered what "not too long" meant in Grenadian language.

The driver stopped at the entrance to a side road filled with gravel.

"We got to wait for the other truck. Maloney is a slow driver," he said as he climbed up on top the hood of the truck and sat down. Rashaun came out with Andria who had just woken up.

"It feels nice and fresh out here," she said as she put her hand up and stretched her body. "This feels good."

"Yeah, my legs were beginning to cramp up in the truck," Rashaun said. He picked up an unknown hard shell nut from the ground and threw it into the bushes. They waited about two minutes before the truck pulled up behind them. The kids came running to Mr. Persaud and hugged him, then went to Andria and did the same. Mrs. Persaud came next and stood next to the truck. The two drivers exchanged greetings, then the one in the truck said good-bye, jumped into his truck, and drove away.

"People, it's going to be a tight fit, but we don't have too much longer to go," the driver said and climbed into the truck. He looked over to see where Andria was going to sit. Mr. Persaud climbed into the passenger side followed by Tim. Rashaun was the first to go into the backseat followed by Andria, Petra, then Mrs. Persaud. Mrs. Persaud took Petra and set her in her lap. She pulled the door shut and the driver started the engine. The driver smiled at Mr. Persaud and asked him if he was comfortable. The other driver had told him that Mrs. Persaud had given him a hundred-dollar tip. The private road leading into the cleansing woman's house was unpaved. Gravels and rocks made the three-quarter mile ride rough and jumpy. Mr. And Mrs. Persaud could barely keep the kids from hitting their heads on the ceiling of the truck.

The driver stopped in front of a heavy metal gate with galvanized covering to restrict a person's view inside. A nine-foot fence that was attached to the gate seemed to extend all around. He turned off the engine and came out of the car. He went to the right side of the gate and said something.

"Okay, folks, this is where we part," he said. Slowly the occupants came out of the truck. The kids seemed tired and restless while the adults looked exhausted. Once they got out of the truck, Mrs. Persaud held both the kids' hands as if afraid they would disappear. Mr. Persaud went to the driver and changed his mind about Coolie people. The driver took one last look at Andria and shook his head. He glanced at Rashaun and exited like his partner before him.

The gate opened slowly as the Americans stood separate and divided. Rashaun and Andria stood to the right. Mrs. Persaud and the kids stood to the left and Mr. Persaud stood directly in front. The woman behind the gate was about six-feet-two-inches tall. Rashaun guessed her age to be about thirty. She wore a white business suit and held a writing pad under her right arm.

"Good morning. I hope you guys had an enjoyable ride coming here," she said devoid of the Grenadian accent. She walked around the group, shaking each person's hand, including the children.

"My name is Ms. Reid, and we are very happy you are here," she said as she started her long strides to the house. Rashaun listened to her, wondering if he had just stumbled onto a private resort instead of a spiritual healer's house. He held Andria's hand as they walked to the house. As they went up the paved path, he noticed a few cages. One was full of white hens, another black cocks, and another a combination of both. The lawn was well manicured and a few mango and coconut trees were present. He looked at the mango tree and noticed ripe yellow mangoes on them, but none on the ground.

"Can we have some mangoes?" Petra asked, looking at on the tree.

"You guys can have anything you want after the ceremony," she said.

"Petra, stop that. It's not nice to ask for something that wasn't offered to you," Mrs. Persaud said, tightening her grip on Petra's hand.

"That's quite all right, Mrs. Persaud. There are plenty of mangoes inside," Ms. Reid said as she walked up the stairs to the large French doors.

"This house is huge," Andria said admiring the house as they walked the stairs.

"Yes, it is," Ms. Reid said. "It has twenty-one guest bedrooms, three kitchens, pool, and an exercise room fully equipped."

"It's a small mansion," Rashaun added.

The Persauds did not say anything. Their minds were preoccupied with what was to come. Ms. Reid led them down a hallway past closed doors into a big room. The room was modernly decorated with three maroon Italian leather couches. The leather on the couches was of a subtle high gloss with worn lines that accentuated the design. Next to each couch were a table and a chair, also made from a deep cherry wood, blending in nicely with the couch. Ms. Reid motioned the Persauds and the kids to one couch, Rashaun and Andria to another one.

"Madam Unida will be in shortly," she said and walked away, closing the door as she exited.

The kids were remarkably quiet as they sat next to their aunt and uncle. Mr. Persaud focused on the door that Ms. Reid had exited. Mrs. Persaud slowly stroked Petra's long hair and Tim held his sister's hand. Rashaun and Andria sat almost huddled together in a room where the temperature was approximately seventy-five degrees. They felt cold and uncomfortable. Neither spoke for fear of interrupting the deafening silence. They felt like children who were told to be quiet or else, even though the "or else" was never said.

The door that opened was not the door that Ms. Reid had exited; it was a hidden door that blended into the walls of the room. The kids were the first to see it, and a little boy about ten years was the first to come out. He had with pale white skin and apparently had never taken advantage of the hot sun. He had blond hair and blue eyes that contrasted sharply with the black gown he wore. He looked around the room not saying a word, then turned to the door he had just opened and made a small bow. It was the signal for the lady of the house to enter.

The lady who entered could have been fifty or a hundred. Age and time had blended in her oval face. There were no lines under the eyes of this woman of the century. For the first time, Rashaun saw someone much darker than himself. Her face was smooth and even toned with a delicate-looking nose and a small mouth with full lips.

Andria did not notice a hint of makeup on Madam Unida's face. She wondered if she was being rude by staring, but she dismissed her thoughts when she saw everyone in the room doing the same thing. Madam Unida was the most beautiful woman she had ever seen. Andria wondered how old she was, but refused to guess because she might insult the lady with her assumptions. Andria watched the form of her face and the size of her nose and lips. Her tooth were white and shining, a feat impossible with dentures. She admired her smooth skin that was as clean as her head, which blended in with her body, making her one even stroke of God's creation. Andria knew she would never meet another woman like her in her lifetime. All of a sudden, she wasn't cold anymore. She felt inner warmth; a comfortable peace had come into the room with her presence. Andria looked at the Persauds. They understood that they were in the midst of a special spirit, a spirit of greatness. Tim and Petra sat there smiling; the first time Andria had seen them smile since they entered the room.

The boy walked up to the desk and chair next to the Persauds and the kids. He lifted the chair out without making a sound. Madam Unida walked to the chair and sat down. The boy stood next to her almost like a guard showing no emotions.

"Welcome to my humble residence. I hope your visit to this island of my birth seventy years ago have been enjoyable and peaceful," she said. As she spoke, her eyes swept over the room, giving each person her complete attention.

Andria understood every word Madam Unida said. She was amazed that she spoke without any accent. Her words glided out of her mouth.

"Mr. and Mrs. Persaud, thank you for bringing your children to receive a cleansing before their life's journey has begun. I understand they had a traumatic experience over which they had no control. Today they will come to that realization; therefore, their past will not be a hindrance to their and your future. The restless spirit of the departed will leave their souls and find solace in their own judgment. Please let them be taken now to be prepared for their freedom." Madam Unida looked at the Persauds then at the boy. The boy turned his head to the right then looked at Madam Unida.

The door that Ms. Reid had exited earlier opened, and a black man and a white woman wearing white robes came in and went to Tim and Petra. Tim and Petra stood almost immediately. Ms. Persaud held on to their hands wanting to go with them. But the black man

155

put his hands gently over the hand that held Petra, and the white woman did the same with the hand that held Tim. Ms. Persaud released the kids' hands and rested her head gently on her husband. He wrapped his right hand around her and looked at Madam Unida. He felt good, and he shared that feeling with his wife.

Andria watched the kids leave with the helpers. She had seen kids afraid before, but there was no fear in these kids' eyes. They smiled at her, and she smiled in return. She looked at Madam Unida, and she knew she could trust this woman with her last breath.

"I feel a lot of love in this room, but I also feel a lot of anger and restlessness of spirit. Andria!" Madam Unida said.

Andria looked at Madam Unida and felt as if this beautiful black woman was reading her whole life story. Andria wanted to answer, but no words came, only a look. She wanted to say yes, but her mouth remained closed. This woman had penetrated her soul. She couldn't feel Rashaun next to her even though he was holding her hand.

"Andria, you need release before you can go on. Your soul is crying like Tim and Petra's souls are crying. You know what it is, but you are powerless to release it. And Rashaun, your anger has been a big part of your success, but now it is destroying you. You are my son in appearance, and I can feel you even more than your mother could. You need to let go of that anger, only then can you really find peace. I will help cleanse your souls because your hearts are pure. I will help you like you two have tried to help everyone who has come close to you. I have no use for monetary gains so this will be free of charge. After I am finished with Tim and Petra, you could let me help you or leave with my blessing. Thank you."

Rashaun and Andria looked at each other knowing they were staying with Madam Unida a little longer.

Rashaun sat on the edge of the bed in his underpants and T-shirt. The clothes he had traveled with were laid out smoothly on the back of the single chair in the room. On the seat of the chair were Andria's clothes except for her bra and panties. Andria was lying on the bed, fully stretched out, looking up at the white ceiling. She had been staring at the ceiling for the past thirty minutes. Rashaun was also in deep thought. They had spoken briefly when they walked into the room, most of it pleasantries and conversation fillers, before they sank deep in thought. Ms. Reid had told them she would come back to take them to Tim and Petra's ceremony. She informed them about the fresh fruits on the table, and if that was not enough, they were welcome to come to the kitchen. Andria had a mango after taking her clothes off, and Rashaun had a banana.

The knock on the door wasn't loud but it was persistent.

"We will be right there," Andria said as she got off the bed and moved to the chair. Rashaun had started putting his pants on at the first knock.

"Good evening, sir, madam," the black lady in a white gown addressed them when they walked out. "This way" she led them down the hall.

The Persauds sat next to each other in the room. Mrs. Persaud was closer to the door than Mr. Persaud, her hands clasped tightly together, looking into the glass; Mr. Persaud was his usual stoic self. Andria was the first to walk in, and she took the seat next to Mrs. Persaud. Mrs. Persaud reached out and grasped her hand briefly. Andria felt her hand warm and clammy. Rashaun acknowledged them and took the only available seat next to Andria. Andria looked into the room and saw Tim and Petra lying on a cot sideways. She could not get a good look at their faces. The room was well lit by two lamps located in the corners. On the wall facing Tim and Petra were cartoon characters from a variety of Disney shows.

Rashaun was the first to hear the music. At first it was the low sound of an African drum. He looked at the others to see if they had heard it too, but they were focused on the kids. The drums became louder and the others started looking around, uncertain of the origin. It was then that he saw him enter, dressed in white this time and moving straight to Tim and Petra. He had a small vile in his hand, somewhat similar to what the pastor used in the church. He went to the end of the cot and sprinkled something on the kids' feet. He knelt at the foot of the cot for a second, then walked to the door and stood with his head bowed.

It was then that she came in, and as her helper before her, she was also dressed in white, her head covered with a white shawl. She walked to the kids and placed her hands on their foreheads. She looked into their eyes and said something incoherent to those in the room. She slowly lifted her hands off the kids' faces reached in her bosom and pulled out a white rag. She wiped the same spot her helper had sprinkled and threw the rag on the floor. She then walked out of the room.

Rashaun and Andria looked at each other with questions in their eyes. For the first time Mr. Persaud had an expression on his face; it was a nasty frown. Andria looked at Mrs. Persaud, tears rolling down her cheeks. It was then that Andria heard the scream. It was loud and piercing. Mrs. Persaud got out of the chair and rushed to the glass, her face anxious and uncertain. Andria quickly went to her and held her around the shoulders. The men dashed to the glass also. The kids had gotten off the couch and were talking. They weren't talking to each other or to the adults who eagerly watched them. They spoke to the blank wall. The adults watched as the kids talked to their imaginary beings. They did not notice Madam Unida coming into the room. She stood behind them as they concentrated on trying to understand whom the kids were talking to.

"Soon it will all be over, and Mrs. Persaud and Mr. Persaud can go home," Madam Unida said.

Andria was the first to hear her and quickly turned around to look. Madam Unida was dressed in black now and so was her helper who stood silent by her side.

"Praise God," Mrs. Persaud said and turned around briefly to acknowledge Madam Unida. Her husband did the same thing, his face much different from earlier.

Rashaun watched as the kids stretched out their hands as if they were hugging someone. They switched sides and did the same thing. They came to the glass partition and waved at the adults in the room, smiling as if in a state of total happiness. No one saw when

Madam Unida's helper had left the room, but there he was with his hands outstretched with black clothing for Tim and Petra. They hurriedly put them on and bolted for the door, hesitating for a second to wave at the blank walls.

After saying good-bye to the Persauds and the children, Andria and Rashaun went back to the room. Ms. Reid informed them that dinner was going to be at seven, and tomorrow they would have their cleansing. When they got back to their room, there were two sets of white gowns laid out neatly on the bed. On the floor were two sets of slippers, one for a man, and the other for a lady. Rashaun was the first one in the shower while Andria went through the bag they had brought just in case they would have to stay overnight. She lifted her head and rolled her eyes when she noticed she didn't have toothpaste or floss. She rummaged through the bag, making a mental note of what she had packed. She could never get Rashaun to pack anything; then again, she wasn't sure she wanted him to. She had seen how he had packed his clothes. For a man who was so neat he sure didn't know how to maximize space in a suitcase. Rashaun came out of the shower, his Barney towel around his waist. Andria laughed. He looked at her then at the towel and joined her in laughter. It was the first time they had laughed together since they came to this place.

"Hey, it's a gift from my niece and I like it," he said. He went to the bed, sat down, and he pulled on the white pants that were left for him. Unlike the gown that was worn in the cleansing, this outfit had a shirt and pants. Andria walked by him with only her panties on. He took the top from the bed and swatted at her.

"You missed," she said and darted into the bathroom. She was pleasantly surprised to find toothpaste, mouthwash, floss, and Listerine on the washbasin. Inside the shower, there was a brand-new washcloth with bottles of body wash, shampoo, and lotion, all of them made by Oil of Solay. She turned the shower on and the warm water fell lightly on her short hair, down her body. It felt good. For the first time, she relaxed. She hadn't even realized that she was so tense. She let the water run effortlessly over her body, finding each corner and crevice to make a stream. Tomorrow was another day, but for now, she was enjoying the tranquility.

Dinner was held in a large hall with a gigantic chandelier in the middle. In addition to the chandelier, there were oval candles on each table. Andria counted at least twenty tables and each was filled with four people. The servers wore white and black shirt and pants according to the table they were serving. There were people from all nationalities, races, and creeds at the tables. The adults and the children all sat together. Andria saw a Jewish couple sitting with a Muslim couple. Andria and Rashaun were led to a table that was occupied by a Spanish couple.

Their escort made the introduction because there were no nametags on any of the people in the room. Andria and Rashaun's dining companions were Jose and Rita Hernandez from the Dominican Republic. The tablecloth was decorated with the different spices that Grenada was so famous for, including the nutmeg and cocoa. The eating utensils were wrapped in an orange cloth napkin. There were four glasses filled with water and a basket with rolls in it.

"I wish we were at that other table," Rita Hernandez said, looking over at one of the tables with the people dressed in black. They seem so happy, talking and laughing without a care in the world.

"Soon, baby, we will get there soon," her husband said, holding her hand in his.

Andria and Rashaun watched the couple and wondered what in their past had brought them here. Rashaun had also noticed the difference in the people sitting at the tables. The tables with the people dressed in black were beaming with joy while the tables with the people dressed in white were quiet and subdued.

"Tomorrow, there will be a whole different crew of people here," Jose said, taking in the view of the room.

"No one stays longer than a day here," Rita said.

"She is blessed," Jose said.

It was then that Madam Unida's helper came into the room followed by his boss. This evening, she and her helper were wearing blue. In sixty seconds, the room was completely quiet. She took her seat at the only single chair and table in the room, located in the front on a slightly elevated part of the floor. She looked over the room with a smile that seemed to unite everyone. Then Madam Unida bowed her head slightly, and the waiters seemed to appear from nowhere. They brought food for every table in the room. On Rashaun and Andria's table were three different platters of fish, steak, and chicken. Each platter contained meat that was stewed, baked, or fried. There were vegetables for the vegetarians, pasta for people who liked Italian.

Now Rashaun realized why the tables were so big. Andria watched him and smiled. She knew he would try every thing that was in front of them.

Madam Unida opened up her hands, and even though Rashaun and Andria couldn't hear her, it was obvious from her movements that she had said enjoy. Immediately there was a clanging of utensils as her guests began their feast. Madam Unida walked. Rashaun, true to his word, took something from every tray on the table; Andria watched his plate piled high with food. Jose also followed Rashaun's example by filling his plate with everything except the fish. The ladies sparingly filled their plates; Rashaun looked at Andria and wondered if she was on a diet. The couples ate quietly making selective statements on the taste of the food. They did not discuss why they were there, but spoke highly of the powers of Madam Unida.

"I would suggest you go to the bathroom first," Rashaun told Andria as he slumped down on the bed. His stomach swirling with the combinations of food he had eaten. He lay on the bed wondering why Andria was taking so long in the bathroom.

"Are you going to be long?" Andria asked as she walked out the bathroom.

Rashaun looked at her, and he saw this smirk on her face.

"Very funny," he said as he squeezed his legs together and headed to the bathroom.

Rashaun was surprised at how sweet the bathroom smelled. He had never gone into the bathroom and smelled shit before. He had started to wonder if Andria ever took a shit. Looking back to the times he had spent with the other women, he couldn't recall going into a stinking bathroom either. After a few minutes on the toilet, he felt very relaxed and started to look around for something to read. There was nothing so he cleaned himself up and walked out of the bathroom feeling ten times lighter than when he went in. Of course, Andria was asleep. He thought about waking her but decided against it. After all, tomorrow was going to be a long day.

The knock on the door came about nine, two hours after the second knock. Andria had opened the door for the first knock, and she was given clean clothes for her and Rashaun to wear for the cleansing. She had to nudge Rashaun for him to go and get ready. The young girl who gave her clothes told her they would be back at nine. It was agreed that Andria would go first for the cleansing.

Rashaun looked at Andria through the glass partition that separated the room. She looked fragile and weak sitting in the center of the room. Earlier on, Madam Unida's helper had come in and given her something to drink. He wondered what it was that they had given her and hoped it was not dangerous. He sat on the lone chair in the room. Then as before he began to hear the drums, he knew that Madam Unida was approaching. She came in as always behind her helper, dressed in white from head to toe like before. She went over to Andria and touched her on the forehead. Andria's body jerked once and sank to the floor. The drums became louder as Madam walked out the door behind her helper. She followed her helper into the adjacent room. Rashaun briefly took his eyes away from Andria to question Madam Unida with his. She walked in, and as her helper stood between her and Rashaun, she redirected his gaze to Andria. Then he saw Andria start to move.

Andria did not know what was happening to her. She had come into the room and sat on the floor as she was told. She had drunk the sweet-tasting substance that the little boy had put to her mouth and waited for something to happen, but nothing did. Her head just felt funny. Then Madam Unida came in and touched her forehead. All of a sudden, her head felt funny and she had to lie down on the floor. It was then she saw him; he was young and handsome like her mother had described. She reached out to touch him, but he said, "No, not yet." She asked him why, but he put his hand to her mouth to silence her. Then her vision of him changed to the one that had caused her nightmares after his death. She saw him and her mother standing over him with blood dripping on his lifeless body. She went around her mother and started to count the stab wounds in his chest. She was young then, about six years old, and her face was expressionless. She shook her father to get him to move, but he didn't. Then she started to cry and pulled on her mother's dress to get her to wake up her father. But her mother wasn't looking; her mother's eyes were directed at the other lady in the room. Andria looked closer and saw her aunt, naked and partially covering her face in the corner. Then the vision changed again, and this time, her father was alive again and he put his hands around her and told her, "Don't cry for me. I'm all right." He hugged her tightly against his big chest and spoke to her the way she had always wanted him to speak to her. He told her what happened, and he told her not to blame either her mother or her aunt. He stressed to her that he was all right, and he would always be with her. He asked her to look at him, and didn't he look good? He didn't want her to have that vision of him anymore. He smiled and she smiled back. He told her he loved her and she was the best thing that happened to him. He told her he loved her mother too. He told her to tell her mother that he is all right and to continue living. "Remember me, my daughter; remember me alive as I am today with you," he said.

Andria got up off the floor and looked through the glass into Rashaun's questioning gaze. She felt as if a large burden had been lifted off her shoulders. She didn't realize that her past was such a large part of her future. She felt tired and weak, as if the cleansing had drained her body, but she also felt a sense of inner peace and resolve. She now realized that the time she had spent with the psychiatrists was helpful, but they could only help so much. She now realized she had hated her mother for killing her father; so many things were clearer for her. She smiled at Rashaun, and she saw his face ease a little. The little boy came into the room and motioned to her to follow him. She waved good-bye to Rashaun and headed out the door.

Rashaun walked back to the room, happy that he knew Andria was okay. Ms. Reid had told him he should change and come back in one hour. As he began to change his clothes, his thoughts were on Andria. He realized then that this was the first time she had been separated from him since they got here. He felt alone without her. As always, the clothes fitted him very nicely. Once he was finished, he lay down on the bed, looking up at the ceiling. It was then that Andria walked in the room. Before he could get up off the bed, she jumped on him straddling her legs around his waist.

"I love you," she said, planting kisses all over his face.

"Hey, what came over you?" he asked getting excited with Andria brushing against him like that.

"I see black is your favorite color," he said.

"Don't you know the saying the blacker the berry the sweeter the juice?" She started to gyrate against him ever so slowly.

"Don't even think about it. I just finished changing my clothes, and I don't think there are enough hours in this day if we get started."

"You are right," she said and quickly got off him.

"Hey, where you going? I still have fifteen minutes, and you know what we can do in fifteen minutes"

"Nope, not today," she said, looking at him, shaking her head.

"You are not right," he said getting up from the bed. He looked at his woman, wishing he could tell her what she had just told him but he couldn't. The last time he had said those three words was a very long time ago. After the incident, he had promised himself never to say those words to anyone again, but he knew he loved her and maybe she could feel that he did. God knew she was the best thing that had ever happened to him in a long, long time.

"I have been sheltered from the cruelty of this world, but Rashaun had to face it from the time of his birth," Madam Unida said as she watched Rashaun in the room.

Andria wanted to take away some of his pain. She had watched him as he ran around the room for almost twenty minutes. Now, he was in the corner, curled up in the fetal position.

Rashaun saw himself once more in his dreams, but this time he was wide-awake. This time the razor-sharp claws were his. He got up off the floor and ripped his clothes off. He felt like his clothes were closing in on him. Then he felt them, the slashing of his skin with the razor-sharp blades. And for the first time, he realized what it was—his skin. Rashaun didn't want to be black anymore; Rashaun didn't want to be the blackest man on the earth. What he wanted was new skin; he wanted to get away from Blacky. His blackness was making him feel ugly and unwanted. All the years he had fought to accept his blackness and be proud of himself were a lie. What he did in essence was cover his shame with false pride. Now he was changing. He had to see what lay beneath the blackness.

Andria watched him, standing with her eyebrows touching the glass. She had wanted to run and stop the blood that seemed to come from every part of his body, but Madam Unida's helper stopped her. No, he said to her. He had to change so he could love himself. He has to realize that his skin was only a covering and it was a beautiful one. He had to love being black.

"But he is bleeding," she objected, "We need to help him."

"No," Madam Unida said, "Rashaun has to live with himself. We cannot live his life for him. I know you love him and he knows you love him, but he has to love himself just the way he is. There is no plastic surgery that will replace the skin, and even if there were, the person will never get one good enough for himself or herself. They will always be looking for a better one. This is Rashaun's problem. He has to deal with it."

Rashaun felt the sweat running down his body. He took his right hand, passed it over his forehead, and looked at it. He kept looking at it hoping it would change to salted water, but it remained blood red. Rashaun was bleeding from the inside. When he saw that, he started to run again. This time he slammed into the walls of the room with a vengeance while screaming at the top of his lungs.

Andria looked at Rashaun, her whole body shaking as if she felt his pain. Madam Unida had just left. She had asked Andria to come with her to get something to eat but Andria refused. She wanted to be there with him, the way he was there for her. She hoped he knew she was there, praying for him and comforting him. She would see him looking at her, but his eyes were cloudy and blank. She wondered if he even saw her.

"Rashaun, look within yourself and accept your beauty."

Rashaun turned, looking around the room to see where Madam Unida's voice was coming from. He had stopped running and had slumped to the ground in exhaustion. Then he saw her naked and as black as he was. Her baldhead reflected the light in the room. And she was beautiful; she was the most beautiful woman he had ever seen.

"Now that you have looked at me, look at yourself," she said.

He turned around, looking for a mirror.

"No, you don't need a mirror. Mirrors only show changes. You have not changed. What lies on your skin is a protective coat for the beauty that lies below. You were given a gift. Close your eyes and let night fall in your mind."

Rashaun did as he was told. When night fell, he could not see himself.

"I can't see myself," he shouted.

"Yes. You can, look within. Forget what they say. You were created in his vision. His vision of beauty, the same way I was. You are his true disciple."

Rashaun wiped the blood off his hands and saw his true self. His skin shone liked an uncut diamond. Priceless and irreplaceable, he was beauty.

"Sun, rain, snow, nor life troubles will have any effect on your skin. Wherever you go, whatever you do, your skin will remain flawless. The only person who can destroy your skin is yourself. And your skin is your beauty. It emulates from the heart. Your heart is black as the night and the night is when we are most at peace. The night is when we make love and life gets its initial creation," she said.

For the first time in his thirty-four years on this earth, Rashaun understood his trials and tribulations.

"Accept yourself and love yourself, and you will see your anger and hate all come from the same place. Stop hating yourself and love yourself, and you will see the difference. You have seen where you were. It's up to you to go where you want, I cannot give you direction but only unblock the path. You have to move on now. Lift that cover off your heart and let love come in with all its magical powers because soon you will be gone. With this said, I must go be thankful."

Andria watched the transformation in Rashaun. The movements of his body told the tale of his distress. Finally he came up to the glass and looked at her, his eyes cloudy no more. It was then she heard the gushing noise and saw the water come down on Rashaun. The water traveled over his body washing the blood from his skin. He was laughing as he played in the water. She liked that. He lifted his hands in the air as if to shout that he was free. His eyes sparkled as he danced in the water that poured from the ceiling. The water quickly became blood from his skin and disappeared in the corner of the room. When the water stopped, the little boy came with a black towel and a set of black clothes. Andria waited for Rashaun to get dressed, then she waved goodbye to him and walked back to the room. Tonight was going to be very special.

Andria looked back at the quickly disappearing island, a speck on the world map, but forever large in her heart. Rashaun was next to her fast asleep, his face relaxed yet his hand held hers tightly.

He had fallen asleep almost as soon as the plane took off. She did not intend to wake him because they had eaten a full meal before getting on the plane. It was the last time they had steam down food on Grenadian soil. She had the recipe in her bag, but Rashaun knew she would never be able to make it the way they did. The recipe depended on too much of a little bit of this and a little piece of that. She took the callaloo and the breadfruit and wrapped it in aluminum foil as instructed; the Manicoo was frozen overnight then put in a plastic bag, folded in an old newspaper then aluminum wrapped. Andria hoped they did not search her bags when she got home. She was hoping Rashaun said those three magic words to her the way she had said it to him the night before after making love. She was disappointed, but hopefully she didn't show it. She knew it had to be on his time when he was ready. He didn't talk to her about the cleansing except to say that it resolved some issues.

Rashaun rubbed his eyes and looked out the window. The clouds lay in all different sizes ahead of them. He was still reeling from the cleansing and what it had brought out. After all these years, he was still suffering from an act of God. He wondered if a person had the choice whether to be born black or white what would they do. If a black person had to choose between being born light or dark skin. Yet, he knew people who made these decisions everyday. A woman meet someone and decided he was too dark to have her baby. The world is very color conscious. No, he didn't have a choice in his color; his mom and dad did that. He had spent almost a third of his life trying to live with their decision. Maybe it wasn't even their decision because he was the darkest of all their children. His oldest sister was lighter than cream. In hindsight, he felt stupid and ungrateful for blaming his parents. He was blessed with birth like everyone else, but he was ungrateful. He had placed so many covers on himself, trying to hide from his blackness. But now all that had changed, and as he looked over at Andria fast asleep next to him, he hoped they could give someone the blessings of birth. He leaned over and kissed Andria on the forehead.

"I love you," he said as the pilot came over the speakers to announce turbulence ahead.

" I love you too," Andria repeated without even waking up from her sleep.

Rashaun came back into the car and closed the door. George looked at him with urgency in his eyes. After Rashaun did not say anything, George put his hands up in exasperation.

"Keep your hands on the wheel," Rashaun said.

"So tell me, how was the trip?" George asked as he sped down Eastern Parkway.

"Excellent, as we told you before. We had a good time," Rashaun answered.

"Come on, Rashaun, you could tell me now that your woman isn't here no more. Enlighten a brother naw. Tell me about the freaks and whores."

"We had a great time. This brother was seriously enlightened," Rashaun said, laughing at George's irritation.

"Here you go again bullshitting. Come on, Rashaun. Did you get a side meal?"

"Actually the food was very good."

"Fuck you!"

"No, George, this trip wasn't about foreign pussy. It was about life."

"You know what, Rashaun? I liked you better when you didn't have a girl. After you came back from a trip, you always had stories about foreign pussy. You remember the girl you fucked when you went to Colombia? She didn't know any English yet you were able to fuck her in about thirty minutes. You know, shit like that."

"That's behind me now. Would you like me to tell you about the cleansing?"

"Does it have fucking in it?"

"No."

"Then hell no, but I know you will tell me anyway."

On their way to the apartment, Rashaun told George about his experience in Grenada. He told him everything about the food, the people, and the cleansing. Of course, George wanted to know what Madam Unida's body looked like being so old. He wondered out loud to Rashaun if fucking her would be a spiritual experience. He asked Rashaun if he thought people like that had had orgasms or transformation. Rashaun asked him if they transformed into what, George told him he didn't have the faintest idea. The other thing George was interested in was the food and the drinks. He wanted to know if Rashaun had brought back anything for the back. He heard that West Indian men drank a number of things for the back to make them fuck longer. George told him about two that he had tried, agony and front-end lifter. They never worked for him so he was wondering if Grenada had something better. Rashaun told him that he didn't go to Grenada looking for that so he didn't know. It was then George told him that he was "absolutely and completely pussy-whipped."

Andria got home and went straight to the shower. The long plane ride had left her feeling exhausted. After the shower, she clicked on the TV to catch up on the latest madness in the Big Apple.

"Same old shit," she said to no one in particular.

Even though she was tired, she did not feel like sleeping so she turned off the TV and went to the phone.

"Hello?" Robin said when she picked up the phone.

"I'm back in the Big Bad Apple."

"Girl, you know the only thing bad in the apple is the black men."

"I thought it was the criminals."

"Aren't they one in the same."

They both started to laugh.

"So how was the trip?" Robin asked, getting straight to the point.

"It was great, the water, the people, the food. We had a wonderful time."

"I bet you guys were getting your freak on in the middle of the ocean under the hazy sun. I know you all freaky like that. I heard a lot of West Indian foods are aphrodisiacs so you guys must have went wild."

"That too," Andria said and started to laugh. Her phone beeped. "Hold on," she said to Robin and clicked the flash button.

"Hey, what's up?" Rashaun asked Andria.

"I'm on the phone with Robin. Can I call you back?"

"You don't have to because I will be going to bed soon."

"I don't know why you didn't just stay over here tonight. I kind of gotten use to sleeping with you next to me," she said.

"Me, too, baby, but not tonight."

"Okay, I'll call you when I'm finished talking to Robin."

"Talk to you," he said and hung up the phone.

"Hi," Andria said as she clicked over the phone.

"Damn, he doesn't want you to breathe. He doesn't know you got friends too."

"Hey, you jealous?" Andria said to her friend.

"You love birds are funny. So tell me about your trip. How was that thing you did with the kids."

"The cleansing you mean?"

"Yeah."

"Well, it wasn't only the kids. We met this amazing woman."

"No, don't tell me you are turning too. I know the black man don't always do the right thing, but you don't have to flip the whole script. There are other men out there."

"Robin, stop being funny."

"Okay."

"Robin, we met this lady called Madam Unida, and she was the most amazing woman I have ever met. It was unbelievable."

"I think I'd better sit down for this. Hold on, let me go get my tea, and I want you to tell me everything."

Andria spent the next hour telling Robin about her trip. She told her friend about meeting her father and talking to him, and about Rashaun bleeding. She told her that Rashaun said "I love you" to her for the first time since they started dating. When Andria finished talking to Robin, she hung up the phone and called her mother. Her mother scolded her for not calling while she was in Grenada and as soon as she came back. Her mother asked her if Robin was more important than her. Andria apologized and told her mother about the trip and the cleansing. Her mother asked her how much Madam Unida charged and how could she go about meeting her. Andria told her she didn't know, but she would find out from the Persauds. Andria got off the phone with her mother and called Rashaun. He was half asleep by then, so they agreed to talk the next day. Robin put the phone down and went to the bathroom to brush her teeth. After that she crawled into her bed. Within minutes, she was asleep. This time she dreamed not about hate and anger, but about love. She dreamed about marriage and a family.

"Yo, she cut me," Tyrone said.

"You want a Corona?" Rashaun asked.

"Yo, are you listening to me?" Tyrone continued.

"I don't know why you bitching. You knew the girl was married," Rashaun said as he put the beer down in front of Tyrone.

"It's not like she cut me for her husband; she cut me for another brother. What happened to me? My dick is too small or what?" Tyrone said as he looked through the Corona bottle. "Do you have a Heiny. That yellow shit is beginning to look like piss."

"Tyrone, your dick got hurt more than you. You still don't understand about women, do you? You got played, take it and move on."

"Yo, man, that was some good pussy. That bitch could throw her legs about fifty different ways. She is a freak; anything goes. No holes barred, and you know I get freaky."

"Yeah, I know how you roll, it's all good."

"Yo, you got any food in this place?" Tyrone asked looking in the direction of the kitchen.

"No, you want to order some?" Rashaun asked.

"Nah, man, I'm going home. I will stop by my mom's house and get a plate." Tyrone got up and drank the last of the beer from the bottle.

"Tyrone, you will never change? Food from your mother and pussy from the women."

"You got it. Once you start getting food from a woman you are fucked. Before you know it, the bitch wants to move in and get married and all kinds of shit."

"So what happens when your mother can't cook for you anymore?"

"You forgot there are West Indian and Chinese restaurants on almost every street corner. I'm out," Tyrone said as he opened up the front door.

Rashaun used the keys Andria had given him to open the door to her apartment. There were two locks on her door, a deadbolt and a regular entry lock. The deadbolt was easy. With two turns of the key he had it open. The regular entry lock was a little bit harder. He fiddled with it back and forth until the cylinder turned. He had called Andria about an hour ago to tell her he was coming over. She repeated to him that he didn't need to call first. He repeated to her that he always called before he went to anyone's house. He didn't like surprises, good or bad. He smelled the baked chicken as soon as he opened the door.

"Andria," he called out.

There was no answer so he walked by the chicken and the rest of the food she had covered on the table. There were two candles burning on the table. After he passed the table, he hesitated, wondering if he should at least take a leg of chicken.

"Andria," he called out again.

Again, there was no answer. As he walked by the bathroom on the way to the kitchen, he heard the shower. He smiled as he took his clothes off.

"Why you took so long?" Andria said as Rashaun entered the shower. "I thought I would catch pneumonia being in the shower so long."

"You are something else," he said, as the water started to pour down his face.

"A very clean something else," Andria said as she took the sponge and started to soap Rashaun down.

"I guess we are eating after."

"Sometimes you are such a genius, Rashaun."

"I guess I am eating twice today," Rashaun said as he took the sponge away from Andria.

"You are a regular Einstein."

"Does this look white to you?" he said, pointing to his penis.

"Just shut up and fuck me."

"As you wish, my lady."

"No! Not my lady today, I want you to fuck me like a sweet bitch." She took his head and shoved it down the full length of her upper body. She turned the water off.

The gym was almost empty when Rashaun got there. He liked it like that. He didn't have to wait on any machine in the process, losing his rhythm. As he walked through he said what's up to the regular morning gym rats, including the sixty-year-old man who had the muscles of a twenty-year-old. Rashaun looked up to him as a

172

hero and hoped one day when he reached that age he would look somewhat like him. The man had told him the secret to his looks was eating right and exercising regularly. He had told Rashaun to always have a goal when weight training and treat it as if it were a second job. The gym was where he did his thinking, just him and his weights. He had left his cellular phone and his beeper in the car. This was his time, and he didn't want any interruption.

He walked to the back of the weight room past the ladies' and men's rooms to a small enclosed area with mats and various stomach-crunching apparatus. He took a blue mat from the pile in the corner and laid it out in front of him. He went through his stretching routine in about fifteen minutes. Today he was doing chest, shoulders, and biceps. He put the two forty five barbells on and lay down on the bench. As he pushed the barbell up and down, he reminisced about the other night. It was the first time he had seen Andria like that. She was absolutely crazy. He smiled as he thought about it. They did almost everything that night. She ordered him to do things they had never done before, everything except anal sex. Nope, she wanted no part of that. She told him some places had a no entry on permanently. They even got into some bondage when she came back with his belt and told him to tie her up. Of course, she didn't have to tell him twice. Damn, it was a wild night. He didn't think he could stay up making love all night but he did. Then when they finally did fall asleep, they slept for about ten hours. Praise God it was Friday. Rashaun finished doing the bench press then went on to incline press. As he pushed the weights up, he realized he wanted to take this relationship a step further. And as the thought came into his head, he put the weights back onto the holder and sat up. He looked around the room to see if anyone had seen his thoughts. Everyone in the room was doing their own thing; Rashaun's thoughts were not on their minds. He had never before been so afraid in his life. The "what ifs" started to come into his mind. What if she didn't really love him? What if she was a closet lesbian? What if she was having an affair? What if, what if, what if . . .

This was his life, it was a short one, and he wanted to make the right decision. He walked away from the bench to the glass partition overlooking the pool. There were three people swimming in the pool but Rashaun didn't see them. Instead he saw the deep clear water with the small waves moving ever so gently. It was there from these waters he made his decision. It was a decision that would change his life forever.

The sergeant arrived on the scene about fifteen minutes after the two rookies sent in the call. He was five feet seven inches and weighed about three hundred pounds. A fifteen-year vet on the NYPD force, he and his partner made an odd match. His partner was a tall Jewish cop who wore his yarmulke under his police cap. A strict orthodox Jew, his parameters were always set. He had become the sergeant's driver about a year ago and during that time a hostile friendship had developed. As the sergeant walked up the stairs of the small two-story attached house, he could see one of the rookies outside with his head bent over. When he reached the top he looked down and saw the vomit on the ground. It was obvious that the rookie had a very heavy Italian lunch or else his guts had fallen out of his stomach. He tried to lift his head to acknowledge his sergeant but instead he puked again, missing the sergeant by a very slim margin. However, he did not miss the sergeant's partner who was following right behind him.

"Damn! Now you gave him an excuse to take another Jewish holiday," the sergeant said. "As if he hadn't taken enough for the year yet."

"Very funny, Bengal," his partner said.

The sergeant walked in through the open door past the living room into the bedroom. The call had come in as a 1013 at this address with the victim in the bedroom. The rookie, in the bedroom, did not seemed as horrified as his partner did; he was standing over a naked black man.

"Sarge, he made the phone call. When I got here, she was already dead."

The sergeant looked from the black man to the naked woman on the bed. He recognized the black man instantly from an introduction from his lawyer friend Rashaun Jones. He liked Rashaun; he was a cool brother.

"You checked her pulse?" the sergeant asked.

"None."

"Any stab or gunshot wounds?"

"No."

"Then how the fuck did she die?"

"My rookie opinion is that he fucked her to death."

"What?"

"That's what he said."

"He said he was mad at her, and he brought her over to talk to her and she started to taunt him about him not being able to fuck and one thing lead to another. He said he was trying to kill her with his dick, but she was enjoying it. He said after they were finished, they fell asleep and when he woke up, he found her bleeding from her vagina. That was when he called us. Sarge, look at him, He doesn't look that big?"

"I guess you don't know nothing about Blackfunk."

"What?"

"Nothing. Let me go outside for a second."

The sergeant issued some orders to his partner then pulled out his cellular phone as he walked outside. He walked to the car and past the rookie cop who was just regaining his composure. He reached inside the glove compartment and pulled out his Casio organizer. He scrolled through dozens of women's names he had collected over the years; it was one of the small benefits of being an officer. He had met Rashaun at the gym when he used to go, but that was past tense now. Time and motivation had ended that activity. Now he was just looking toward retirement. Five more years and he could walk away with a gun and a nice retirement account. After being on the job for over fifteen years, he cherished having the gun more than the retirement package. He and his cop buddies sometimes joked around about how crazy one must be to walk the streets of New York City without a gun.

"Rashaun, this is Bengal." He gave everyone his last name, a bad habit from the job. "One of your boys is in trouble."

Rashaun hung up the phone and sat back on the edge of the bed. He felt numb and weak as if the air had been taken out of his lungs with a vacuum. Bengal didn't say the name of the dead woman, but he had a good idea who it was. As far as Rashaun knew, Tyrone was only fucking one married woman now, Andria's friend, Judy. Rashaun contemplated whether he should call Andria or go to the precinct. He called Andria then called back Bengal who informed him they had completely ID'd the girl in the bed. It was Judy.

Rashaun sat there looking at her, wondering if he should say something. He had tried holding her, but she pushed him away. When he had first told her, she went into a rage, screaming and crying. Then she started beating his chest with her hands. Then she pushed him away and sat down staring at the floor. He knew in times like these he should say the right thing or say nothing at all. At this time, he didn't know what the right thing was so he kept silent. The phone rang interrupting the sadness in the air.

Rashaun went to the phone and picked it up. It was Robin's tearful voice on the line. He told her that Andria was not able to talk, but he'd give her the message. She asked if she should come over, but Rashaun said no he would stay with her. He stayed with Andria for the next two days, taking time off his job to be with her. They visited Judy's parents and expressed their condolences, and Andria spent some time playing with Judy's child. No one talked about how Judy died or the impending trial of the man arrested in her death. Instead, they spoke about the good mother she was and how much her husband loved her.

Rashaun and Andria also visited Steve, Judy's husband; he was distraught over his wife's death. They barely caught him at home, because he was spending most of his time with his parents. He asked Andria if she knew Judy was having an affair with Tyrone. She lied and told him no. He asked her if there was something wrong with him, was he doing something wrong? She shook her head repeatedly; there was nothing else she could do. Rashaun stayed away from their conversation, turning his head when he saw Steve crying in Andria's arms. He believed there were some things in life a man should not see another man do. Andria offered to come over and help him clean the place up, but Steve refused; he wanted to spend the time closing out the memories with his wife.

After Rashaun left, Andria sat down on the couch in front of the TV. She was looking at the Fox TV show. Usually that show made her laugh, but it wasn't causing the same reaction today. Instead she was thinking about her friend Judy, of the laughter and the tears. She loved her friend. Judy had a way of making life full and open. There were no boundaries in her life and no time for regret. Judy knew one way to live life—go out and live and let the chips fall where they may. Andria would think twice and three times before she did something, but not Judy. She would just go with the flow. It didn't matter where that flow would take her, whatever happened she would deal with it. She once told Andria she didn't believe in religion because she couldn't follow someone else's path. She had to do what was right for her and whatever happened, happened. It was as if she knew that her life would be short. She tried to do as much as possible every day. She traveled three times as much as Andria, and men, she could write her book on them. Judy had lived in her short life, she really had. Andria smiled when she thought of the different things Judy had told her she did. Yes, Judy burned the short candle very fast.

The light seemed to have stopped burning when he entered the cell. It was his second visit with Tyrone. It didn't matter how many times he had gone through these gates, he could never get use to it. It frightened him, the same way his friend was frightened in there now. The officer had walked with him to the gate and had positioned himself outside when Rashaun went in. Rashaun looked at Tyrone, the silly smile had departed from his face. The dim prison cell and the cost of despair had made him age way beyond his thirty-three years. He looked up from the cot he was sitting on when Rashaun walked in.

"What's up, my brother?" he said with a forced smile showing his teeth.

"Everything's cool," Rashaun said as he greeted his friend with a firm handshake.

"How is everyone on the outside?" he asked making it seem like if there were plane apart.

"Everyone is cool as far as I know." Rashaun answered.

"You have seen her baby?" Tyrone asked.

"Yeah, she is okay."

"You know, I never met her child. We started fucking right after she had the child. She never wanted me to see the child. She always kept it straight up. Yep, straight up fucking, nothing else."

"That's good sometimes," Rashaun said, trying to add something.

"Yeah it's the life we live, no complications." He sounded sad.

"Well let me get to why I asked for you to come here today. I need your help. I don't know if you heard but I fired my lawyer."

"You want me to recommend someone for you?"

"Not exactly."

"I don't like the way that sounds. You not going to try to do anything stupid like represent yourself, are you?" Rashaun asked searching his friend's face for the answer.

"No, I am not stupid. I don't know the law so I am not going to fuck with it. However, if I get sent up for twenty-five years then maybe law will be in my future." He cracked a faint smile. "I don't know. Maybe I deserve to be sent to prison for the rest of my life."

"With that attitude you will."

"This brings me to my reason for asking you to see me today. I want you to represent me. If I am going to be set free or sent to jail, I want the person who helps decide my fate to be someone I trust and respect. I know I'm asking a lot because it might cause some static at home with your woman, but I want you to please consider it. I don't want an answer now. Take your time, go home, and think about it. I am not sure how I'll pay your firm because as you know I don't have much money. And presently my parents are trying to mortgage their house to come up with the one-hundred-thousand-dollar bond."

Rashaun looked up at the iron ceiling that held his friend prisoner. He wasn't sure what to say, but most of all, he didn't want to let him down. For the first time he was questioning his professional ability to represent a client. He knew if he took the case, he would have to explain it to Andria, but somehow he knew she would understand. But could he win the case? He looked at his friend who was silent for the first time since Rashaun had entered the room.

"The last time I came to visit you, you didn't tell me what happened that night. I want you to tell me now and include what you told the cop," Rashaun said as he leaned back on the wall of the cell.

" I had told you that Judy said that it was over, right?

"I remember."

"Well, she called me up and said she wanted to come over and get an umbrella she left. Bullshit, exactly. Well, I said 'fine, come over. I'm not doing anything.' She came over wearing this little miniskirt and shit. I played it cool; I didn't make a move, waiting to see what she would do. I gave her the umbrella and she asked me if I wasn't going to offer her a drink or something. Then she started about me being a sorry-ass nigger who couldn't fuck and that's why she left my ass. She told me my dick was small and I couldn't use it, that's why I couldn't have a woman; the bitch went off. Now you know I don't have a small dick."

"Tyrone, you're getting a little too personal."

"You know what I mean. Man, by the time she finished talking, I wanted to kill the bitch. Then she kept taunting me, pushing her ass in front of me and telling me I couldn't handle it. I think that was the time I ripped her clothes off and threw her on the bed, and even then she was still taunting me, calling me Pokemon and all that shit. Man, that was the first time I had ever seen my dick so big. I swear, it was like a transformer. Shit was just added on. Man, I fucked that girl with the intention of killing the bitch. You remember when we were talking about Blackfunk? I had never experienced that shit until then. When I woke up, my dick was all swollen and cut up and bleeding. It was then that I noticed her on the bed, and I called the ambulance who called the cops."

"You told the cops what you just told me?" Rashaun asked.

"Kind of, they saw her ripped clothes and all that, but there were no marks on her body."

"How do you know that? Did you look for any?"

"Judy always takes care of her body. She is always as smooth as silk."

"I don't know about this case, Tyrone. You have taken Blackfunk to another level. I will have to think about this case and get back to you. Give me the name of your ex-lawyer and I will talk to him."

Tyrone gave him the name; they said their good-byes and Rashaun walked out of the jail. As he walked to his car, a yellow cab stopped beside him and he waved it away. This world was always changing. God knew he had no idea what tomorrow would bring.

"Finally, praise the Lord," Rashaun's mother shouted as she put the rice on the plate.

"Mom, I said I am going to ask her to marry me. It doesn't mean that she will say yes."

"Boy, you are a fool. Why wouldn't she say yes? You are handsome, mainly because of me, of course; you are educated with a profession that makes lots of money. You have a heart bigger than the ocean and you are very responsible." She put the food in front of him.

"Mom, you make me sound like an ad for the United Negro College."

"Boy, you got my blessing. I think you found a good woman in Andria so go on and make me some grandchildren. I have waited long enough for that day, but first eat your food. Soon you won't be coming here for food anymore."

"I doubt it, Andria knows me better than that. My mom's food will always be the best," Rashaun said as he took the fork and started eating.

"I have to call my brothers and sisters and tell them. They will be so happy. They never thought you would ever get married."

"Mom, can you wait until I ask her first? I'm asking her this weekend, then I will call you and tell you what she said."

"I'll wait," she lied, smiling.

"Please, Mom," Rashaun said, knowing that she would be on the phone two minutes after she saw his car drive away. He smiled and continued to eat.

Rashaun took Andria's hand and walked up the stairs to Robin's house. Robin and her husband had bought one of the beautiful colonial-style houses with six bedrooms and huge living and dining rooms off Flatbush Avenue. Andria loved the house, and she told Robin so every time she came over. Robin had invited them to dinner. Andria did not know what the special occasion was, but she had never turned down an invitation from her friend. It was the first time she had gone out since Judy's death.

Rashaun kept putting his hand in his pocket to make sure the little box was still there. He had bought the ring at Bloomingdales for six thousand dollars. At first when he walked into the store the sales people ignored him as he stood in front of the diamond showcase. But when he took his coat off, the salespeople came running over to help him. He was wearing an $800 Armani suit. They showed him a few rings until he settled for the one in his pocket.

Andria rang Robin's doorbell and stepped back. She waited twenty seconds before ringing it again.

"Where is she?" she asked Rashaun.

"I haven't the faintest idea," he answered.

"Do you think something is wrong?" she asked as a look of concern came over her face.

"Maybe they are in the kitchen," Rashaun suggested.

"Let me use your cell," Andria said.

Rashaun reached into his pocket for his cellular phone.

"Andria!" Robin called out. "Sorry about the wait, but we were in the kitchen getting dinner together. Come in. Hello, Rashaun." Robin winked at Rashaun as he walked by her. She led them through the hallway and down to the living room.

"Where is the child?" Andria asked.

"Asleep finally." Robin answered. "Honey," Robin called out to her husband.

As they entered the dimly lit living room, there was a massive shout of surprise.

Andria was in shock as she looked at the group that had gathered on the living room floor. She saw a crowd of her friends and some of Rashaun's, including the one she didn't like; the one they called PMF.

"Surprise what? It's not my birthday."

"Oh no," was the response from the crowd.

"Then what could it be, Rashaun?" Robin asked as she turned to him.

It was then that Andria turned to Rashaun and saw the little box in his hand. Her mouth opened and stayed that way for at least thirty seconds.

"What?" she asked, her eyes starting to well up with tears.

Rashaun got down on his knees and opened the box; the diamonds sparkled off the gold ring. "Andria, will you marry me?" he asked, looking into those beautiful eyes that started to drip tears of joy.

Andria's heart was beating a mile a minute when she dropped to the floor, her hands encircling him as the tears flowed freely from her eyes. "Yes, I will," she whispered in his ear. "Yes, I will," she repeated. She moved her head away from his shoulder and grasped his face in her hands. Slowly, she started to kiss him, her tongue reaching deep inside his mouth, her hands holding him close.

Rashaun heard her say yes the first time, but he wasn't sure of what he heard. When she repeated it, a burden was lifted off his shoulders. He didn't realize it, but he was nervous and shaking until her words made him the happiest man in America. He didn't have any backup plans if she had said no; maybe he would've died. He slipped the ring onto her finger as she held him, her warm body touching his, tears rolling down her face. His heart had doubled, and for the first time in his life, he was living for two.

"We didn't hear you?" Robin shouted.

"I will, I will, I will!" Andria shouted back, taking her lips briefly off Rashaun's.

"Let me propose a toast to Andria and Rashaun," George said, lifting his glass filled with crystal champagne.

Robin ran down to the table, grabbed the three glasses of champagne, and brought them back to Andria and Rashaun who had finally stood. She gave each one of them one and held hers up high.

"Cheers," George said aloud as glasses started to touch.

"I'm going to kill you for not telling me anything," Andria said to Robin as she and Rashaun stepped down into the living room to greet their friends.

"He must have spent al least five thousand bucks on this ring," Sharon said, turning the ring around on Andria's finger.

"Damn, girl, you got a good man there," Paula, said as she filled up her champagne glass with cristal. "Look at all this he set up. Do you know how much this must have cost to cater?"

Andria had stopped listening to her friends and quietly walked to the corner of the room. Robin saw her leave and knew what was on her mind.

"You wish she were here, don't you?" Robin said as she slipped her hand over her friend's shoulder.

Andria turned around, tears coming from her eyes. "I miss her. She had started to like Rashaun even though she thought he was a little stuck up."

"I'm sure she would have been very happy for you," Robin said.

"Robin, why did she have to die now? I hate Tyrone," Andria said and turned around as the tears flowed more freely.

"Congratulations." A woman about twenty years old extended her hand to Andria.

Andria wiped her tears with a tissue and extended her hand to the woman.

"Thank you, and you are?" Andria asked.

"I'm sorry, my name is Maxine, I'm Lance's girlfriend. By the way, have you seen Lance and the other guys?"

"I'm not sure, but I could bet they are outside talking nonsense," Robin said to the woman that looked too young to be holding a champagne glass in her hand. "If I were you, I would wait until they come back in."

"Thank you. This is a really beautiful house you have here. I hope to own one like this when I graduate from college. If you don't mind me asking, how much did it cost?"

"I really hate to talk about my house on Andria's special occasion so let's not get into it. Call me sometime and I will tell you about it. Thanks," Robin said and took Andria's hand and walked away.

"She is so young," Andria said as they stopped at the buffet table to get some shrimp cocktail.

"I remember those days. I thought they would last forever. Now I'm looking at thirty-two. What happened during that time, Andria?"

"I keep asking myself those same questions, and I keep sounding like a broken record. Did Rashaun have something to eat?"

"Wow, there you go sounding like a wife already," Robin said. "You don't want to spoil him this soon I'm sure he knows where the food is, and if he is hungry, believe me, he will find it."

"I guess I'm getting a little bit carried away, aren't I?"

"Yes, you are. Now let's go hear one of Paula's sob stories," Robin said as she pulled Andria by the arm and steered her over to the group of women in the corner of the room.

"Timing, timing means everything," Pedro said as he adjusted himself on the uncomfortable stool. He looked around to see if anyone else had difficulty with this cave man way of sitting. Even Peter was comfortable with his legs swinging freely off the ground. Rashaun had his stretched way out in front of him. Only Robin's husband seemed to have similar difficulties.

"I hate these fucking stools. They give you absolutely no back support. We saw them online and they looked so good. Robin warned me not to buy them. Of course, I wouldn't listen, told her it's a man thing and look at this now," he said, rocking unnaturally on the stool.

"Yeah, the bullshit we say and do to keep up our masculinity," George said.

"On the serious tip, Rashaun. I hope you know what you're getting into. Marriage isn't a joke. It takes a lot of work and a major commitment on both sides. I have to say, though, that I never regretted getting married. After a while, you want something more from life than the in and out," he said, finally getting to a spot on the chair where he was comfortable.

"Not me, no marriage for me. Too many of these women are hookers and players. I know women, and I wouldn't trust them as far as I can see them. My philosophy is simple, fuck them and leave them exactly where you met them," Lance said a little bit of bitterness in his tone.

"You know what I say you give women too much freedom, and they walk all over you. I see some guys letting their women get away with all kinds of shit. Respect is the key to a good relationship; if a woman respects you, she won't try certain things. You have to establish that respect from the beginning, then they won't bring half of the bullshit to you," Pedro said.

"Spoken as a true Jamaican," George said, "and you guys don't eat pussy neither. Bullshit, when you marry a woman get ready for changes. The bitch is gonna change, like it or not. What you have to do is learn to deal with it. You got to ignore certain things and make an issue of others. This marriage shit isn't easy, my man. I say you get yourself an outside shit, and when the stress gets too much, you go and get a little relief. But you got to keep moving with that side thing otherwise you get stuck and she becomes worse than your wife. Before you know it, you have a kid, and you're paying rent two places."

184

"Spoken as a true modern married man," Rashaun said. "I don't think I want to go that route."

"We will see," George said, shaking his head.

"What you got to say, Peter? You've been married a few months now," Rashaun said.

"It's okay, Peter. You can talk, your wife is not around. You don't have to ask permission," Lance said.

"Tell me it isn't so, Peter," George said, looking at Peter like a judge to jury.

"He is just saying that because my wife makes most of the major decisions. I let her do that. I'm just not good at certain things," Peter said, wondering why they had to bring him into the conversation.

"You pussy," Lance said, looking at Peter angrily.

"Thanks for the advice, guys, but I think I will take it as it goes," Rashaun said, swinging around in his chair.

"You are going to miss a lot. Man, I went to this party the other day; it had about eighty brothers and about fifty sisters in there. And everybody was fucking; you go from one female to another, nonstop, just pussy all over the place. And me, I'm going to stay with one woman for the rest of my life? The same ugly pussy every time I wake up and go to sleep? I don't think so," Lance said, his eyes declaring his passion.

"There comes a time in a man's life when he has to move on, a chance to advance. There are only so many women you can fuck before becomes redundant. To fall in love and commit to someone has great rewards," Robin's husband said, his words penetrating the ears of the men who were gathered.

"Good luck, guys, I will remain how I am. I will go from woman to woman until Viagra is useless to me. Then I will spend the rest of my life going over the memories of a well-spent time on Earth," Lance said, smiling as a memory came into his head. "Well, guys, got to go. There is this young girl inside that promises to do a lot of things with me tonight."

"Can you elaborate?" George asked, wondering about the potential of the girl.

"Shut the fuck up, George!" Rashaun said as he got off the stool.

185

"What you need to do is ask your woman if she would sleep with another woman," Peter said softly.

"What you mean ask her if she would eat pussy?" George said.

"Who gives a fuck? The bitch want to eat pussy let her eat pussy, just make sure she invite your ass," Lance said in a nonchalant way.

"Not when she is your wife," George said. " I have no problem with a woman eating pussy. Shit, it's the best turn-on in the world. Imagine a woman going down on another woman and her ass all cocked up in the air. If that don't make your dick hard, Viagra can't help."

"I'm with George. Give me a pussy-eating woman anytime. That means she has friends who are pussy eating, too, so you get two for the price of one," Lance said. "Look at the young girl who came with me today. She had been with a woman. I have no problem with that. Actually, I'm trying to get her to invite her friend over for a threesome. Shit, like I said, if you guys haven't tried that, it's fucking wicked," Lance said, rolling his eyes.

"The owner of the house isn't saying anything," George said to Robin's husband.

"If my wife told me she was thinking of eating pussy, it's simple—the marriage is over. I can't argue with her, I can't convince her not to. It means she is going in a completely different direction than me. I can't take her to Pussy Anonymous." Robin's husband said, his voice steady and controlled.

"It's not always that easy when you love somebody," Peter said.

"Love does not make everything okay. I have had threesomes, but if Andria had told me she had been with another woman, we would not be here this evening. There are certain things that are a simple no. I believe once you been down a road, you have a tendency to go down that road again. I am not going into this marriage to try to change Andria. I doubt I will ever be able to do that. Whatever she is, she is. If she's been with another woman or is thinking about experimenting, there isn't a fucking thing I could do about it."

"I say we all get together and fuck our brains out," Lance said. "The more the merrier. I have no feelings for those bitches and

186

whores, I encourage eating pussy. You guys have to learn to let go, give your woman freedom to explore different things. What you guys scared of anyway? Afraid she won't want dick anymore?"

"Lance, I think the last woman you ever cared about was your mother," Rashaun said.

"You damn right and she will remain the last," Lance said. "I am not going through the drama with any of those bitches out there."

"On that uplifting note, I think we should go join those ladies," Robin's husband said.

"Bitches you mean," Lance said under his breath.

"Too much Cristal in there to go to waste," George said.

"My young thing must be looking all over for me," Lance said as he headed inside.

Robin's husband put his hand on Rashaun shoulder.

"Man, you are doing the right thing. When you find the right one you've got to do the right thing. And from what I have known about Andria, you've got the second prize," he said.

"Who got the first?" Rashaun asked looking at him.

"Me, of course. My Robin will be singing to me for the rest of my life." He grinned as they walked back into the living room. When they got there and Rashaun saw Andria next to Robin he smiled.

"I think I got the first," he said to Robin's husband.

"What first? What were you and Robin's husband talking about?" Andria asked as she took his hand.

"We were just b-s-ing," he said. "Let's go and thank the people for coming."

"Why didn't you tell me about the videotape?" His fists were clenched and eyes red.

"I didn't know they would find it," Tyrone replied.

"I told you before about videotaping shit," Rashaun said, moving around the room, "but your ass wouldn't listen."

"Man, I thought with videotape a woman could never accuse you of rape. The shit is proof that it was consensual."

"Now the proof is going to hang you by the balls."

"I didn't know," Tyrone said.

For the first time Rashaun saw the bags under his friend's eyes. Tyrone had not been sleeping. His parents had just gotten the money to bail him out when the DA received the tape and went back in front of the judge. They asked that his bail to be revoked. Rashaun argued against it, but the judge sided with the DA. It was a terrible blow to Tyrone, and he had cried when Rashaun told him on the phone.

"How much is on the tape?"

"I think almost everything."

"Did you say anything about killing her on the tape?"

"I can't remember."

"Did you curse at her or threaten her?"

"I can't remember, I might have."

"I hope not, for your sake."

"Rashaun, how did I get here? All I did was take a little bit of pussy. Damn, I've never hurt anyone in my life. I never did. Now I am looking at spending the rest of my life in jail. For what?" Tyrone screamed. "For a piece of another man's pussy! This shit isn't right! This shit just isn't fucking right." And for the second time in a few weeks, Rashaun watched a grown man cry like a baby. He sat down on the hard jail bed and put his hand around his friend's shoulder.

"It's going to be okay," he lied.

He stayed for another half hour, talking to his friend about the case and everything that been happening on the outside. Then he walked back over to the district attorney's office to meet the new DA handling the case and to get a copy of the tape. Rashaun had been the opposing lawyer in so many of the state prosecutions, he was sure he would know the new district attorney. Even though they work on opposing sides, there was no animosity among them. He sometimes had lunch with them and always went to their Christmas parties.

He said hello to a few DAs and lawyers as he walked up the Supreme Court steps. He saw a few cops who he also had dealings with and he greeted them as well. He went into the small office that six district attorneys occupied. He stopped one who he knew from a previous trial and asked him who was the district attorney on his case.

"That's okay, John I will handle it."

Rashaun heard the voice and did not get up or turn around. His blood started to race through his veins. His palms became clammy and wet. He felt sick, but didn't feel anything coming up in his throat. She walked past him and closed the door. She sat down and he still did not look at her. Instead, the video started to replay in his head. He saw her smiling with his friend. Taking her clothes off as if he was her man. Then he saw them, him ripping into her like a worthless piece of meat. And she was enjoying it. His friend taking the blood and using it as lubricant, and all the while the hate and anger burned in his eyes. Rashaun closed his eyes tightly so that the memories would stop coming. He hoped she didn't see him do that; damn, he was nervous and angry. Maybe if he hadn't seen the video he would not have hated her so much right now. Maybe she should of died like Judy did from the Blackfunk.

"Hello, Rashaun" she said with a big smile on her face. "It's been a long time."

For the first time since she came in he looked at her. She hadn't changed much; her face was angelic as before. The white suit she wore couldn't hide the tremendous body it covered. He looked at her face without saying a word. The memories kept flooding his head. He didn't want to be there.

"How have you been?" she asked.

He kept looking at her not saying a word. His skin felt hot, and small beads of sweat ran down his forehead.

"What are you doing here?" he managed to say, his voice barely audible.

"I am the new senior district attorney and I have the case."

"Why are you doing this to me?" he asked, his voice hoarse with anger.

"Doing what?" she asked.

"Ignorance was never bliss with you so don't try it now."

"Rashaun, are you still upset about what happened between us all those years ago?" she said, her eyes mirroring his. "I said I was sorry. You didn't deserve that."

"Sorry? Bitch, you changed my fucking life!" he said, his voice loud and angry.

"Rashaun, you are shouting. Can we talk about this over dinner? My treat. I promise."

"I don't want to talk to you about anything except this case," he said, regaining control of his voice.

"Okay, if that's the way you want it. I was young then and I said I was sorry. You have a new life and I have a new life." She opened the big manila envelope she had put on the table.

"That's it?" he asked.

"Yes, he incriminated himself on the tape," she said as she pushed it to him. "And as you know, videotapes tell the whole story. You know what I mean?"

Rashaun snatched the tape off the table and put it in his briefcase. He got up, turned around and started to walk to the door.

"Still so much anger. See you in court."

He didn't want to answer her. He didn't want to see her for the rest of his life, but as life goes, he wasn't given a choice. Eventually one must face the pain and deal with it. For the next few months, Blackfunk would be with him twenty-four hours a day.

The cab ride to his apartment was a short one; he barely saw the actions of the big city. While in the cab, he took the video out of his briefcase and looked at it. The label read evidence 1289: the state of New York vs Tyrone St. James copy. Rashaun turned it over a few times then put it back into his briefcase.

"Hi," she said as she put her hands around him and gave him a kiss on the cheek. He took her hand, walked over to the living room, and put his briefcase down. He held her hand swinging it ever so slightly. The engagement ring glittered on her finger.

They walked over to the terrace. He looked beyond Brooklyn to the city of Manhattan. He held her around the waist as the clouds in the sky started to move. The thunder came loud and furious as he held onto her.

"Do you promise?" he asked.

"Till death do us part," she said and turned around and kissed him again, this time on the lips. He returned her kiss with the passion of a drowning man taking her lips, her tongue into his mouth, and then laid his head on her shoulder. A few teardrops fell from his eyes as he looked at the turmoil in the sky. There was a storm coming, and it was dark and vicious. However, he wasn't running this time; this time he would stand up and fight.